Forever Would Be Nice

Karen Legasy

Yellow Rose Books
by Regal Crest

ISBN 978-1-61929-436-3

First Printing 2020

9 8 7 6 5 4 3 2 1

Original cover design by AcornGraphics

Published by:

Regal Crest Enterprises

Find us on the World Wide Web at
http://www.regalcrest.biz

Published in the United States of America

Acknowledgments

Thank you to Regal Crest Enterprises for believing in and publishing my story.

I would like to acknowledge Humber College for its gem of a Correspondence Program in Creative Writing. Many thanks to author Kim Moritsugu (*The Showrunner, The Oakdale Dinner Club, The Restoration of Emily*, etc.). Over the course of several months, Kim provided invaluable writing guidance and mentorship that helped to shape *Forever Would Be Nice*, which was initially entitled, *The Visitor From Iceland*.

Michaela Lynn, I feel so fortunate to have had you as my editor. It has been a pleasure working with you on this book. Your suggestions, edits, and comments have certainly helped make the story a much better read. Thank you☺

A lot of credit goes to Cathy Bryerose and all of the folks at Regal Crest Enterprises for bringing stories like this to print. The world is a much better place because of you. Thank you☺

A wholehearted thank you to Pam for your constant support in life, and with all of my writing projects. Our trip to Iceland in 2015 was just so wonderful, almost magical as we shared the journey of this story together. I am so grateful for having you at my side for the last twenty plus years. Being with you forever would be nice.

I'd like to thank the Canadian Embassy in Iceland for inviting us to march with them in the 2015 Reykjavik Pride Parade. What a thrilling experience!

I would also like to acknowledge Jeff and all the fun times we had together. You taught me so much, and Scott was born from this. I miss you and hope that you are resting in peace.

This book would not be possible without you, the reader. I hope you enjoy the story, and your armchair travels in Canada and Iceland. Thank you for reading.

Dedication

To Mom. I miss you so much.

Acknowledgments

Thank you to Regal Crest Enterprises for believing in and publishing my story.

I would like to acknowledge Humber College for its gem of a Correspondence Program in Creative Writing. Many thanks to author Kim Moritsugu (*The Showrunner, The Oakdale Dinner Club, The Restoration of Emily,* etc.). Over the course of several months, Kim provided invaluable writing guidance and mentorship that helped to shape *Forever Would Be Nice,* which was initially entitled, *The Visitor From Iceland.*

Michaela Lynn, I feel so fortunate to have had you as my editor. It has been a pleasure working with you on this book. Your suggestions, edits, and comments have certainly helped make the story a much better read. Thank you☺

A lot of credit goes to Cathy Bryerose and all of the folks at Regal Crest Enterprises for bringing stories like this to print. The world is a much better place because of you. Thank you☺

A wholehearted thank you to Pam for your constant support in life, and with all of my writing projects. Our trip to Iceland in 2015 was just so wonderful, almost magical as we shared the journey of this story together. I am so grateful for having you at my side for the last twenty plus years. Being with you forever would be nice.

I'd like to thank the Canadian Embassy in Iceland for inviting us to march with them in the 2015 Reykjavik Pride Parade. What a thrilling experience!

I would also like to acknowledge Jeff and all the fun times we had together. You taught me so much, and Scott was born from this. I miss you and hope that you are resting in peace.

This book would not be possible without you, the reader. I hope you enjoy the story, and your armchair travels in Canada and Iceland. Thank you for reading.

Dedication

To Mom. I miss you so much.

Book One

Chapter One

THE SUN WAS beginning to rise when the power went out. The air was muggy and the sky was going to be clear for another day. Six scorchers in a row and another five forecasted. We had been warned about possible power outages with the extra demand for air conditioners. Now here we were.

I had gotten up at five-thirty on this Wednesday morning to beat the humidity of the day and jog around my neighborhood. I was drenched within the first few minutes of my run. Scott, my best friend and housemate, hated the heat and would be upset with the stickiness.

The streets were quiet except for a few dedicated dog walkers. I nodded as we passed, each of us absorbed in our own electronic worlds. Mine included Melissa Etheridge and her *Fearless Love* album. It wasn't that I was fearless about love. It was more that I had given up on it. The tunes were catchy and I needed something to get my adrenalin going so early in the morning.

The neighborhood was a quiet residential area in Ottawa with big trees and large lots, but not so big houses. That's mainly what had appealed to me when I'd bought my house five years ago. I also liked the location because I could be in the heart of the city in fifteen minutes in good traffic.

The annoying pain in my right hip started and I had to stop running. Jogging was a new thing for me. It was part of my weight loss plan.

Over the winter I had put on almost ten pounds. They showed up one morning when I stepped on the scale because I didn't want to believe it when I struggled to do up my freshly washed jeans.

Drastic, I told myself. I'd have to take drastic measures to stop this. The next time I stepped on the scale, I had gained another five pounds. I shrieked and made the mistake of telling Scott when he asked what was wrong. I became his *Butterball* Pumpkin.

I was walking now. My route was fairly short, but I had yet to conquer running it non-stop. The walking stretches were getting shorter though. I started to trot again.

Today was garbage day. One house had a big heap and at the

side of the pile was something I wanted—bamboo ski poles. They'd be perfect with my new snowshoes I'd bought at a spring clear-out sale with every intention of heading to Gatineau Park next winter.

I slowed down, although it wasn't as if I was sprinting in the first place. I wanted the poles, but I didn't want anyone to see me taking them. I also wanted to finish my loop before running with the poles. I sauntered by.

As soon as I passed the poles, I regretted my decision. I almost turned around, but suddenly a dog walker appeared out of nowhere so I continued on.

I had been watching the curb for a few months now because almost every year someone cleaned their garage and threw out a pair of bamboo ski poles. They would be perfect with their big baskets for all of the snowshoeing I was planning to do. I suddenly found myself jogging faster to finish my loop and get back to the poles before they were gone. The garbage truck often came early.

By the time I got to my driveway, my mouth was feeling dry so I stopped in for some water. Scott stood in the kitchen as I reached into the cupboard for a glass. I didn't pay him any attention because I expected he would be there, making his breakfast.

"Somebody finally put out a pair of bamboo ski poles." I took a gulp of water, waiting for Scott to comment. He would know what I was talking about because he knew it was garbage day and that I'd been on the hunt for the poles ever since I'd bought my snowshoes. "I'm going to go get them now." I took another drink, but still no comment.

I turned around and looked at Scott. He clutched the letter that I'd found in our mailbox the day before. It had been handwritten, addressed to Scott, with no return address. He'd been out late so I left it on the small shelf where he always kept his keys. Scott's hands were shaking and his neck was red.

"What is it?" I put my glass on the counter.

"It's from someone who says he's my biological father," Scott said. "He wants to meet me."

Chapter Two

SCOTT HAD BEEN adopted close to forty years before when he was three months old. He had no knowledge of his birth parents and never seemed to care about knowing who they were. I, on the other hand, was fascinated with who they could have been, and whether or not he had any siblings.

"You're kidding." I regretted the words as soon as they were out of my mouth. As if he would kid about something like that. "When does he want to meet?"

"Today." Scott was slightly hunched and gripped the letter with both hands.

"Who is he?"

His hands shook as he stared at the page. "Someone named Ari Agnarsson."

I heard the distant garbage truck and had a vision of it eating my bamboo ski poles. I didn't know what to do. I couldn't run out on Scott at a moment like this, but if I didn't, my poles would be gone.

"Where does he want to meet?" I pictured the truck getting closer.

"Somewhere downtown. He suggested one of the coffee shops on Bank. He said to text him if that's okay."

"Why now? Why today? Doesn't he know you have to work?"

"Fuck work. I couldn't concentrate on anything." Scott threw the paper on the counter. "Will you come with me?"

"You want me to go with you?" I hadn't meant to shriek. "Of course I will."

"Thanks." Scott hadn't seemed to notice my tone, or that I was giving up the bamboo ski poles. "I don't know if I want to meet him."

"Oh Scott, you have to. Can I see the letter?"

He picked it up and shoved it at me. It was one paragraph, neatly printed in blue ink, and requesting to meet as soon as possible. It was signed Ari and there was a cell number with an area code I didn't recognize.

"What do you think, Bebs?" Barbra was my first name, but my friends called me Bebs. I was named Barbra Ethel Burnaby. The Barbra came from Barbra Streisand because my mother was a huge fan. Ethel was my paternal grandmother's name and Burnaby was my family name. If I were a dog, I'd be a mutt, a mixed breed. I couldn't lay claim to being Italian, Polish, French, or even Indigenous. I had a bit of all of them in me, but not enough to feel like I belonged anywhere.

Scott edged over to the coffee maker, which still had no power, and tried to turn it on. "Fuck."

"Can I see the envelope?" I reached out. There had been no return address, but I wanted to look again in case I'd missed something.

Scott fondled the envelope before handing it over. "There's nothing much on it."

It had the same blue ink printing as the letter and in addition to our address, the words: *To Scott Pullman, private and confidential please.*

"I think you need to text him," I said.

"He's probably still in bed." Beads of sweat had formed on Scott's forehead and were starting to roll down his cheeks. Could there have been some tears in the mix? "I'm sending a message to say I won't be at work today and then I'm having a shower." Scott bolted out of the kitchen.

I didn't have to send a message to work since I no longer had that kind of job. My position as an architect with the federal government had recently been eliminated so I'd decided to leave rather than find another job within.

When I had joined the government fifteen years ago, straight from university, I had big plans. I saw myself making a difference in the world—tackling climate change head on and helping to design buildings that didn't waste energy. South facing windows, super insulation, airtight with proper ventilation, and environmentally friendly building products—the whole gamut— it seemed so simple. But of course budgets and politics always came into play and there was little room for changing the world. Now here I was, fifteen years later, standing in my kitchen without power because of climate change.

But I had big plans now. My dad's former company, BB Construction, was going to specialize in certified passive houses, if I could revive it. Baxter Burnaby, my dad, started BB Construction almost forty years ago when he met my mother. He had been retired for two years now and as the company was a one-man operation, it retired as well. All I had to do was convince my dad to let me bring him and his construction company out of retirement. I wanted to give it new life by designing and building passive houses. I also had to convince my parents to loan me enough money to get it started, a much easier task had he been greener in his thinking, and if I'd been more like my sister, Mary.

Chapter Three

I SPOTTED ARI as soon as we entered the coffee shop. He was sitting by himself at a corner table and looked just like Scott, except older and greyer. He still had a full head of hair. Scott would be pleased because he was always so afraid of becoming a bald old guy like my dad.

When Ari noticed us, he stood to reveal a tall handsome man and it became obvious where Scott got his good physique. A lot of it must have been genetics because Scott didn't exercise all that much and wasn't into lifting weights. He did like riding his bicycle though.

"Hello." Ari held out his hand to Scott.

Ari's face was red and so were his eyes.

"Hi." Scott extended his hand then pulled back after a quick shake. I felt tears and a tightening in my throat. Scott was in shock. We had taken my car because he wasn't in any condition to drive.

"Thank you for coming." Ari wiped what could have been a tear from his cheek then turned to me.

"You must be Scott's wife?" He smiled and extended his arms.

"No, she's not my wife. This is Barbra." Scott never called me Barbra.

"I'm sorry." Ari's cheeks reddened. "Your friend then?"

"Yes, we're friends." I shook a warm, firm hand.

"We live together," Scott said, hands jiggling change in his pockets.

I knew by Scott's softening tone and hidden eyes that he wanted Ari to think we were a straight couple. We had been living together in my house for close to five years. Scott had been in a long-term relationship with his partner, Stephen, and needed a place to stay when it ended. I had just bought my house and was living in it by myself so I was happy for the company and someone to share the costs.

We were both still single. I didn't think I'd ever find my Ms. Right and it was like Scott had become my Mr. Right. We had the perfect marriage—there were no vows and there was no sex. And we could play the happy heterosexual couple at times like this.

"Please, sit down." Ari motioned to the empty chairs at the

table. "What can I get you? My treat."

Scott and I both requested iced tea. I wasn't sure if I was going to be able to drink it, but at least it was something cold. The power had come back on shortly after Scott had gotten into the shower. I was able to have a pot of coffee ready by the time he returned. I made a full pot of ten cups that we finished off by noon.

"Holy shit, he looks just like you," I said as Ari was getting our iced tea.

"Do you think so?" Scott's lips were white and his neck was red.

"Yes. You look so much alike it's almost uncanny. He has to be your birth father."

Scott and I had discussed the possibility that this wasn't his biological father. The letter seemed surreal, so out of the ordinary.

"I wonder what he wants?" Scott fidgeted with his hands on the table.

"Give him a chance." I said. "I think there were tears in his eyes."

"Where do you think he's from?" Scott scrutinized Ari as he paid for the iced tea.

"I don't know," I said. "It sounds like he has a slight accent, but it's hard to say."

Ari returned to the table and sat down. "I am so happy you are here." He focused his eyes on Scott and his expression was soft with a hint of a smile. "We have lots to talk about, yes?"

Scott's expression was harsh and his voice shook when he spoke. "How did you find me? And why now?"

"It was not easy finding you," Ari said. "I didn't even know you existed until a few months ago."

"You didn't know about me?" Scott shook his head. "I find that hard to believe."

"It's true." Ari sipped his coffee, both hands wrapped around the mug the way Scott often held his. "It wasn't until I found the letter."

"What letter?" Scott straightened, crossing his arms.

"It's a long story." Ari put his mug down and leaned into the table toward Scott. "I had a box full of old papers that had been laying around for years. When I finally looked through it, I saw an unopened letter addressed to me from Canada, Ottawa. It was from your office of services for children." Ari paused. "It must have come in the mail when Anja and I were going through our divorce many years ago."

"Who's Anja?" Scott shuffled in his seat.

"She was my wife for a short time and we weren't talking very much to each other back then. Anja had thrown all of my papers into a box and gave it to me when I left." Ari paused then let out a big breath before continuing.

"I didn't care about anything during that time. I put the box of papers away and forgot about it until a few years ago when my sister, Katarina, was cleaning up around the house and wanted me to go through it. So much time had gone by and I still didn't like thinking about the past. I put the box out with the garbage."

Ari's attention shifted toward the window where two passing dogs growled at each other and tugged at their leashes. When he brought his eyes back to Scott, the corners of his mouth were raised. "Katarina brought the box back in. She emptied all of the papers on the floor in front of me one night when I was watching the television. Katarina knew it was a bunch of papers from my time with Anja. She had been nagging at me for years to go through it. She thought there could be something important. I thought she was crazy."

Scott played with his phone.

"And now here we are," Ari said. "If it wasn't for Katarina, we would not be meeting."

Scott looked up. "It doesn't make sense."

"I didn't want to believe it either," Ari said. "I didn't think it was possible until I saw pictures of you."

"How did you get pictures of me?" Scott glared.

"The computer," Ari said. "Katarina helped me. When we put your name on the Internet and saw your pictures in Facebook, I knew you were my son."

"How did you get my name?"

"I tracked it down through your office of children's services. It took almost two years, but another letter finally came in the mail and gave me your name."

"What about my mother? What do you know about her?"

"You have her eyes. I never thought I would see those eyes again." Ari hunched over the table and wrapped both hands around his now empty mug. "Your office of children's services told me she died soon after you were born." Ari wiped a tear. "I wish things had been different and we could have had the time to get to know one another. But we were so young and lived a world apart."

"How did she die?" Scott asked.

"She was killed in a bad accident," Ari said. "She was hurrying to cross the street and was hit by a big truck."

"And where were you?" Scott's arms were on the table.

"Back home in Reykjavik."

Chapter Four

WE TALKED ABOUT the fact that Ari was from Reykjavik. I felt stupid because I wasn't sure where Reykjavik was. I felt even denser when Scott knew right away it was the capital of Iceland.

Ari had been born and raised in Reykjavik and still lived there. He had been married to Anja for less than a year before they split up. He now lived in the same house he grew up in and shared it with his younger sister, Katarina. She too was not married.

"What was my mother's name?" Scott asked. We were drinking coffee again. It had been my treat this time. During intimate conversations like this, I would have preferred a glass of wine, but coffee was the next best thing.

"Ginny." Ari smiled. "She told me it was short for Ginette. She had the most beautiful blue eyes that were like twinkling stars."

So that's where Scott got his blue eyes.

"What was her last name?" Scott leaned into the table.

"Belanger," Ari said. "I only learned that a few months ago when I found out about you."

"If you didn't know her last name," Scott said, "how did she know yours?"

"She must have copied it from my Passport when I slept."

"So I was the product of a one-night stand? My mother was a hooker?" Scott flung his hands in the air.

"No, no, not at all." Ari's head wagged back and forth. "Your mother was my little angel. I was skating when my blade hit a crack in the ice and I fell face down."

Scott's forehead furrowed. "You were skating?"

"Yes. I was skating on your Rideau Canal here in Ottawa." Ari smiled. "It had been a dream of mine to skate on it, the largest skating rink in the world."

"You came all the way from Iceland to skate on the Rideau Canal?" Scott asked, his lips crooked.

"Not exactly." Ari chuckled. "I was on my way home to Iceland and Ottawa was a one night stop over."

"So it was a one-night stand then." Scott crossed his arms again.

"It wasn't like that." Ari looked as if he were going to reach out and touch Scott's arm, but instead ran a hand through his hair. "When I fell on the ice I wasn't hurt, but my nose was bloody. I had been by myself and disoriented because it was dark. I let myself lay there for a minute then all of a sudden I saw a white flash from your mother's skates. She stopped and asked if I needed help. I was so embarrassed being rescued by a girl."

Scott breathed heavily though his nose, his face expressionless.

"I had just turned nineteen," Ari said. "Hardly a man, but that's not how I felt. I had been on a journey of sorts I guess you could say. I needed to get away from Iceland and explore the world. For me, the world was the United States. New York City. On my way back home I wanted to give myself one last treat. I stopped in Ottawa so I could skate on your canal."

"It sure sounds like you got a treat," Scott said.

"Yes, and now I have another treat sitting right here in front of me." Ari's eyes were wet again. "A son. I always wanted a son."

Scott stared at his silent phone.

"Your mother's spirit was with me every night after that." Ari dug in the front pocket of his jeans for a tissue. "That is why my marriage to Anja didn't last. I am sure of it. Getting on the plane that next morning is the biggest regret of my life. I could never forget my sweet Ginny. I guess you could say she was a free spirit and I thought I could be like that too."

"So you just left and that was it?" Scott's eyes went to Ari.

"No, not at all. I tried hard to find her. I even came back to Ottawa, but it was like she never existed. We didn't have Facebook in those days—just the phonebook. And there were no Ginny's listed. I spent lots of time skating on the canal and hoping to see her again. I ran out of money after three weeks and had to return home to Reykjavik. I told myself that she had forgotten about me and was probably with somebody else. If only I would have known. I would have brought the two of you back to Reykjavik." Ari was crying. Scott squirmed in his seat.

"So much time has been lost," Ari said, "and now I finally get to meet my son just when I am dying."

Chapter Five

ARI TOLD US he had stage four cancer. Melanoma. I never would have thought someone could get skin cancer in a place as cold as Iceland. We offered for Ari to come over to our place, but he declined, saying he was tired and needed to rest.

It was my night to go to my parents' house for dinner. I tried to get Scott to come too, but he said he needed some alone time to absorb things. I understood.

Dinners at my parents' place were usually just like old times. Ever since she retired, my mother insisted on giving her two girls a break during the week. My sister, Mary, and I usually came on our own. Mary was married to Jonathan, a busy heart surgeon who never had time to come. Scott was always invited too, but he seldom accepted.

Mary was three years younger than me and had been married to Jonathan for ten years. I was still waiting to become an aunt. Mary and Jonathan had put their careers ahead of having kids.

Mary was a lawyer and a stellar one at that. She was naturally good at everything and even though I was the older sister, Mary was the role model. She had always been a high achiever and I knew she'd be on time for dinner. Mary got her name because our mother loved the Mary Tyler Moore show. Fond memories of sitting in the living room with my mother and watching Mary Tyler Moore drive her Mustang at the start of each episode made it my dream car.

My parents' house was the one Mary and I grew up in. It was a two-story, four-bedroom home that my father built, but he didn't really maintain it the way you'd think a carpenter should. Our mother had to get after him to do the little repairs when they became something bigger. Despite all of this, the value of their property had soared over the years and I think that's why my mother let him get away with slacking off.

I was late for dinner by the time I stood at the bottom of the stairs in their small front entry. I could tell by the clanging of utensils on plates that they had already started eating. I stuffed their house key into the front pocket of my dark green cargo shorts then stopped by the powder room to wash my hands before making an entrance into the dining room.

"Barbra, you're late," my mother said. Her wavy shoulder-length hair was dyed auburn, as she liked to call it, but it usually looked orange to me. A retired high school English teacher, she was always correcting us. I remembered being in high school and hearing students refer to her as Mrs. Ruthless Burnaby. She wore a lime green floral patterned sundress over her slim sixty-two year old figure.

"Sorry," I said as I reached for my plate, which had been set on the table.

"Wash your hands first," my mother said.

"I just did." I served myself some spaghetti and sauce from the stovetop then sat across from Mary.

"How come you're late?" My dad stuffed a piece of garlic bread in his mouth then licked his thick fingers. He wore a faded grey T-shirt that stretched across his belly and was almost the same color as the patch of short stubbly hair that circled his completely bald scalp. "Your mother's been working hard all afternoon to get this meal ready."

"Sorry." I said. "I lost track of time. It's been quite the interesting day."

"Well, you should hear about my day," Mary said. "We had to take Barbie to the vet this morning." Barbie was her three year-old Bengal cat. "She could hardly move and didn't want anyone to touch her."

"So was it five hundred bucks?" My dad chewed as he spoke.

"Dad," Mary mocked hitting at him.

"Baxter, let her finish," my mother said.

"Barbie had a reaction to one of the vaccines she got from the vet yesterday."

All eyes were on Mary as she delicately picked at her pasta.

"Well, if the vet caused it, I sure hope you didn't have to pay." My dad took a drink of his red wine. "Wouldn't you agree with that, Ruth?"

"How's the poor thing doing?" my mother asked, patting Mary's arm.

"She seems to be okay now, but it sure was scary this morning."

"You're spending way too much time and money on that cat." My dad's fork clanged against his plate. "When are we going to get grandchildren? Eh? I don't know what's wrong with you girls."

"Well you know what's wrong with me," I said, my teeth clamping together as I readied for the attack.

"I don't understand you." This time it was my mother who

spoke and may as well have wagged a finger the way she glared at me. "Scott is so handsome and you've been single for how many years? I would have thought the two of you would have gotten together by now and given us a grandchild."

I didn't say anything because I was used to it. I loved my parents and knew they meant well, but sometimes I couldn't understand how they could have been my parents in the first place.

"Tell us about your interesting day." My mother eyes were still on me. "Did you manage to find a job?"

She didn't get it. I didn't want to find a job. I wanted to create my own.

"No." I took a big bite of garlic bread and chewed as I spoke. "Scott met his dad today."

"What?" My dad used the back of his fist to wipe spaghetti sauce from his lips. "I thought they weren't talking. Did his parents come for a visit?"

I stuffed my mouth full of spaghetti, sucking it up through my lips until my cheeks were full. All eyes were on me now.

"No." I had a hard time speaking and had to pause to chew and swallow. "I mean his birth father."

"You mean his real dad?" My mother looked at me, her green eyes like tennis balls.

"His real dad lives in Vancouver," I said. "How can you say that someone who didn't raise him is his real dad? His real dad is the one who raised him." Scott probably would have contradicted me on this, not having had any contact with his adoptive father in over twenty years, but I felt the need to correct my mother on something.

"Okay, Barbra", my father said, "you know what your mother means."

"It was so weird," I said. "Scott just found out this morning and we met his dad this afternoon."

"How did he know it was his biological father?" Mary asked, her tone almost sarcastic.

"I knew for sure as soon as I saw him," I said. "He looks just like Scott except about twenty years older."

"Is he gay too then?" My father's pitch was a bit higher than normal.

"No he's not." It was time for me to leave. I quickly told my family about our visit with Ari then redirected the conversation back to Barbie. I left as soon as the dishes were cleaned up.

Chapter Six

WHEN I GOT home, Scott was sprawled out on the white leather couch with the TV remote resting on his chest. It was his favorite position. There was a tennis match on and he loved watching tennis, especially the male players.

"How was dinner at the Flintstones?" He didn't look up, but I knew by his tone he was doing okay. He sometimes referred to my parents as Fred and Wilma because he felt they still lived in the Stone Age. He referred to Mary as Pebbles. Princess Pebbles, to quote Scott. When he was on his Flintstone kick, he would call me Bebs-Bebs, instead of Bamm-Bamm.

"Same as usual." I plunked down in the large red recliner beside the couch. "What did you get up to?"

"Isn't it obvious?" Scott turned his palms upward as he motioned toward the television.

"Are you going to work tomorrow?" I closed my eyes.

"I have to. Not everyone is as lucky as you." Scott was jealous of my current situation. Although he was good at his job as a policy analyst in the federal government, he would have rather not worked. He was always trying to dream up ways of supporting himself without having to work. He even asked me to marry him one time when he was drunk and was complaining about his job. He said that it would be perfect. He would look after the house while I went to work. If only my mother knew.

"I am so looking forward to sleeping in tomorrow morning," I said.

"What do you have to be tired about?"

"It can be exhausting at my parents' place."

Scott's eyebrows were raised when I opened my eyes. He flapped his lips. "Getting a free home-cooked meal should hardly be considered exhausting." He sat up, took a gulp of water and swirled it around his mouth before swallowing. "Speaking of family, what do you think Ari wants?"

"To get to know you. I think it's as simple as that because I didn't get the sense he's a complicated man."

"So you're saying my dad is simple?"

"Well, he is your dad after all," I said. "Who would've thought you'd have Icelandic genes. You can have an icy glare though. I'm sure that's where you get it from."

"Did you tell your parents?" Scott leaned forward, always interested in my parents' opinion, whether likeable or not.

"Do you really want to hear what my dad asked?" My jaw tightened.

"He wondered if my dad was gay, right?" He sighed.

"And can you believe that my mother still thinks we should be a couple so they can have grandkids?"

"Why would my dad be gay and not him?"

"Because you're a guy and I'm not." If either of our fathers were considered simple, I'd say it was mine.

"He wants to get together again tomorrow," Scott said. "I told him we could do dinner."

"Okay. Do you want to bring him here?"

Scott's eyes shifted to mine. "Would you mind?"

"Of course not. I also think it'll be good for you to out yourself to him and see how he reacts."

"He'll probably be on the next plane out of here." Scott leaned back into the couch.

"I think he's more with it than that. Besides, I won't allow my dad to come around while he's here."

"Hey, wait a minute." Scott straightened up again. "Maybe it might be good for the old Baxter to meet my dad. Or the other way around."

"Why's that?" When Scott referred to my dad as the old Baxter, I knew what he really meant to say was the old Bastard and even though sometimes I referred to my dad that way, I got on Scott's case every time he did. We both settled on the old Baxter.

"Maybe if he sees the old Baxter accepting us, it'll be easier for him."

"I wouldn't say that either of my parents have fully accepted us," I said. "And you also don't know Ari. He could be a bigger Baxter than my dad. He could be a real ass...I mean Arihole with this. Hey, that kind of works."

Scott laughed. "Maybe it might be fun to see the two of them together. I wonder what Baxter would say to him?"

"I think my dad would be quiet at the start. He usually doesn't say much until he knows he can control the conversation."

"It's going to be hot out again tomorrow." Scott rubbed his hands together. "Maybe we could put on a barbecue. What do you think?"

"You want me to be here too?" I already had plans.

"Why not? It's your house, after all."

"I don't know if it's a good idea to have my dad here," I said. "Why don't you and Ari use the night to have some bonding time with just the two of you. Besides, I'm having dinner with Mary tomorrow night."

"Perfect." He clapped his hands together. "We can invite Mary too. We'll have one big family dinner."

I knew it was my mother's choir night and she never missed it. I wouldn't have to invite her so it might be tolerable. "I suppose you want me to get things ready while you're at work?"

"Of course." Scott smiled. "I'll pay for everything."

"You're not planning to out yourself, are you?"

"What's the hurry? Let's just let things unfold tomorrow night and see what happens."

"Okay then," I said, "maybe I'll out myself to him."

"Hmmm." Scott rubbed his chin. "That might work."

"If I do that, you know my dad will out you then?"

"You're right," Scott said. "Maybe we shouldn't invite the old Baxter after all."

"Are you kidding?" I said. "My dad may have his faults, but he can be useful sometimes. This way you won't have to stress about outing yourself. It'll be done for you." I stood up and headed toward the kitchen. Scott followed.

"There's only one problem." I reached for a glass as I replayed the whispered dinner invitation when our mother left the room. "I got the sense Mary wants to talk to me about something. She may not want to come here for dinner."

"You just saw her tonight." Scott leaned against the kitchen counter, blocking the sink I wanted to access. "If it's that important, I'm sure she'd have talked to you about it tonight."

"Maybe she didn't want my parents to hear."

"You could have gone for a drink afterward," he said.

"She had to meet Jonathan. He keeps her on a tight leash." I never liked my brother-in-law and his slick way of charming my parents with unnecessary compliments.

"That doesn't sound good." Scott shifted so I could access the tap. "And what about old Johnny Boy? Do we have to invite him too?"

"Nope." I took a drink. "Mary said it would be just the two of us."

"That's good." Scott never liked him either, sensing disdain whenever they talked. "Where's Johnny Boy going to be?"

"Working I imagine. I'll have to check with Mary to see if

she's okay with this. It's not often that Mary has time to herself and as I said, it seemed like she wants to talk to me about something."

"Well, whatever it is," Scott said, "it can't be as important as this."

Chapter Seven

AS I PULLED up in front of Mary's monstrosity of a house, I wondered if I should have bought a convertible. I loved my ruby red Mustang, but when there was no rain I longed to go topless. I wanted to feel free and look cool—especially as I pulled up in front of Mary's.

Mary had agreed to come to the barbecue. She had always been fascinated with the fact that Scott was adopted and was curious about Ari. I imagined Scott was right and whatever she wanted to talk to me about wasn't as important as this.

Mary had been watching for me and motioned at the window that she'd be out in a minute. As usual, she was rushing. I rolled down my window and turned the engine off. It was another scorcher.

Scott had already picked up Ari and they were at the house, bonding I hoped. My dad seemed pleased to have been invited. I told him I'd pick him up after getting Mary.

"Sorry!" Mary called out as she slammed the front door shut and hurried to lock it.

"No problem. Take your time." I started the engine and closed my window. I nudged up the air-conditioning and watched Mary sprint down the driveway. She wore a pink long-sleeved sweater set and navy twill shorts. Her delicate sandals were much dressier than the sports ones I normally wore.

Mary got in, shut the door, and put her purse at her feet before reaching for the seat belt. "Dad will be upset if we're late."

"I imagine he's still sitting in his favorite lawn chair with a beer in his hand. If I had a truck, we could just lift him into the back and he wouldn't even have to move."

"What time are we supposed to be there?" Mary was distracted and kept fidgeting with her purse. She pulled her sweater closed at the front and held onto the edges as though she was cold.

"Are you okay?" I slowly pulled away, fearing something was up.

"Me? Why? Why would you ask?"

"You seem stressed or something," I said.

"Do I? Everything's fine." She stared out her side window.

We drove a few blocks in uncomfortable silence so I put the

radio on. A Jennifer Nettles song was playing—"His Hands." I turned up the volume and hummed along to the tune, especially the chorus. The song had a cheery beat, but not so cheery subject. It was about domestic abuse but I liked the tune and never really thought about the significance of the words.

"Please turn that off!" Mary's voice shook as she dug a tissue out of her purse and wiped her eyes.

I silenced the radio and swerved to the curb, my heart pumping with dread. "Mary, what's going on?"

"I'm sorry," she said, "but that song..." She blew her nose and stifled a sob.

"Oh my God, Mary, is Jonathan beating you?"

No reply. Just more tears.

"Fuck." I pounded the steering wheel. "How long has this been going on?"

Mary sobbed, her face buried in her hands. I didn't know what to do. I felt like I should put my arm around her or something, but it was awkward in the car. I put a hand on her shoulder. "You're staying with me tonight."

"I can't." Mary shook her head.

"Okay, then we're driving to the police station." I put the car in drive but kept my shaking foot on the brake.

"No, please don't." Mary wrenched her face out of her hands, reddish green eyes glaring at me. "No one will believe me. And he'll have me disbarred."

"He can't do that." I eased the car into park.

"Yes he can and I know that's what'll happen. He's a top-notch surgeon for fuck's sake." Mary never swore.

"He's a top-notch prick for fuck's sake." I felt like yelling. "Anybody who touches my little sister is in big shit with me."

I heard a text come into my phone, which I was trying to balance on my lap. It was from Scott, wondering where we were.

"Okay, here's what we're going to do," I said. "I'll call dad and say something came up and I won't be able to pick him up tonight."

"No, don't do that," Mary said. She straightened up and blew her nose again. "Let's go. I'm not going to let this ruin everyone else's evening."

"We can't ignore this." My stomach churned with dread.

"Don't worry about me." Mary forced a smile. "I'll be okay."

"Of course I'm going to worry about you." I hit the steering wheel again. "And just wait 'til I get my hands on that fucking prick."

"Barbra, I can handle this on my own." She tapped my arm. "And please don't tell anyone, especially Mom and Dad. Now let's go. Dad will be wondering where we are."

Scott sent another text full of questions marks. I quickly responded with a *C u soon* then pulled away from the curb to pick up our dad. I didn't know what else to do.

My dad was sitting on a lawn chair when we pulled into the driveway, just like I had predicted. The house was starting to look a bit run down on the front. It wasn't anything that a coat of paint and a few new windows couldn't fix, but that's just how it was with my dad. He was a good guy though and would never hit our mother, or us.

I got out of the car in time to hear my dad groan as he struggled out of the lawn chair. He staggered toward my car. I hoped it was from stiff leg muscles.

"I bet you wish you bought the convertible, eh?" His comment was followed by a weather report then a few words on how dry his lawn was looking. I stood at the opened passenger door while Mary climbed into the back seat. My dad wasn't used to getting into the long low seats of the Mustang and it was always a challenge for him to get his seat belt sorted out.

Back in the driver's seat, I caught a glimpse of Mary in my rearview mirror. She looked fine. I wasn't feeling fine though. Our dad, totally oblivious to what had just happened, rested his arm on the passenger door and tapped his fingers. He was in a good mood.

"So what do you think we'll talk about?" He didn't wait for an answer. "I suppose we could ask him about Iceland. Never been there, except through TV, and can't say I'd ever want to go. It must be so cold. And it's so far away from everything. Scott should consider himself lucky he grew up in Canada instead of Iceland."

As annoying as my dad was being with his finger tapping and nattering on, I was relieved for him to do all of the talking for the moment.

"Barbra, your neck is all red." He was looking at me. "So are your ears. You got too much sun. What were you doing out in the sun anyway with this heat?"

I snapped back to the moment and out of my fantasy of beating the shit out of Jonathan. It was just in time too because I was turning into my driveway. I parked beside Scott's car. "They beat us here."

"Good," my dad said. "I hope dinner's ready because I'm

starving." He struggled with his seat belt then grabbed onto the door and frame to get out. "With this hot weather, it seems like I can't get enough to drink. I sure hope you have some decent beer, Barbra."

"I think I might have one too," Mary said as she climbed out of the back.

I needed one also, but I was the designated driver. I didn't know how I was going to get through the next few hours.

Chapter Eight

ARI AND SCOTT sat on our cozy but somewhat rickety deck under the shade of a large patio umbrella that sheltered a plastic dining table. Scott jumped up, almost knocking over his chair. "You made it."

"Of course," I said. "Traffic was bad."

"The traffic was fine," my dad said. We had walked around the outside of the house into the backyard. "The girls were slow getting to my place. That's why we're late."

"Ari," I said, "I'd like you to meet my dad, Baxter Burnaby."

"Hello, Baxter." He struggled to get up, but then just held out a hand as my dad shuffled onto the deck. "I'm Ari Agnarsson."

"Boy, you sure look like Scott." My dad slapped his hand into Ari's.

"And I can see that Barbra looks like you," Ari said.

Scott smirked. He liked to tease and say that if I cut my hair any shorter I'd look just like my dad.

My dad hovered over Ari because Ari's attempt at standing didn't work. He was sitting in an awkward corner between the deck railing and the table, but if he'd been standing, he would have hovered over my dad.

When Ari noticed Mary, he made another attempt to stand and this time managed it. He offered his hand to Mary. "You must be Barbra's sister, Mary. Scott told me that you would be joining us. It is very nice to meet you."

"It's so wonderful to meet you too, Mr. Agnarsson." She could be so charming, even in distress. Their hands slid into each other.

"Please, call me Ari." He covered Mary's hand with both of his before letting go and reclaiming his seat. "I can't say that Mr. Agnarsson was my father, as you Canadians would say, but it still makes me feel old."

"You were adopted too?" My dad's forehead creased as he looked at Ari.

I noticed Mary backing away toward the patio doors.

"No, not at all," Ari said. "My father was Mr. Agnar Jonsson."

"Oh, so your parents weren't married," my dad said as he sat beside Ari.

I was starting to feel awkward, but Ari didn't seem to mind.

He put his arms on the table and leaned forward. "We do things a bit different in Iceland." Agnar was my father's given name. That is why my last name is Agnarsson. You see? I am Agnar's son. My grandfather's name was Jon Sigurdsson. My father was Jon's son, or Agnar Jonsson.

"Sounds confusing." My dad tapped his fingers on the table.

I had lots to learn about Iceland.

"My son would be called Ari's son or Arisson." Ari continued.

"Scott Arisson." I looked at Scott who was still hovering by the patio doors and noticed that Mary had already disappeared inside. "It has a nice ring to it, don't you think?"

"Sure, whatever. Ready for a beer, Baxter?"

"I thought you'd never ask."

"Jeez, Dad, we just got here." I inched toward the patio door.

"Hey, I was getting thirsty waiting in the hot sun for you to pick me up."

When Scott handed my dad a beer, I snuck into the house in search of Mary. I found her in my bedroom, sitting on the edge of the bed with a fist full of tissues.

"I'm sorry, Barbra. I just need a few more minutes to get a hold of myself. And please, don't let anyone, especially Dad, know there's anything wrong."

"How long has this been going on?" I sat beside her.

"Things haven't been good for a while now. I don't know what to do." Mary buried her face in her hands and started sobbing again.

I wasn't used to seeing Mary cry and we never had a touchy feely sister-type of relationship. I didn't know whether to put an arm around her or tell her to stop crying. I felt I should say something other than the profanities about Jonathan whirling around inside my head.

"Scott has a friend who works at a crisis center. I can get you her number."

"I can't call anyone," Mary said. "Jonathan will find out and he'll kill me."

"Did he actually say he'd kill you?" I jumped up, fingernails digging into my palms.

"He didn't say that, but it's how I feel sometimes." Mary blew her nose then stood. "We should get back out there."

"How can you let him get away with this?" I struggled to keep my voice low. "We need to tell the police."

"They're not going to do anything." Mary said. "It'll be my word against his. I have to figure this out myself." She pushed past me and walked out of my bedroom then straight into the bathroom. I heard the click of the door lock.

I went into the kitchen where Scott was waiting for me. His eyes were bulging. "What's going on?"

"Shhh! Mary doesn't want anyone to find out."

"Find out what?" Scott whispered.

"That Jonathan's beating her." I could hardly get the words out through my clenched teeth.

"No way." Scott's jaw dropped.

"She just told me." I grabbed a few bowls from the fridge. "That's why we were late. I want her to stay here tonight, but she won't." I yanked off the plastic covers. "There's no way I'm letting her go home." The bathroom door clicked open. "Don't say anything and let's get back out there before she finds us talking about it."

The two men were laughing when we got outside. It was as if they had been the best of buddies for years. My dad was like that. He had lots of experience making friends out of strangers over a beer or two or three.

"Who's ready to eat?" I put the bowls on the table then went over to the sizzling barbecue. I had prepared some salads earlier in the afternoon and Scott barbecued chicken breasts.

"You know I'm starving," my dad said as he stood. "And I'll have another beer with my dinner, but first I need to go inside to make room for it."

"Ari, what can I get you to drink with dinner?" I let Scott deal with the barbecue.

"I will just have water and can get it myself, thank you." He got up with ease from what had been his awkward corner. I was sure my dad had pulled the table out to give Ari more room. He could be good at fixing things when he wanted to be.

We ate out on the deck. There was a light breeze forming and the hot sun had lowered so the temperature was pleasant. The dinner conversation was easy and jovial with a flow that jumped from subjects like the news, weather, Iceland, and Ottawa. Then Mary outed Scott.

"So Scott, how's the float for the gay pride parade coming along?" Mary was so used to Scott and me talking about our lives that it mustn't have occurred to her that we hadn't yet said anything to Ari about us being gay.

Scott's face drained and bulging eyes of discomfort looked at me to get him out of this. I froze.

"Did you decide to call it Pink Pedals?" Mary continued, oblivious to what she had just done. Ari had a slightly open mouth.

Mary finally clued in when Scott said nothing. I didn't know what to say either. What could I possibly say to rescue the situation? My dad ended up coming to the rescue.

"I can't wait to see it." He broke the awkward silence. "Ari, you'll have to come with us if you're still in Ottawa for the parade. My wife, Ruth, and I usually go down to watch the parade. It's too bad she couldn't come tonight, but she won't miss her choir for anything. She's been going to it for years now and likes to sing with the other women."

Ari smiled at Scott. "I would love to. I think my sister, Katarina, would like to be here too. She usually participates in the Reykjavik Pride activities."

Interesting. Scott's aunt was a lesbian.

Ari paused then continued when no one else spoke. "So tell me, Scott, what is this Pink Pedals that you are working on?"

"Oh it's nothing, really." Scott's face had regained some color. "A few friends that I cycle with are putting together a float for the parade."

"And will Barbra be part of the Pink Pedals too?" Ari looked at me and smiled.

It didn't take him long to figure me out. "I haven't decided yet."

"Mary's husband is a heart surgeon, you know," my dad said. There was a pause as I think we were all expecting him to say something else to go along with the statement. He didn't.

"Oh," Ari said. "And where is he tonight?"

"Working," my dad said. "He's a busy guy, eh Mary? Always helping others."

I got up and collected plates. "Coffee anyone?"

Mary stood too and grabbed a few bowls of salad before disappearing inside. By the time I got into the kitchen, Scott following close behind with the salt and pepper, Mary was rushing toward the bathroom.

"I can't believe she did that," Scott said.

"Keep your voice down," I whispered. "She's under a lot of stress."

"Aren't we all?" Scott flung a tea towel into the sink.

"Look, you could have had some long drawn out outing process. I think the way it worked out was perfect. Kind of like ripping off a bandage, don't you think?" I loaded the dishwasher.

"I hardly think being outed by someone can be compared to taking off a bandage."

"If you're going to stand there, at least make yourself useful and put on the coffee. This is for you and your dad, after all." Scott's pouting irked me because I now had bigger things to worry about than his ego. I didn't know what to do about Mary. Could she be crying again? Or maybe she was just using the bathroom.

"I'd better check on Mary."

"You're coming back out there, aren't you?"

I ignored Scott and approached the bathroom door. "Mary, are you okay?"

"I'm fine." Mary opened the door as she was pulling her sweater on. I caught a glimpse of a blackened bruise on her right arm.

"Did Jonathan do that to you?" I reached out, but she grabbed my hand and wouldn't let me touch her.

"Why didn't you tell me Ari didn't know about Scott?" She brushed past me and headed toward the kitchen. Scott was still there.

"I'm sorry, Scott." She touched his arm. "I didn't realize you hadn't said anything to Ari yet. I feel so stupid for outing you."

Scott moved toward Mary and put his arms around her. "Don't worry about it. And I'm so sorry for you too."

"Sorry about what?" Mary's eyes flashed to me.

"Let's go back outside." I pushed them toward the patio where my dad and Ari were having another comfortable conversation on the weather.

Ari stood when he saw us. "Scott, you have to work tomorrow and I am getting tired. If it wouldn't bother you, I should head out now."

"Sure, whenever you're ready."

I was relieved Scott didn't coax him to stay longer because I was anxious to get some time alone with Mary.

"It was nice meeting you, Baxter." Ari looked down as he shook my father's hand. They were both standing now.

"The pleasure was all mine," my dad said. "Barbra, I'm ready to head out now too."

Ari turned to me. "I am so happy that you and Scott are taking care of one another." He stretched out his arms and pulled me into a bear hug. "I can see that you have a good life here. Thank you for the nice dinner and company."

"You are very welcome," I said, tapping his back.

Ari released me then turned to Mary and took her hand in his. "It was so nice to meet you, Mary. I hope we will see each other again."

"I'm sure we will." Mary smiled.

"Bebs, I can give your dad a ride home too if you want."

"That would be great." I really wanted to talk to Mary and with our dad around I was sure she'd try to find a way out of it. I was determined to not let that happen.

Chapter Nine

AFTER THE GUYS left, Mary quietly helped tidy up. I opened a chilled bottle of white Chardonnay and poured us each a large glass. I hoped it would help her relax so she'd tell me what was going on. It would also be my excuse as to why I couldn't drive her home.

I had managed to coax Mary into the living room with the wine. We were both sitting on the couch.

"Mary, you really need to get some help. This isn't acceptable."

"I can handle Jonathan." She sipped her wine.

"No, you can't. Just look at your arm. Here, let me see it again." I leaned over.

"Barbra, please don't." Mary pulled away.

My hands were shaking so I put my glass on the coffee table to keep from spilling it. "Does anyone else know?"

"No." She glared at me. "You told Scott, didn't you?"

"I can't keep something like this to myself."

"You have to." Mary sighed. "Jonathan and I'll get through this. It's very stressful for him at the hospital. He lost a patient the other day, you know. He was performing a double bypass and the patient went into cardiac arrest. He blames himself."

"That doesn't give him the right to take it out on you." I tried to stop clenching my teeth. "What he's doing to you is wrong and you're putting yourself in danger. You need to report him to the police."

"I can't do that." Hair flailed as she shook her head. "I won't do that. I like my house, and I like my lifestyle. I'm not going to risk losing it all."

"You're risking your life for a big house?" In addition to having the salary of a surgeon, Jonathan had family money. "I can't believe you're saying this."

"Everyone loses their temper once in a while." Mary closed her eyes. "Jonathan is human, that's all."

"No, he's not. Well, maybe he's human, but he's certainly not a good one in my book. Besides, you're a successful lawyer and can afford stuff on your own."

"Not in the neighborhood we're in now. And what kind of lawyer would I be if I couldn't handle this on my own? I'd be so embarrassed if my colleagues found out."

"Embarrassed? If *anyone* should be ashamed by this, it's Jonathan. Not you. I'm sure your colleagues would support and even admire you for standing up against the prick."

"I don't think they'd believe me." She gulped her wine.

"Of course they would." I wanted to scream.

"Everyone loves Jonathan and thinks I'm so lucky to have him. Even the neighbors all think he's the best. It seems like every time I see one of them, they comment on how good a guy Jonathan is."

"Why would you want to stay in your house with stupid neighbors like that?" I took a sip of wine as I waited for a response that didn't come. I softened my tone. "What's going on with you? I don't understand how you can let him get away with this."

"I don't want to lose everything." Mary played with her phone. "I don't want to be disbarred."

"He can't get you disbarred. He may be a high and mighty hero of a shit surgeon, but that doesn't give him the power to have you disbarred."

"I gave it to him." She hit a fist against her forehead. "I was so stupid."

"What do you mean?" Mary always followed the rules when we were growing up. It couldn't be that bad.

She shook her head. "I falsified some legal documents that would have brought charges against one of his friends. Actually it wasn't really a friend of his. It was a head surgeon during Jonathan's residency who had gotten into trouble and heard Jonathan was dating a lawyer. It was about ten years ago when Jonathan and I were trying to get established in our professions. It certainly helped Jonathan with his career. As for me, it did nothing but undermine my work with guilt and fear of being caught. I didn't want to do it, but I was so in love with Jonathan. He would do anything for me so why wouldn't I for him?"

Mary twitched then grabbed her phone. "Shit, it's Jonathan. I have to take it."

She answered before I had a chance to react. I felt like grabbing the device and throwing it through the window.

"Barbra and I are just sitting here talking. Okay." She put the phone back in her lap. "He's on his way to pick me up."

"You can't go with him. I won't let you."

Mary stood, clutching her phone and empty wine glass. "I have to. Please don't make this any harder than it already is." She hurried into the kitchen.

I put my face in my hands and closed my eyes. I had to think. And fast. I didn't want to put Mary in more danger than she already was, but I was pretty certain she'd choose Jonathan over me if I caused a scene. Where was Scott and what would he do? I looked for my cell then realized I had left it in the kitchen.

I almost bumped into Mary as she scurried around, trying to decide what to do with her empty wine glass because the dishwasher was full.

· "Just leave it on the counter," I said. "I'll deal with it."

"Thanks for the dinner." She picked up her purse. "Please don't let Mom and Dad know." She kept looking out at the street. "I'll be okay and I don't want you to worry."

"Of course I'm going to worry. You're my little sister and I have to take care of you." I put my arms around her. The returned hug was stiff and short.

My phone was blinking. There was a text from Scott saying he'd stay away until I gave him the okay to come home. I started to write a reply.

Jonathan had pulled into the driveway without me noticing. Mary was out the door and gone before I even had a chance to say goodbye. I hit Scott's number.

"Hey."

"Mary just left with the prick."

"You let her?" Scott was chewing something.

"Where are you?"

"Sitting in the park around the corner. I was waiting to hear from you. I didn't want to interrupt anything but it sounds like I should have come home to talk some sense into the two of you."

"What do you mean the two of us?"

"Well you just let her go."

"I know, I know. What else could I do? She refused to stay and I was afraid she'd side with the prick if I confronted him."

"I suppose you want me to come home and fix things?"

"I need to figure out what to do next. You're always good to bounce ideas off of."

"More like your voice of reason, I'd say. See you in a bit."

I went to the living room and sank into the couch. Another glass of wine and phone in my lap, I had an uneasy feeling about Mary. How could I have just let her go? I wished I could tell my parents about it, especially my mother, but that was out of the question because Mary didn't want them to know.

I didn't have to wait long before Scott pranced into the living room. "Our dads really seemed to hit it off." He plunked down in the red recliner. "Your dad wants Ari to meet your mother. We're going over to your parents' place on Saturday night for dinner."

"Does my mother know?"

"She probably does now. So what did Mary say? What's happening over at the palace?"

"She didn't go into a lot of detail, but I noticed a big bruise on her arm."

"I wondered why she kept a sweater on the whole time. It was boiling out on the deck."

"I don't know what to do." I grabbed my phone. "I'm going to send her a text to make sure she's okay."

"I wouldn't. Old Johnny Boy is probably monitoring her messages."

"You're right." I dropped it back into my lap and moaned. "I can't even send her a text."

"There's not much you can do."

"I have to get her to leave the prick." I pounded the arm of the couch.

"Well you might have the chance to work on her again Saturday night because your dad wants Jonathan to come to the dinner with Mary. I think he wants my dad to see his wife and his other daughter's husband. At least he sure made a point of talking about them on the way home."

"You just gave me the perfect reason to call Mary. I'll check in to see if they got their invitation yet."

Mary's phone rang five times then went to voicemail. "Shit. She's not answering." I didn't leave a message. "Let's go for a drive past her place." I jumped up.

"And do what?" Scott didn't move.

"I don't know. See if Jonathan's car is there and if there's any lights on." It was starting to get dark.

"And that's going to tell you?"

I dropped back down on the couch. "You're right."

"Of course I am. Why don't you just try to forget about it for now? You can't help her if she doesn't want it. All you can do is be there when she needs you."

"What if it's too late? I'd never forgive myself."

"Forgive yourself for what?" Scott leaned forward. "You've done nothing wrong and everything you can do right now."

"I could kill the prick." I knew I really couldn't, but it felt good to say it.

"Yeah right. As if you'd do that."

"I know." I paused. "How did you think things went tonight?"

"I'm just so glad it's over." Scott straightened. "It's a good thing we invited your dad. I couldn't believe your sister though."

"She did you a big favor."

"How?"

"You no longer have to agonize over outing yourself," I said. "Who knows, maybe she even took some of the pressure off Ari. Don't you think it was the perfect opportunity for him to out his sister?"

"I bet you'd like to meet her." Scott stood and started toward the kitchen. "What are you drinking?"

"There's a bottle of white wine in the fridge." I followed him into the kitchen.

"Did Ari say anything more about his sister on the drive home?"

"No. We talked about his cancer though." Scott's tone saddened. "He told me it's spread to his liver and spinal cord. It doesn't sound good."

"I'm so sorry to hear that." We emptied the bottle of wine then sat out on the deck, in the dark.

"He's got to stick around." Scott leaned back in his chair. "I'm thinking about taking a leave from work so I can spend more time with him."

"Did he say how long he's in Ottawa for?"

"No and I didn't ask. I don't want to know when he's leaving. I just want to know that he's here now."

Scott's family history was complicated. I knew he considered me family and I was touched, but it was nice to see him starting to open up to Ari. Scott had left home when he was seventeen because his adoptive father wouldn't accept that he was gay. He seldom spoke about that time in his life and I didn't push him. My family and I kind of adopted him and he was always included in family activities if he wanted to be.

"Where's he staying?" I wanted to support Scott in whatever way I could and was prepared to let Ari share the basement.

"He found himself a place in a rooming house downtown. He said he's paid for the month."

"And then after that?" I asked.

"He didn't say. But you know, Bebs, I was thinking maybe he could stay with me, in the basement. What do you think?"

Scott knew me so well. "Do you think you could handle that?"

"Sure, why couldn't I?" He reached for his wine.

"What if you get really close to him and then you lose him? Could you handle that?"

"He's not going to die, you know." Scott stiffened. "There are all kinds of treatments for cancer. It may be tough but he'll get through it."

"I would think he'd have to be home in Iceland for treatments," I said. "I wonder how he arranged things to come to Canada with such a condition? I'm sure he wouldn't have any health care coverage if something happens to him here."

"I don't know and I don't want to know." Scott's chair scraped against the deck as he stood. "I think I'm ready for bed. It's been a long day."

I stayed outside a bit longer, thinking of Mary and wondering about Ari's sister. What did she look like and was she single? When I finally did get into bed, I had a long restless night of tossing and turning.

Chapter Ten

I TIMED MY morning jog to finish right after Scott left for work. Pondering my professional future and what I wanted to do with the rest of my life was on my agenda.

I showered then made myself a coffee and two slices of toast with peanut butter and jam for my ritualistic breakfast. The table on the back deck beckoned so I grabbed my computer and sat outside.

The morning air felt fresher than it had all week. A light breeze played with the corners of my paper napkin and a few clouds shaded me from the sun. A pair of female cardinals landed in the ceramic birdbath on the lawn, splashing around and playing together in the fresh water that Scott must have added before leaving for work.

Life with Scott was good, we were family, and he would never do anything to hurt me. Where would things go now that Ari was in Scott's life? I liked living with Scott and hoped things would stay the same. I bit into a piece of toast and it tasted good, like it did every morning.

I continued watching the two cardinals as wings flapped, water droplets sparkled, and feathers ruffled in the shared bath. The last time I shared a bath I was so in love. That was six years ago and I didn't think I'd ever get over it.

A red male cardinal swooped down and perched on the edge of the birdbath. In an instant he was gone and so was one of the females. The remaining bird sat still in the water as though trying to figure out what had just happened.

I could relate to the now lonely bird. In my case, it was another female dressed in red that had swooped in and Ellen, my life partner of five years, followed her away.

I wondered what Ellen was up to these days. She had moved to Vancouver with her new lover, but I heard the relationship had ended and Ellen was back in Ottawa. Would she ever try contacting me again?

I opened up Facebook and although we weren't friends, I had found Ellen's page many times before. Her privacy settings were fairly strict, but my heart always palpitated when I saw her profile picture. It came up right away again this time and she smiled back at me. Ellen's long brown hair I had loved playing with was still in a ponytail. It was always so soft and left my fingers smelling like her lilac shampoo. My heart melted, but my head throbbed because I knew I shouldn't be thinking about her.

Scott would be upset if he knew I was thinking about Ellen again. When he had moved in with me, my break up with Ellen was still recent and I was messed up. I had been so in love with her and thought for sure she felt the same about me. I was even starting to think about having a child and raising it with Ellen.

Scott had helped me move on with my life, or at least get out of the deep depression I was in. We helped each other during that time because Scott was also reeling over his break up from Stephen. Stephen had cheated on Scott many times and with many different partners. Scott finally walked out on him after coming home early one afternoon and catching Stephen having sex with one of the guys on their volleyball team. Stephen tried for months to get Scott back. He told Scott the different partners were just fuck buddies and didn't mean anything. Scott was stronger than I would have been if Ellen had tried to get me back.

Ever since Stephen, Scott would not commit to any relationship. He'd had his share of dates and flings, but nothing serious ever came of them. He once told me that he didn't have a very strong sex drive and figured that's what broke up his relationship with Stephen. He could have a relationship without sex, but he couldn't have one without trust.

Ellen's picture was mesmerizing with her toned abs and tanned skin. I couldn't stop staring. I wondered what it would be like to see her again. Ellen was a police constable with the Royal Canadian Mounted Police and had told me she loved the adrenalin rush her job sometimes gave her. I longed for an adrenalin rush of my own.

I could always send her a quick message to say hi and see if she responded. My heart rate picked up. No. I couldn't do it. I exited Facebook and started surfing for information on developing a plan for the construction business I wanted to start.

I found a template and looked at the type of information I needed to include. I wanted to help fight climate change by designing and building super insulated houses. I would also offer services for renovating existing houses to bring them up to the passive house standard. It would be a hard sell because the cost of retrofitting an older house to become super-insulated was almost prohibitive. It was much more gratifying for most homeowners to put out extra money for sexy things like a granite counter top or marble flooring rather than triple-glazed windows.

It was kind of like buying boring, practical underwear that nobody saw but could make all the difference if it fit properly and provided comfort. That kind of underwear just wasn't sexy, unless of course it was on Ellen.

I hoped my dad would help out with the sales and marketing part of the business, but first I had to convince him. I planned to use his name and years of experience to promote my company. I also wanted him to help retrofit my house to the passive house standard. My retrofitted house would be my sales model and the standard clients could strive toward. I planned to take training and get professional certification for designing and building passive houses, but my dad had a lifetime of experience in construction. It would make a perfect rebirth of BB Construction as a family business. If only my dad would go for it and my mother would let him. Even Mary could get involved as our company lawyer, should the need ever arise.

The lonely cardinal played in the birdbath, as though waiting for the other female to come back. I clicked on Facebook again and just had to type an E in the search field to bring up Ellen. I clicked on the message box and typed in "Hi" then rushed to delete it, but my pinky finger somehow brushed across the keys and the message was sent. Shit. My heart pounded. There had to be a way to retract the message.

Too late as Ellen instantaneously replied with a phone number and request for me to call her. Like now? What would I say? I had to try three times before dialing the correct number. She answered on the first ring.

"Hey, Bebs." Ellen sounded thrilled to hear from me. "Is that you?"

"Hi." Beads of sweat tickled my forehead.

"I've been thinking about you so much, Bebs." Was she really? "I wanted to call, but didn't think you'd ever want to hear from me again."

"I heard you moved back to Ottawa." Stay calm.

"Can you believe it? I didn't think I'd ever move back here, but shit happens and things change."

Tell me about it. I should just hang up.

"It's great to hear from you," she said, her voice sounding sincere. "What are you up to these days?"

I didn't want to talk to Ellen about my life. I was curious about hers though. "I've been very busy with things. And you? Still with the RCMP?"

"Yes. I'm a sergeant now." Pride in her tone.

"Good for you." I'd always loved seeing Ellen in her red uniform. "Congratulations."

"Gee, thanks. We should get together for coffee. Are you at work now?"

"Sort of." She didn't have to know I was unemployed at the moment.

"I'd really like to see you. Are you able to meet for a coffee over lunch?"

No. Don't go there. "I might be." I felt like the lone cardinal was flapping around inside my stomach.

"How about noon? Would that work for you?" She sounded so chipper.

"Sure."

We agreed to meet at a coffee shop in the west end of the city at a convenient location. What had I just done? If only I were in a stable relationship and could show Ellen that I'd moved on with my life. My relationship with Scott, although comfortable, didn't qualify. I'd dated over the years since Ellen and even had a few relationships, but none of them lasted. No other woman ever grabbed at my heart the way Ellen had.

The rest of the morning was a write-off because I couldn't think about anything else other than all the possibilities that could come out of my meeting with Ellen. I felt excited to see her again, but I was still so angry with her and now with myself for contacting her.

Ellen stood in the parking lot, leaning against a shiny black SUV with tinted windows when I pulled up. Her skin was indeed tanned and dark sunglasses hid her beautiful brown eyes. She wasn't in uniform and wore a sleeveless blue T-shirt with navy cargo shorts and sports sandals. Her arms were toned and the muscles in her legs matched. My T-shirt wasn't sleeveless and my arms matched my legs too, but not Ellen's. Our cargo shorts and sandals matched though.

"Wow, nice car," Ellen ran her hand across the hood of my Mustang as I stepped out onto the pavement. "I love the color. When did you get it?"

Oh that ponytail, how I wanted to touch it again. "A few months ago."

"It's so good to see you, Bebs." Ellen wrapped her arms around me and pulled me into a firm hug that lingered. I inhaled the familiar lilac shampoo and wanted to cry tears of joy, mixed with sadness and anger.

"Let's go inside," Ellen said. "I'll buy you a coffee."

Buying me a coffee was the least Ellen could do. I looked for a quiet table in a corner as Ellen ordered. The last time I was in a coffee shop, Scott and I were meeting Ari. I wished Scott was with me now, but I knew he never would be.

Friends used to call us Bebellen because we were always together, joined at the hips. Our friends stayed Ellen's friends after the breakup because most of them were with the RCMP. Ellen dumped me for another constable in the RCMP. Donna. I had heard they became known as Donnellen. I don't know what I would have done if it hadn't been for Scott.

"Two cream and one sugar, right?" Ellen placed the coffee in front of me.

"You remembered."

"Of course I do." Ellen sat down, her ponytail over her right shoulder, and locked her brown eyes with mine. "There are lots of things I remember about you."

"How long have you been back in Ottawa?" Breathe.

"It's been two months." Ellen let go of my eyes and sipped her coffee. "I kept hoping we'd run into each other because I was afraid to call you after everything, you know."

Ellen dropped her eyes to the table, and I knew she was waiting for me to respond. I wanted to sip my coffee and act as though she really meant nothing to me now, but I was too afraid to pick up the mug in case she saw my hands shaking.

Ellen finally moved her eyes back up to mine. "Are you with anyone?"

"No." I looked down. "And you?"

"No." She sighed. "It's been lonely the last while. I hope we can at least be friends."

She said at least. What did that mean? Could we ever be more than friends again? Was she still interested in me? "I'm here, aren't I?"

Her hand reached across the table and covered mine with that familiar warm touch. It felt nice. "I'm so glad you are. How are your parents?"

I didn't move my hand. "They're doing great. Both are retired now and loving it."

"And Mary?" Ellen took her hand away. "Do she and Jonathan have any kids yet?"

"Not yet." Jonathan, miserable prick that I wanted to clobber. Ellen had no doubt they'd still be together. "And your family? Are they all fine?" Ellen's parents and one brother lived across the country in Victoria, so I hadn't known them as Ellen had known mine.

"Yeah they're great, but they weren't happy to see me move back to Ottawa."

"I guess they wouldn't be." Neither would my family.

"I hope you're happy I moved back." Ellen's eyes met mine again. "I'm sure glad we've reconnected."

"I don't know how I feel." But I *did* know. I was delighted I'd screwed up and the message got sent after all. "Do you have the day off?"

"Not really," Ellen said. "I'm flying back to Vancouver later this afternoon."

My heart dropped.

"I have some meetings out there next week," she said. "I decided to go out for the weekend and tidy up a few last things to complete my move back here."

Was she leaving a mess? "Oh, I see." I risked picking up my coffee, grasping the cup with two hands. "How long will you be gone?"

"A week. I fly back next Sunday. Maybe we can have dinner on Monday?"

"Maybe." No, I have to move on.

"So what have you been up to? Which government department are you with these days?"

"I'm no longer working for the government."

"No kidding. I thought you were a lifer."

"I was." I was referring to our relationship.

"What happened?"

"Shit happens and things change," I said.

"Where are you working now?"

"I'm going out on my own. I want to start my own company so I can call the shots."

"Wow, Bebs. That sounds exciting. Are you going to offer consulting services in architectural design?"

I hadn't thought of that angle. "I'm exploring a number of possibilities. And you? What brings you back to Ottawa?"

Ellen smiled. "My promotion to sergeant and a chance to work on the human trafficking file."

"Sounds interesting."

"It's scary, shocking actually." Ellen looked at the big black sport watch on her left wrist. "Sorry to cut this short, but I have to head out to finish packing and get to the airport."

"Sure." I stood up.

"I knew we wouldn't have a lot of time, but I really wanted to see you today." Ellen followed as I walked toward the exit. My legs felt heavy and my breathing shallow.

When we got outside, I waited to see what Ellen would do. She put her arms around me and brushed her lips against my cheek before resting her head on my shoulder.

"We'll talk later this week," she said.

"Enjoy your flight." I couldn't think of anything else to say. Not while standing in a parking lot with shaking knees and a fear of what might happen if her lips got anywhere near mine. I pulled out of the hug.

"See you around," I said.

I could still smell Ellen's lilac shampoo as I drove away and knew I'd have to take another shower when I got home.

Chapter Eleven

I NEEDED TO talk to someone about seeing Ellen. Mary would have to do since I would never tell Scott. She could keep a secret and I wanted to check in on her anyway. I dialed Mary's cell as soon as I got home, but it immediately went to voicemail. I redialed a few minutes later. Voicemail again. She picked up on my third try.

"Hi. What's up?"

"Do you have time to chat?"

"What happened?" She sounded concerned.

"Nothing." I paused. "I saw Ellen today."

"Oh no. She's back in Ottawa?"

"Yes." I kept an eye on the kitchen window in case Scott came home early. "We had coffee together."

"Oh, Barbra, don't get tangled up with her again."

"We just had coffee," I said. "She's on her way to Vancouver right now."

"Good riddance. I hope she doesn't come back."

"She's moved back. By herself."

Mary paused. "And how are you feeling about that?"

"I don't know." I pinched myself to make sure I wasn't dreaming, that I'd really had coffee with Ellen. And she wanted to see me again.

"Does Scott know about this?"

"Of course not. He'd be furious."

"So she called you?"

"Sort of."

"Please don't tell me you called her."

I stayed silent.

"What were you thinking?" Mary's voice was calm.

"I don't know," I said. "Are you in the office?"

"No. I'm working from home. Why don't you come over for a swim? Jonathan won't be here until later tonight."

"Is that okay?"

"Of course it is. I'm not on a leash or tied up or anything."

"Don't make light of Jonathan hitting you. How was he when he picked you up last night?"

"Good actually. He surprised me with tickets to Paris in September. And he says he's looking forward to dinner at Mom and Dad's tomorrow night."

"Nice guy. Don't be fooled by that."

"You're a fine one to talk," Mary said. "Maybe Ellen didn't hit you, but she sure did her share of damage."

"I know. That's why I need someone to talk to."

"Grab your suit and come on over."

The doorbell on Mary and Jonathan's house had a majestic sound to it. It reminded me of a Disney movie with a princess and a castle. *Beauty and the Beast* came to mind.

Mary opened the front door and led me into a large, bright entryway with a silver grey marble floor bordered by a stately oak staircase leading to the second story. Barbie, Mary's Bengal cat, circled her feet.

"Good timing because I just finished up my last file for the day," Mary said. "We'll head right out to the pool. What can I get you to drink?"

"I'd like a strong shot of rum, but since I'm driving, I'll take a cold diet cola without the rum if you have any."

The pristine pool beckoned on this blistering Friday afternoon. I approached the edge and looked at the mermaid on the tile bottom. Ellen and I had enjoyed a private swim with her one scorching summer evening while Mary and Jonathan vacationed in Europe. Ellen had joked about having a threesome in the pool and I thought it was funny, until Ellen left me for Donna shortly afterward. I came to hate the sight of that mermaid I had secretly named Donna and would spit in the pool every chance I got.

"Barbra, did you just spit in my pool?"

Whoops. "Sorry, I got a bug in my mouth."

"Go ahead and dive in, but don't drown yourself." There was a time after Ellen that Mary had been seriously worried I might do something like drown myself.

"Not a chance." I did a cannon-ball jump into the water and let myself sink as close to the bottom as I could before kicking Donna in the face and re-surfacing. "The water's perfect. It feels so refreshing."

Mary was in the pool now too and swam up to me. "So what's going on with you and Ellen?"

"Nothing." I quickly scanned for any visible bruises, but there were none other than the fading one on her arm.

"Okay, let me rephrase my question," she said. "What's going on with you? Why would you even give Ellen the time of day?"

"I was curious, I guess."

"You *guess?* Barbra, you can't guess about Ellen. You can't go back there."

"I know."

"So what happened? Why did you call her?" Mary swished her arms in the water.

"It's complicated. She wants to have dinner."

"Please don't tell me you're thinking about it."

"It's been six years and I still haven't gotten Ellen out of my system." I kicked my legs to keep from sinking.

"Well then maybe you need to take a good laxative." Mary's lips puckered. "Considering the shit she put you through, you must be so bunged up it's a wonder you can do anything."

"What about you and Jonathan?" Water splashed as I moved my hands. "He's putting you through shit and you're not leaving him."

"That's different."

"No it's not. Ellen may have cheated, but she never laid a finger on me. Has Jonathan ever cheated on you?"

"No. Never."

"How can you be so sure?"

"I just know he'd never do that. He's trying, you know. I didn't ever see Ellen try to get you back."

"People make mistakes. It's not like I was perfect either."

"You never would have cheated on Ellen," Mary said.

"Cheating isn't in my genes." I leaned back and closed my eyes.

"How did you feel when you were with her this afternoon?" Mary sounded like our mother. "Maybe you weren't cheating with her, but you were doing something you don't want Scott to know about. How would you define that?"

"I don't know." I dunked my head to cool off. "It's not like Scott and I are married or anything."

"You know that trust is very important to Scott. I think you need to tell him you saw Ellen."

"I will, but I don't think the time is right." I needed a change of subject. "He has enough on his mind with Ari."

"Ari seems like such a nice man," Mary said. "Do you think he's going to die soon?"

"I hope not. I think he's helping give Scott more purpose in life. Scott's so used to focusing on himself, but now there's Ari to think about."

"This time Scott won't be around to pick up the Ellen pieces like the last time."

"I know, I know. Maybe I just had to see Ellen again to know what it would be like."

"How does she look?"

"Great. She's a sergeant now."

"It sounds like you're still drooling over her. I'm worried about you."

"I'm worried about me too."

"You really need to stay away from her." Mary turned our mother's look-a-like eyes on me.

"Please don't tell anyone about this." I felt like a misbehaving child.

"I won't," she said. "And especially not Mom and Dad."

My mother never liked Ellen because they both battled to control me while my dad saw that she made me happy. When she stopped making me happy, my father teamed up with my mother to insist I forget all about Ellen.

I didn't stay at Mary's for supper. I wanted to get home and flop on my bed to relive my meeting with Ellen and convince myself I was going to take Mary's advice and not let Ellen back in my life. Once there, I grabbed my computer and brought it to the bedroom with me. Ellen had sent me a Facebook friend request along with a short message saying how happy she was to see me again.

I ignored her friend request and opened up my music library. Hidden in my playlist was an old Joan Armatrading song, "The Weakness in Me." The first time I heard the song, Ellen and I were at a Melissa Etheridge concert in Montreal. I had been so in love with Ellen and I found it such a sad song. I never imagined I'd end up listening to it over and over again through inconsolable tears.

After Ellen left me, I wanted so much to be the weakness in her. Each time I had tried reaching out to her, which Scott referred to as stalking, I hoped she'd see her mistake and reach back. Instead she picked up her new life with Donna and moved across the country to Vancouver. I finally realized the real weakness was in *me* and that I was the one breaking down a little bit more each time Ellen rejected me.

If nothing else, my meeting with Ellen was vindication because she had finally reached back. I deleted her friend request.

Chapter Twelve

SCOTT BELTED OUT the words of a song from the *Sound of Music* to announce he was home from work. He liked to sing Barbra Streisand songs to tease me about my name but often got the music of Julie Andrews and Barbra Streisand mixed up.

I was still in my bedroom thinking about Ellen and trying to decide what I was going to wear to dinner at my parents' place. "Get it right," I shouted. "That was Julie Andrews, not Barbra Streisand."

"Oh yeah, I forgot." Scott chuckled.

"My mother would never forgive you for a mistake like that." I went to the kitchen, wondering if Scott would forgive me for a mistake like contacting Ellen.

"You're such a funny girl." Scott's words were garbled. He leaned against the counter, a bottle of roasted peanuts in his hands. "Guess what?"

"I don't know. You tell me." I really wanted to tell him about Ellen.

"My boss gave me the go ahead for a leave of absence." Scott wiggled his hips. "I'll take the next two weeks as vacation and then I can have up to three months off without pay."

That was just what I needed—Scott hanging around all day or wanting me to spend time with him and Ari. "Good for you. What are you going to do over the next few months? Go to Iceland?"

"No way, that's for sure. As much as I hate this heat we've been having, I'm not freezing my buns off in Iceland."

"What about when Ari heads back there?" Maybe I'd have to go to someplace like Iceland after seeing Ellen.

"He's not planning to go back for now. We had lunch today and talked about his plans. He wants to stay in Ottawa and get to know me."

"What about his treatments?" I needed some treatments of my own. Head treatments.

"He told me he's taking some pills for now."

"Pills? What kind of pills? Pain killers?" I could use a few of those.

"I don't know," Scott looked at the floor, his shoulders slumping.

"He told us he has stage four cancer," I said. "I'd think he'd be getting some kind of chemotherapy. Didn't he say anything about that?"

"He didn't say and I didn't want to pry." Scott sighed then looked up. "Let's focus on something more positive. Why don't we go out for dinner to celebrate tonight?"

"Celebrate what?" Seeing Ellen?

"The start of my holidays, of course."

"You only have two weeks of holidays. The rest is without pay. You need to start watching your money."

"Party pooper."

"More like a reality check," I needed one of my own. "You don't want the hills to be alive with the sound of debt."

"I'll just borrow from Ms. Money Bags here."

"I hardly think so. I don't have a job now, remember?"

"You got a package though."

Yes, and the brush of Ellen's lips against my cheek.

"Which has to last me for at least a year," I said. And the rest of my life for Ellen's lips against my cheek because I couldn't let it happen again.

"Well, we should do something tonight."

"The grass needs cutting." I opened the fridge and looked inside to see what I could grab to eat. "We could have an omelet for dinner."

"It's too hot to cut the grass and I'm not in the mood for an omelet. I think I'll bike downtown and grab something there. Why don't you come with me?"

My phone rang. "It's Mary. Hey, Mary, what's up?"

"Hello, Barbra." My heart skipped a beat when I heard the prick.

"What's going on?" I looked at Scott and mouthed that it was Jonathan.

"Can't I call my sister-in-law?"

"Where's Mary?"

"She's in the shower."

"Why are you using her phone?"

"What's with all the questions? I don't have your number programmed into mine so it was easier just to use hers."

"Why are you calling?"

"Good to hear from you too," he said.

"Sorry." Not really. "I was expecting it to be Mary." Scott moved closer and tried to listen in.

"I promised your mother we'd bring a cake for dessert

tomorrow." A nasal inhale. "Could you be a sweetie and pick it up from the bakery for me? Mary and I have a golf game and won't have time."

Fuck you. "Sure, I guess."

"I noticed you called Mary three times this afternoon," he said. "What's up?"

"Nothing." Bastard. "I just wanted to talk to my sister."

"Good. I'll text the details later." Jonathan ended the call.

"Prick." I moaned in anger. "Can you believe him? He wanted to know why I called Mary this afternoon."

"I heard," Scott said. "So, what's up?"

"The hair on the back of my neck." I slammed the phone down on the counter. "Can't I call my sister?"

"It sounds like a bike ride might do you some good."

"Go ahead if you want to eat downtown." I closed my eyes in an effort to calm down. "I'll save my money and have a cheese omelet." Scott and I split the grocery bill to make things easier. It was much cheaper for me because he often ate out and left the food to either go bad or be eaten by me.

"Think of the calories you'd burn with a bike ride downtown," Scott said. "Or are you planning to be a butterball pumpkin for Halloween?"

Had Ellen noticed I'd put on weight? "There'll be a lot less calories in an omelet than in whatever you're going to eat. Besides, I went for a jog this morning when you were still in bed and then a swim this afternoon at Mary's."

"How's she doing?" He lingered at the stairway to the basement.

"She seems fine. She told me she and Jonathan are going to Paris in September."

"Paris, nice."

My phone rang again. "It's my mother."

"I'm out of here," Scott said. "See you later."

"Hi. What's up?"

"Have you talked to Mary today?" Concern in her voice.

"Yeah I was just with her. Why?"

"I called over there this morning and it sounded like she'd been crying."

"Did you ask her about it?" How could I have missed that? Damn Ellen.

"Of course I did. She told me she's fighting off a cold. How could she be catching a cold with this hot weather we've been having? Something's not right."

I wanted to tell my mother, but I couldn't betray Mary just like I knew she wouldn't say anything about Ellen. Ever since Mary and I were kids, we always stuck together and never tattled on each other. Mary had kept secrets many times for me, especially when I was a teen and struggling with my sexuality. I did some stupid things, but Mary never told.

"Well?" My mother was waiting for me to say something.

"Was Jonathan with her?"

"She didn't say. Why? Is he off today?"

"No, but he called me not too long ago and asked if I'd pick up a cake at the bakery for him. He said he promised you he'd bring one for dinner tomorrow."

"Yes, isn't that thoughtful of Jonathan." She was oblivious. "Mary is so lucky to have him."

"He's lucky to have her."

"Barbra, what's that tone about? What's going on?"

"Nothing. I'm just tired."

"Tired? What do you have to be tired about? It's not as if you worked all day."

"In fact I did work today," I said. "I spent the morning working on a business plan."

"It sounds more like a hobby to me," she said. "You're thirty-eight years old. Don't you think it's a bit late to start a business? You should be thinking about making money to save for your retirement since you just gave up a good pension."

"My job in the government was cut. It's not like I just quit it on my own."

"You could have tried harder to find another one and stayed in government. Your father and I still can't believe you walked away from such a good pension."

Grrr. "I'm not thinking about retirement because I still have a long career ahead of me."

"It's time you got a bit more serious about life. You had a good career and the years will go by fast. I'm so glad I have my pension now." She snapped her tongue. "If it wasn't for my pension, your father would still have to work."

Are you finished? I didn't say the words out loud. I learned many years ago not to do that. "I have to go. Scott's waiting for me."

"Oh, what are the two of you up to?"

"We're biking downtown for dinner."

"That sounds like fun," my mother said. "It's still hot out so be careful you don't get sun stroke."

"I will. Love you. Bye."

"I love you too, dear. Bye."

Scott came back into the kitchen just in time to hear that I was biking downtown with him. "You'd better hurry up and change." He smirked.

Chapter Thirteen

NIMBUS CLOUDS, BIG and fluffy with various shades of grey, swirled across the brilliant blue sky they were starting to hide as I drove to the bakery. It was just after one o'clock on Saturday afternoon and I was in my Mustang by myself. Scott had taken his car to get Ari and we'd meet at my parents' place. I felt exhausted after a night of tossing and turning. I kept thinking about Ellen, worrying about Mary, and stressing about seeing Jonathan because of what I might say or do. I had visions of picking up the cake and throwing it at him in front of everyone. I could never do it for Mary's sake and for what Ari might think of me after a stunt like that. If only my mother knew what was going on, she'd grab the cake and hurl it at Jonathan herself.

When I got to the bakery, it occurred to me Mary probably didn't even know about the cake otherwise she'd have managed to pick it up. Jonathan liked to get all the credit for things like bringing a fancy cake to my parents' dinner party.

By the time I'd left the bakery, the sun was totally hidden and a few clouds were starting to look like blackened bruises. Kind of like the bruise I saw on Mary's arm.

Mary's white Mercedes SUV was parked in our parents' driveway when I pulled up to the curb. I wondered if Jonathan had bailed in the end. I was trying to spot figures through the living room window when an approaching vehicle blasted its horn and I almost dropped the cake. I flung my head around to see Scott's BMW pulling to the curb, two bobbing heads inside.

"Good one." Scott laughed as he got out of the car.

"Very funny." I felt like throwing the cake at him.

"You looked like you were spying," Scott said. "Are you afraid to go in or what?"

"Nice to see you again." Ari squeezed my shoulder. "What have you got there in the box?"

"Oh nothing," I said. "Mary's husband asked me to pick up a cake for him."

"That's right." Jonathan had slithered up beside me and took the box. "Thank you so much, Barbra. You're a real sweetie of a sister in-law."

I backed away as Scott stepped forward to introduce Ari. "Hey, Jonathan, I'd like you to meet my birth father, Ari."

"It's nice to meet you, Ari." Jonathan juggled the cake box with one arm as he held out the other to shake Ari's hand. "My wife, Mary, has told me a lot about you."

"Oh, the doctor surgeon," Ari said. "I have heard a lot about you too."

How much had Scott told Ari about Jonathan?

"What's going on out there?" My mother's head hung out the front door. "Come on inside. Barbra, make sure all of your windows are closed because it's going to rain."

"They are." Thunder rumbled in the distance as I entered the freezing house with the blasting air conditioner.

Mary and our dad sat in the living room. He was in his rocker recliner, holding a bottle of beer, while she perched on the couch, glass of water in hand. My mother and Jonathan were in the kitchen, dealing with the cake.

"Hey." My dad got up. "Come on in." He held out his hand to Ari. "Here, take my chair. Barbra will get you a beer."

"Hello, Baxter." Ari shook my dad's hand. "The couch is good for me. Nice to see you again, Mary." He shook her hand then sat beside her.

"I'll take Baxter's chair," Scott said.

"Oh no you won't." My dad dropped back down. "Barbra, get Scott a beer too, eh?"

"Do you have anything hot to drink?" I asked. "It's freezing in here."

"What do you mean it's freezing?" My mother had come back into the living room. My dad jumped up from his chair again.

"Ari, this is my wife, Ruth."

Ari stood to move around the coffee table.

My mother extended a hand across it and smiled at Ari as though he were some exotic creature. "The visitor from Iceland. I've heard a lot about you. It's a pleasure to meet you."

"The pleasure is all mine." Ari grasped my mother's hand.

"I can see where Scott gets his good looks." My mother liked to flatter.

"Oh you are too kind." Ari released my mother's hand and sat back down. He didn't say anything about me getting good looks from anyone.

Jonathan returned to the living room and resumed his place on the other side of Mary.

"Jonathan," my dad said. "How's your beer? Are you ready for another one?"

"Sure, why not. Mary's driving today." He let the remaining

foam from his glass slide into his mouth.

"Barbra, bring another beer for Jonathan too," my dad said.

My mother pulled out a few chairs from the dining room table then relaxed in her rocker recliner and looked at me. "If there's none left in the fridge, we put some in a cooler in the garage."

I nodded and went into the kitchen. Scott was right behind me. I swung open the fridge door and scanned for beer. There were none. I slammed it shut then stomped toward the back door to access the garage.

"Is everything okay in there?" I pictured my mother stretching her neck toward the kitchen.

"There's no beer in the fridge," I said. "I have to go out to the garage."

"Do you need some help?" My mother's chair squeaked as though she were getting up.

"No. I'm fine. Scott's here to help me." I stepped outside before she could say anything more.

The red and white cooler sat on an old wooden table that my mother often used when preparing plants for her small vegetable garden or putting seed into her many bird feeders. My mother took care of the garage. It was tidy and everything had its place. There was even a large mat that covered the floor and their new looking, but older Camry was securely parked near the front of the garage.

"Wow, this place looks cleaner than our house," Scott said. "Don't you wish you'd taken after your mother more than your father?"

"Not really." I opened the cooler and grabbed four bottles of beer. "Although there have been times, especially since finding out about Jonathan being such a prick, that I wish I was more like her and could make life miserable for him."

"He doesn't look like such a prick right now." Scott stood beside me, his eyes wandering around the garage. "Hey, look over there. A pair of bamboo ski poles."

"Where?" I put the beer down.

"They're hanging on the wall just above the front of the car. Maybe your parents will give them to you so you don't have to go garbage picking."

I had forgotten my mother had a pair of bamboo ski poles. She used to go cross-country skiing and even led the cross-country ski club at school for a few years. But that all stopped about twenty years ago when she fell while skiing and broke her right ankle. My mother was furious about her broken ankle and blamed the skis. She wanted them gone, but my father thought they were still good and that maybe Mary or I would use them. It all had come to a head on garbage night.

Mary and I watched from my upstairs bedroom window as our dad made the treacherous journey down the driveway to put the skis in with the garbage. It had been freezing cold and our dad didn't want to go outside, especially after a few beers, but our mother just wanted the skis gone.

Our dad emerged from the garage, juggling the skis to keep them from getting caught between his legs. He had on his brown plaid flannel slippers and could hardly stand because he was sliding all over. Mary and I had almost peed ourselves laughing as we watched him do a near face plant in the snow then hurl the skis toward the garbage pile.

Scott had lifted the bamboo poles off their hook and was studying them. "These would be perfect for you. I'll leave them down and you can ask your mother if you can have them. In the meantime, we'd better get back. Jonathan is waiting for his beer."

"That prick. I'd love to take one of those bamboo poles and shove it right up his ass."

"I think for today you'd better just stick to giving him a beer."

"Oh I'll give him a beer all right." I grabbed one of the bottles and shook it before we went back into the house.

I took the cap off the bottle I didn't shake to make sure my dad got that one. Scott handled his and Ari's beer. I shoved the unopened bottle toward Jonathan.

"Aren't you going to open it for me?" Jonathan looked at me.

"You're a big strong surgeon." I sat down on one of the dining room chairs and could feel my mother's eyes on me.

Jonathan put the bottle down on the coffee table without opening it. They were in the middle of a conversation about Ari's cancer and Jonathan was talking as though he knew everything about melanoma. Mary looked in good spirits as she wore a short sleeve cotton blouse and had no signs of new bruises amidst the goose bumps on her arms. I would have bet she wished she had that sweater from the other day with her now. I was starting to eye the fleece blanket that hung over the back of my mother's chair.

"What are they giving you for treatment?" Jonathan asked Ari. "Actually I'm surprised your doctor even let you come to Canada right now."

"I have had some radiation," Ari said. "I'm in between treatments to give my body a rest. When I get back home, I will start the chemotherapy. "

"Oh," my mother said, "when is that? How long are you here for?"

"I am not sure yet." Ari looked at Scott. "I want to have some time to get to know my son." He turned back to Jonathan. "I hear you and Mary are going on a big trip this fall."

Jonathan's prick of a mouth formed a smile. Most people considered him handsome, but I always thought his mouth was a little too small for his face. His neatly trimmed black mustache did nothing to make it look any bigger. He put his right hand under his nose and spread his thumb and index finger to the ends of his mustache as though holding it in place then turned to Mary. "Yes, I'm taking my Mary to Paris."

His Mary. My ass. She's Mary, period.

"I'm so excited." Mary smiled at Jonathan and put a hand on his knee. She seemed sincerely happy and they looked like the perfect couple. I wanted to gag, but then I thought of Ellen and what it would feel like to put my hand on her knee.

"I always wanted to go to Paris," my mother said. "You're so lucky."

My mother certainly wouldn't have said that if Ellen were to take me to Paris. But then again, my mother knew about the pain and suffering Ellen had put me through, but she didn't know about Jonathan. Yet.

"Now, Ruth, you could've gone to Paris if you wanted to," my dad said.

"Oh yeah, sure, by myself. Paris is a such a romantic city and you expect to send me there by myself."

Jonathan picked up his beer and twisted off the cap. Nothing happened at first, but as he held up his glass and readied to pour, foam flowed up from the bottle and into his lap."

"Dammit," he said.

"Oh my gosh!" My mother jumped up, grabbing the fleece blanket off the back of her chair and rushing over to Jonathan's aid.

"Watch the carpet," I said. I could feel vibrations coming from Scott's chair.

"Barbra, go in the kitchen and get some paper towels," my mother said.

"Barbra, you should've opened the bottle in the kitchen," my dad said.

Jonathan stood up and it looked as if he had peed himself. His ears were red and his hands had formed fists. My mother leaned over the coffee table and tried to pat the front of his pants with her fleece blanket.

"It's fine, Ruth." He grabbed the blanket from my mother and glared at me before scurrying out of the room toward the upstairs bathroom.

I looked at Mary. Her mouth hung open and her eyes raced back and forth.

"Barbra, aren't you going to get the paper towels?" My mother stood in front of the coffee table, studying the puddle of beer that had formed on it. "It's going to run onto the carpet."

"Oh yeah." I shot up from my chair and tried to catch Mary's eyes as I made my way to the kitchen. She would've known I'd planned for Jonathan's beer to overflow because she knew me. Her eyes usually sent me sparkles at times like this, but all I saw were her black pupils. What had I done?

When I reached for the roll of paper towels on the kitchen counter, I looked out the window and noticed that the rain had started. That meant we'd be stuck inside for the rest of the visit. That was just what I needed.

My mother grabbed the roll of paper towels out of my hands when I got back into the living room and began soaking up the beer. Ari and my dad had also noticed the rain and were commenting on the coming storm.

"There could be flooding," my dad said. "We're supposed to get a lot of rain."

"Yes, I heard we are going to get a big thunder and lightning storm today," Ari said.

"It'll be good for the heat we've been having." My mother spoke as she headed to the kitchen, juggling the beer soaked paper towels.

There was a bright flash of lightning and then silence. Everyone was getting ready for the thunder.

Jonathan walked back into the living room. "Mary, get your purse. We have to leave. I just got a page from the hospital. One of my patients is having trouble breathing."

Thunder boomed and then silence again.

"Gee, that's too bad," my dad said after a short pause. "Mary can stay here and Barbra can drive her home."

"No, she can't," Jonathan said. "Mary's my designated driver."

"What's this?" My mother came back into the living room

and looked at Jonathan. "You have to leave already?"

"Yes, sorry, Ruth but duty calls. Thank you for the blanket, but I'm afraid it smells like beer now. As I guess I do too. Mary will have to bring me by our house so I can change before going into the hospital."

"Mary can come back," I said. "After all, we have a nice dessert to eat."

"We'll see," Jonathan said. "She might have to wait for me at the hospital."

"I'll call her and check in to see if she's coming back," I said. "It would be a shame for her to miss dinner with us. And you could always take a cab."

"Barbra," my mother said, "let Jonathan and Mary sort it out. We hope the two of you can come back for dinner. Jonathan we understand how important your job is and that somebody's life may depend on you right now." My mother gave Jonathan a hug.

My dad got out of his chair and gave Mary a hug. "Come back for supper if you can." He let go of Mary and grabbed Jonathan's hand. "Thanks for coming, Jonathan. Go save someone's life now."

Gag.

"Oh the cake," my mother said. "What are we going to do with the cake?"

"Eat it, of course," Jonathan said as he hurried to put on his shoes. He was trying to escape.

"Let me cut you and Mary each a piece before you go." My mother rushed to the kitchen.

"Never mind." Jonathan said. "We don't need any."

My mother came back into the living room with the cake on a platter. The cake was decorated to resemble France's flag with white icing in the middle, blue on the left, red on the right and a chocolate Eiffel Tower in the center.

"It's gorgeous," my mother said. "Thank you, Jonathan."

"You're welcome, Ruth. We really have to go now."

"Let them go," my dad said.

"Yes, sorry," my mother said. "Darn, look it's pouring out there now. You're going to get soaking wet. I'll get my umbrella and Barbra can hold it over you on the way to the car."

"Thank you, Ruth," Jonathan said. "You're so kind."

"Jonathan can run," I said. "He's already wet. I'll help Mary though."

The rest of us stayed for a relaxing dinner inside while the storm raged outside. I ended up eating one too many pieces of the cake and left my parents' feeling stuffed and guilty because I couldn't stop thinking about Ellen.

Chapter Fourteen

THE FOLLOWING WEEK was uneventful. I was proud of myself for not responding to Ellen's attempts to contact me. Scott spent his first five days off work acting as a tour guide, showing Ari many of the city's attractions. They really seemed to enjoy each other's company and were getting closer each day.

I touched base daily with Mary and was beginning to think maybe Jonathan had smartened up and wouldn't hit her again. Mary was convinced of it and seemed happier than ever.

I wasn't feeling happier than ever. My life felt as if it were going nowhere and I doubted my ability to put a good business plan together that clearly articulated what I wanted to do. The problem was that I hadn't yet talked to my dad about his part in my business plan because I was too afraid he'd say no.

Maybe Ellen was right on the mark when she'd asked me whether or not I was going to offer consulting services in architectural design. Ellen always had a way of stimulating me. I could call my consulting firm BB Architecture and have some business cards printed up. That might work.

It was Saturday morning and I was sitting out on the deck with my computer and a coffee. Scott had been out late the night before with some friends and was still in bed. There was another Facebook friend request from Ellen and I was feeling more fragile than I had been all week. My fingers hovered over the keys as I tried to get the strength to delete it, but I couldn't stop myself from accepting it.

Ellen's world opened up to me. There she was again, in her brilliant red uniform, looking sexier than ever. I could hardly breathe.

"What are you up to?" Scott rubbed his eyes, still wearing the T-shirt and shorts he must have slept in. I hurried to close Ellen's Facebook page.

"Nothing."

He sat down and rubbed a hand through his hair. "I feel like shit."

"That's too bad." Scott obviously hadn't seen Ellen on my screen because if he had, the shit would have been about me.

He sighed. "I promised Ari I'd pick him up this morning and take him to Black Rapids for lunch. I just can't do it. I probably still have way too much beer in my body to drive anyway."

"Would you like me to pick up Ari and take him to Black Rapids?" I felt the need to do a favor for Scott so he might cut me some slack when he found out about Ellen. Black Rapids was a beautiful picnic area at one of the lock stations along the Rideau Canal so this wouldn't be too hard on such a nice day.

"That'd be great." He covered a yawn. "I'll give you money to buy something for lunch. I owe you for this."

I watched Scott shuffle into the house for his wallet and wondered how big of a debt Ellen would become.

ARI WAS WAITING for me at the front of his rooming house when I pulled up. He seemed okay to spend time with me. I was content to be distracted from Ellen and her Facebook page that I couldn't wait to explore.

"Hello, Barbra." He smiled and waved as he approached my car. "Good to see you."

"Hey, Ari. Jump in."

He buckled himself into the front passenger seat with ease. He wore clean, but faded, blue jeans, a black T-shirt, hiking shoes, and a new red Canada ball cap.

"This should be fun," I said. "I haven't been to Black Rapids in years." It had been over six years, actually. I hadn't been to Black Rapids since Ellen and I broke up. We used to meet there for lunch when she worked on summer weekends.

"I am very interested to see one of the locks on the Rideau Canal system in operation," Ari said. "Scott said there should be some boats going through today. You are so kind for taking me and I thank you."

"It's my pleasure." The last time Ellen and I were there, I had the feeling something wasn't right. She was quiet and I had to keep repeating myself. Ellen broke up with me a few days later and I always wondered if she'd meant to break up with me then and there at Black Rapids.

Ari and I found a picnic table near the water's edge. There were other people around, but the park wasn't packed, making it the intimate setting I remembered.

"How are you feeling these days, Ari?" We were eating our lunch.

"I am so happy to be getting to know Scott."

"I mean with your health? How are you feeling physically?"

"I get by." Ari took a bite of his sandwich wrap and looked

out over the water as he chewed. I waited to see if he would add anything more, but the pause persisted.

"Ell...I mean Ari, what's really going on?" Shit, did he catch that?

"I cannot go through chemotherapy again." His eyes were weary. "Scott doesn't know this. We don't say much about my cancer. I think he is afraid to ask and it's good that you are not afraid to ask. I can see that you and Scott really care about each other."

"What'll happen if you don't have chemo?"

"I will die. My doctor told me that."

"You can't do that to Scott. I won't let you." My voice shook with sadness.

Ari chuckled. "You know, Barbra, I think you and my sister, Katarina, would get along just fine. From what Scott has told me and seeing you now, I think you and Katarina are very much alike."

"Please don't change the subject. What do you mean you can't go through chemo again?"

Ari watched a few mallards in the small bay. "This cancer just won't leave me. Taking the chemotherapy was hell the last time and I cannot do it again."

"When was that?" So he'd been through this before. My heart sank further.

"Ten years ago." He was calm, as though just talking about the ducks.

"Oh, Ari, there have been so many advances in cancer treatments in the last few years. You can't give up now."

"I hope you and Scott will meet Katarina one day." He stood up and squished his empty sandwich wrapper. "Katarina is very angry with me right now. She didn't want me to come to Canada."

A small cabin cruiser had approached the locks and Ari strolled over to have a closer look. I wondered what the state of Ari's mental health was right now? Had Scott noticed any of this? What was Ari thinking? I got up from the table and made my way over to the edge of the lock to stand beside him.

"This is so fascinating," Ari said. "It's amazing how they can drain the water out and make it like the boat is going down some stairs. The trees and the water are so beautiful. There's nothing like this back home."

"When are you planning to leave Scott and head home?"

"I know you will take care of Scott after I'm gone," Ari said.

"Just like Katarina has taken care of me."

Ari stifled a gasp and grabbed at his stomach. "I think I'd better sit down again. Can you help me to the table, please."

"Are you okay? What's going on?" I grabbed his arm and we shuffled back to the picnic table.

Ari dropped down on the bench. "Give me a minute please."

"Do you need to go to the hospital?" My heart felt as if it were in my throat.

"No, that's not necessary." His voice was strained. "I'll be okay once I catch my breath."

I stood beside Ari ready to grab hold, expecting him to topple over at any minute.

"The cancer is in my stomach now," he said. "The pills were working to stop the pain. I don't know what's happened."

"We should get you to a hospital." I reached for my cell to call Scott.

"No, no. I will be fine." His breathing was heavy as he put a hand over my phone. "There's nothing they can do for me there. Once I get back to my room I will take another painkiller. I just need to rest for a bit now.

An awkward silence ensued as I finally sat on the bench beside him. "Where did your cancer start?"

"In my left shoulder." He shifted it toward me. "They tried to dig it all out, but I guess they missed some."

"How did you get skin cancer living in a place like Iceland?" It didn't make sense.

"I was stupid." Ari chuckled. "I wanted a nice tan, darker skin. I was tired of looking like a ghost all the time. I went to the tanning salons and now I believe that's what caused it."

"There's all kinds of trials out there now," I said. "Advancements are being made every day. Did Jonathan have any ideas?" Ari's situation sounded desperate.

"No. He is a heart surgeon and not an oncologist. There is a big difference."

Tell me about it, the smug prick. "So what are your next steps?"

"To walk to the car so I can get back to my room and rest." Ari struggled to his feet.

"That's not what I meant." I grabbed onto his arm.

"I know," Ari said. "We will talk later about this, okay? For now, let's just enjoy this beautiful day while we head back."

Chapter Fifteen

ELLEN'S FACEBOOK PAGE was full of posts about her love of swimming, showing she was still passionate about the sport. It wasn't surprising, given her athletic physique that was turning me on as I sat on my bed exploring her site. What was surprising was that she was still a Facebook friend with Donna and there were a lot of pictures of the two of them together on different vacations, full of smiles and sexy poses.

Looking at the photos was like playing with hot and cold taps where I couldn't seem to get the temperature right and kept getting either doused with boiling or freezing water instead of a nice warm mixture. When I heard Scott in the kitchen, I went out to see what he was up to.

"You're home," Scott said. "How'd it go with Ari?"

"Good." How was I going to tell Scott about what happened? "He liked Black Rapids and it was nice to have a chance to chat with him on my own."

"What did you talk about?" He popped a few cashews into his mouth.

"Different things." I opened the fridge and stared inside at the almost empty shelves. There was nothing to snack on, not even any cheese, so I shut the door. "How are you finding him?"

"Okay. Why?" He closed his eyes and sighed. "I need to sit down. Let's go out to the deck."

"Can you handle the sun?" I imagined he had just crawled out of bed and he still looked pale. "It's bright out there."

"It's bright everywhere," Scott said. "I'll bring my sunglasses."

"I hope your sunglasses aren't rose colored when you're with Ari." Might as well just jump into it. "I think he seems to be just letting himself die."

"I don't get that sense. He keeps telling me he's feeling great and hasn't felt this good in a long time."

We were sitting on the deck now and I was watching out for the cardinals, but they were nowhere in sight and the birdbath was dry.

"He told me he's not going to have any more treatments," I said.

Scott had his elbows on the table and dropped his head into

his hands. "Maybe I was just trying to forget about his cancer. He always says we have so much time to catch up on."

"I think it's more about having so little time left. Has he told you anything about his sister Katarina?" I was curious.

"He said they've become really close over the last few years since living together in the same house they grew up in. Can you believe it? They still live in their childhood home."

"Are their parents alive?" I couldn't imagine living with mine.

"No. They both drowned in a boating accident about twenty years ago."

"How tragic." The thought of losing my parents like that was gut-wrenching. "How did it happen?"

"Ari told me his father had a small fishing boat and his mother loved to go out to sea with him. He said they'd often go out for a few days at a time. This one time an unexpected storm came up and they never came back. A search party found their capsized boat, but their bodies were never recovered."

"Poor Ari and Katarina." I fought back tears. "Were they living with their parents then?"

"No. Katarina was living in California and Ari had his own apartment."

"California. That's interesting."

"Ari said Katarina left Iceland when she realized she was a lesbian. She headed to San Francisco because she figured that was the place to be. She met a woman there and ended up staying for fifteen years until they broke up and Katarina moved back to Iceland. Ari was living in the family home by himself and she moved in with him."

"Maybe we should try contacting her to see what she thinks." I wondered if she knew his mental state?

"I'm not going behind Ari's back." Scott's head swayed against his hands.

"I think you should. He's taking painkillers."

"I didn't know that." Scott looked up, eyes hidden behind sunglasses.

"He was in a lot of pain this afternoon." I cringed at the memory. "He told me the cancer's moved into his stomach."

"Fuck. I didn't think it was that bad."

My phone vibrated and I saw Mary's number on the screen. "Mary's calling. Or maybe it's Jonathan." I answered.

"Barbra." Mary was crying.

"What's wrong?" My heart hammered.

"I think I broke my arm."

"How? Are you at home? Where's Jonathan?"

"I'm at home. Can you take me to the hospital?"

"I'll be right there. Have you called the police?" I mouthed Jonathan's name to Scott.

"No." She almost yelled. "I don't need the police. Can you just come?"

MARY'S CAR WAS the only one in the driveway when I got to her mansion. She struggled to let me in while cradling her left arm with her right hand. Her hair was a mess and her cheeks were tear-stained. She wore a white bathrobe and there was no sign of Barbie.

"What happened?" The prick hit her again.

"I fell in the bathroom upstairs when I was getting dressed."

Yeah right. "Where's Jonathan? Does he know about this?"

"He's gone out. Can you help me put on a blouse? I can't move my left arm and it hurts like hell?"

"Was Jonathan here when it happened?"

"Yes." Mary started to cry again. "We were arguing and I don't even remember what started it. All I remember is Jonathan grabbing me by my arm and yanking it behind my back before throwing me toward the bed."

I followed Mary upstairs to her bedroom. The room was a mess and I noticed a lamp knocked over on the floor. "This is unacceptable. We need to call the police."

"No, please don't." She grabbed onto my arm. "I need to think about this first."

"There's nothing to think about." I pulled away in anger. "Your prick of a husband needs to be charged."

"Barbra, please let me handle this." She could hardly speak through her sobs. "I thought I could stay a few nights at your place."

Yes, at least I could get her away from the prick. I touched her shoulder. "Let's grab some things now so we don't have to come back. Tell me what you need and I'll pack a bag for you."

"We'll have to bring Barbie too," Mary said. "I think she's hiding somewhere downstairs. The poor thing."

I dropped Mary off at the hospital emergency room and left her there by herself while I brought Barbie to my place. We chose a hospital that Jonathan didn't frequent just to make sure we wouldn't run into him. It turned out Mary's arm just had a sprain and we were finally able to leave.

Scott and Ari were sharing a pizza on our back deck when we got home from the hospital. I had texted Scott to let him know Mary would be staying with us.

"How are you doing?" Scott asked Mary.

"Not as bad as I thought. It's only a sprain." She chirped her response, oblivious that I'd told Scott what had happened. "I thought for sure it was broken." Her arm was in a sling, she had been given some painkillers, and we hadn't eaten yet.

"A sprain can be very painful," Ari said. " Both of you come sit down and have some pizza."

"Thank you," I said, eyeing a big slice with a mixed cheesy topping.

Ari got up and pulled a chair out for Mary and I sat beside her.

"Apart from your arm," Scott's voice lowered, "how are you doing?"

"Feeling stupid," Mary said. "I can't believe I fell like that when I was getting out of the bathtub."

Scott flashed his eyes at me, eyebrows raised. What could I say?

"I'm glad Barbra was able to help me because Jonathan was at the hospital." She reached for the smallest slice. "Mmm. This looks good."

"I hear you and Barbie are going to be staying with us for a while," Scott said.

Mary paused before responding. "Yes. Where is she?"

"I put her in the spare bedroom where you'll be staying," I said. "She was sprawled out on the bed when I left and should be fine because I put out some food and water along with her litter box."

"I'll check on her just to make sure she's okay." Mary got up and went inside.

"What's going on?" Scott asked.

"I don't know what to do." I shook my head. "She doesn't want to go to the police and you just heard her blaming herself."

"What do your parents think?" As much as he mocked my parents, Scott valued their opinion.

"They don't know anything about this. I'm dying to tell them but Mary has forbidden me to say anything."

"Poor Mary," Ari said as he started to get up. "From what Scott has told me, I believe she is scared. I think it's time I go back to my room now."

Mary went to bed early and I was anxious to have some time by myself. Ellen was still on my mind. She could give me a police perspective on Mary's situation. It was just the excuse I needed to convince myself that contacting her again was the right thing to do. I went to her Facebook page and spent the next few hours getting lost in her world.

Ellen had suggested dinner on Monday, but I wanted to talk to her before then. I sent a note offering to pick her up at the airport on her return the next day then went to bed.

Chapter Sixteen

I LOOKED UP and spotted Ellen. She was at the top of the tall escalator in the arrivals area of the Ottawa airport that travelers rode down to claim their baggage. She noticed me right away and gave a big smile. I grinned back, but the closer she got, the harder I found it to keep my smile. What was I doing?

"Hey, Bebs, thanks so much for picking me up." Ellen pulled me into a smothering hug.

"How was your flight?" As if I cared.

"Long. I'm glad to be back in Ottawa. And I'm especially glad you're here to pick me up." She blew a kiss into my ear.

I pulled away, my stomach in knots. "Do you have lots of baggage?" Other than your baggage with me that's getting in the way right now.

"Just one. I've gotten really good at packing over the years and managed to squeeze everything into one suitcase. This is just like old times." She patted my back. "I can't believe you're here."

I couldn't believe it either. "Something's come up and I was hoping to pick your brain as a police officer. I didn't want to wait until tomorrow." The words sounded pathetic now that I was saying them, but she didn't seem to think so.

"Sure, anytime." Concern in her voice. "What's up?"

"I'm trying to help someone." We stood off to the side and away from the crowd around the luggage belt. "Her husband's physically abusing her and she doesn't want to go to the police."

"That's hard." Ellen's eyes moistened. "Do you want me to talk to her?"

"No, but thanks for the offer." She could be so sweet and caring. Sometimes. "I was hoping you might have some advice on what I should do."

"She needs to file a complaint with the police."

"She refuses to involve the police."

"Why?" Ellen's voluptuous lips teased.

"Her husband's job." My knees shook. "He has a position of professional prominence."

"So what?" Ellen leaned closer, her lips almost brushing my ear and tingling my spine. "Some of the worst offenders are doctors, lawyers, and even police officers. How do you go to the police if your violent partner is a police officer?"

Hmm. What did that mean? I had never heard what happened between Ellen and Donna.

The awakening baggage belt jarred into action and suitcases started to spit out. Ellen hustled into the crowd, readying to grab her bag as soon as it passed by. She stood slightly hunched and frowned. Was she thinking about Donna?

"Is your friend safe right now?" We were in my car driving toward Ellen's place.

"Yes," I said. "She's out of the family home."

"She's at a shelter?"

"Not really, but she has a place to stay."

"Don't kid yourself, Bebs. Safety in situations like this has nothing to do with being in or out of the family home. Are there children involved?"

"No." Just Barbie.

"That's good. Whenever I've responded to a call of domestic violence, it's the kids that get to me. They have such big eyes full of fear and hatred, especially when we have to take them from their parents for their own safety. I hope you're keeping safe in all of this, Bebs."

"I can handle myself. Besides, I won't hesitate to call the police if I feel at all threatened."

"It could be too late then. Don't get caught in the middle of someone else's problems. I wouldn't want anything to happen to you."

"I'll be fine."

"I love this car." Ellen caressed the front dash and central console with neatly manicured fingers that had once touched me like that.

I stomped on the gas pedal to give a quick thrill through sudden acceleration.

"Wow, I love the sweet sound of that engine." She giggled. "I could just sit here and drive away with you right now."

Was Ellen flirting with me? "So how was your week in Vancouver?"

"I really enjoyed the conference."

Donna had probably been there.

"Will you come up for a coffee?" We were in front of Ellen's apartment building.

"I can't. I already have plans." I wouldn't let myself go anywhere near her apartment with just the two of us.

"Are we on for dinner tomorrow night?"

"I don't know yet," I said. "There's a lot going on so I'll let you know tomorrow."

"I figured you were busy when I didn't hear from you all week." Ellen lifted her bag from my trunk. "Thanks again for this and good luck with your friend." She gave a weak smile then rolled her bag into the building without offering another hug.

It was late afternoon when I got home. Mary was cuddled up on the couch with Barbie and a book. Her arm was still in a sling.

"Why aren't you sitting outside on a nice day like today?" I sat in the red recliner.

"I wanted to sit inside with Barbie." She kneaded the cat. "She got spooked yesterday. Where were you?"

"Where's Scott?" She didn't need to know where I was.

"He's gone somewhere with Ari. Were you with Ellen?"

Damn. "Sort of. I picked her up at the airport. She's back from Vancouver."

"Great. Don't you think we have enough going on right now?"

"I know." I flopped back and hung my feet over one of the arms of the chair. "I didn't spend a lot of time with her. I just wanted to pick her brain since she's a police officer."

"You didn't tell her about Jonathan, did you?" Mary straightened.

"Of course I didn't, but I did talk to her about your situation without giving any details. She said the same thing I've been telling you. You need to go to the police."

"I already told you that's not an option."

"Have you heard from the prick today?"

"While you were out with the bitch?" Mary paused to let her stinging words sink in. "Yes. I told Jonathan I'd be staying with you for a few days. He says he's sorry and understands if I need a bit of time."

"Are you going to tell our parents now?"

"Of course not." Mary massaged Barbie, gleaming every time she looked down at the purring cat.

"What are you going to tell them about staying here?"

"They don't need to know I'm staying here. I have my cell so it's not like they'll know I'm here if I talk to them on the phone."

"Our mother already suspects something's up. She called me the other day and told me it sounded like you had been crying when she talked to you on the phone."

"Oh, that was so hard. Jonathan had been upset with me for not buying the right kind of toothpaste when she called. I answered just so Jonathan would stop yelling."

"The right kind of toothpaste?" Her life must be hell.

"It was more about the flavor. Jonathan can't stand toothpaste that tastes like wintergreen. I knew that, but I just forgot."

"Hey." Scott had come home and flopped down on the couch beside Mary. He reached to pet Barbie.

"How's Ari today?" I asked.

"He seems off." He gently massaged the purring cat. "We went for a walk downtown along the canal and he was quieter than usual. We weren't out long before he wanted to go back to his room for a nap."

"That doesn't sound good," I said. "Are you going to check in on him later?"

"Yes. I told him I'd stop by after supper and we could go somewhere for an ice cream cone."

"Oh look," Mary said. "Mom and Dad just pulled up. Scott, please don't let them know I'm staying here okay?"

"Sure, but what are you going to say about Barbie being here?" Scott glanced at me.

"I'll figure something out," Mary said. "Please just play along with it."

My mother came in first, carrying a small container of raspberries. "Hi, Barbra. Your father and I were out for a drive to the market and thought we'd stop by to drop these off."

"Mmm. They smell so good." I met them at the door. "Thanks."

"Mary, you're here too." Our dad stepped inside. "What happened to your arm?"

"And why is Barbie here?" my mother asked. "Mary, what's going on?"

"Nothing. I slipped getting out of the bathtub yesterday and sprained my arm." She stood up and went over to our mother, cradling Barbie with her good arm. "Say hi to Grandma. Barbie was sick this morning so I didn't want to leave her alone."

"The poor thing." My mother patted Barbie's head then shot her green eyes to Mary. "How could you have fallen getting out of the bathtub? You're too young for that."

"Mother," I said, "anyone can fall getting out of the bathtub. It has nothing to do with age."

"Barbra," she said, "someone as young and agile as Mary shouldn't fall getting out of the bathtub."

"What's everyone doing inside on a nice day like today?" my dad asked.

"Barbie didn't want to go outside," I said.

"I can't believe you're letting that cat call the shots around here," he said.

"Baxter," my mother said, "Barbie's not feeling well."

"Then just leave the damn cat in the house."

"Are you able to stay for a little visit?" I asked. My parents were standing in the front entryway. "We can always move out to the backyard."

"Oh no," my mother said. "I just wanted to drop off the raspberries. It's too hot to sit outside."

"Then come in and we'll stay here," I said.

"It's way too hot in here," my dad said. "What's wrong with your air conditioner? Doesn't it work anymore?"

"I prefer not to use it if I don't have to," I said. "It's not that hot in here."

"It's like a sauna in here. Ruth, let's get back in the car where there's air-conditioning."

"Scott, how's Ari today?" my mother asked. "Surely he's not sitting in his room all by himself on such a nice day."

"He's napping." Scott had gotten up and was standing with us by the front door. "I'm going to take him for an ice cream cone after supper."

"How nice," my mother said. "I wish one of our girls would take us for an ice cream cone sometime."

"Okay, Ruth, let's get going." My dad started out the door. "This ice cream cone is starting to melt."

Scott and I stood in the doorway and watched as my parents backed out of the driveway. My dad was at the wheel and my mother waved as they drove away.

"That was nice of your parents to bring some fresh raspberries," he said.

"Yeah it was. You can bring some of them to Ari later on if you want."

"Thanks. I sure hope he's feeling better because I don't know what to do."

"He needs to go to a doctor," Mary said. Like she was a fine one to talk.

"He won't," Scott said. "He told me he doesn't have any medical coverage while he's here."

"Oh, Scott," Mary said. "He has to go back to Iceland as soon as possible. You might have to go with him."

"I know. I'll talk to him about it tonight and start looking into it tomorrow."

Maybe I could go too and get away from Ellen. Mary would have to come as well because I couldn't leave her alone with the prick.

Chapter Seventeen

I RACED AGAINST impending rain on my dull Wednesday morning jog. An overnight wind had reduced the humidity and blown in black clouds that were accompanied by distant rumbles of thunder.

The last few days had been busy with helping Scott organize for a trip to Iceland. The first problem was that Scott's passport was about to expire so he couldn't leave the country even if he wanted to. Mary's and mine were up to date.

Ari slept a lot and kept to himself. Scott looked more discouraged after each visit with Ari.

Jonathan had been trying to win Mary back with flowers, chocolates, and dinner invitations. She seemed to be coming to her senses, realizing it was time to move on from the prick and her big house. I didn't know where my senses were because I couldn't decide what to do about Ellen.

I hadn't received any flowers or chocolates from Ellen, but I had gotten another dinner invitation to her apartment. It came in the form of an e-mail just as I left for my run. Mary would berate me if I accepted and I didn't even want to think about what Scott would do.

It was garbage day again and I spotted another pair of bamboo ski poles as I rounded a corner. They were sticking out of the top of a yard waste bag. I veered to the curb and yanked one pole out of the bag. It was missing its bottom basket. I shoved it back in then tugged on the second pole, maneuvering its still intact basket through the maze of little twigs and weeds. There was a small crack in the bamboo shaft, but nothing that a piece of duct tape couldn't fix. I took it because with the sound of the approaching garbage truck, I knew it was now or never.

Pole in hand, I raced against the rain that had started to splat on the pavement. When I got to my street, the downpour turned torrential as I sprinted toward the police car in my driveway.

I clutched the bamboo ski pole when I got in the front door, heart pounding with dread. Scott sat on the couch, head in hands and crying. Mary and a male police officer were consoling him.

Mary approached me and whispered through tears. "It's Ari. He died. They found him this morning at the rooming house."

"What?" This couldn't be true. He couldn't be dead.

"It looks like a suicide." Mary murmured.

"Are you sure?" Not Ari. No way. Tears touched raindrops on my drenched skin.

"He left a note." Mary handed me a few tissues.

"A note?" My head was buzzing.

"Yes. Scott has it." The flowers on her cotton housecoat blended into psychedelic blobs.

I leaned against the wall and bent over to prevent my weak legs from collapsing. "What does it say?" How could he do this?

"He didn't want Scott to watch him die. He left contact information for his lawyer back in Reykjavik."

I started to wobble. Mary grabbed my arm, took the bamboo ski pole from me, and led me to the couch.

"Oh, Scott," I said. "I'm so sorry." I sat down, put my head on his shoulder, and cried along with him.

"We were just getting to know each other and now he's gone again." Scott could hardly get the words out as he sobbed.

"I'm here for you." I put my hand on his and squeezed while Mary led the police officer to the door.

"I have to let Katarina know," Scott said. "Will you help me Skype with her?"

"Of course I will."

Katarina answered on the first try. I struggled to keep it together, focusing on the woman on screen to block out tears. She had shoulder length blond hair, a light complexion, and appeared to share her brother's good looks. I could see some resemblance to Scott as well.

She gave me a beautiful smile until her eyes shifted to Scott.

"It's Ari, isn't it?" Her face crumpled.

"Yes." Scott started to sob and couldn't speak. He shoved the computer in front of me.

"I...I'm so sorry to have to tell you this, Katarina, but Ari has died." What if some stranger was telling me that Mary had just died?

"Oh no." She cried out. "How? What happened?"

"It looks like suicide." My insides were ripping out as I felt her pain.

"I should have known. Why did I let him go?" Katarina buried her face in her hands and bawled.

My heart went out to her. I longed to reach through the screen and offer a consoling hug. The most I could offer was to cry with her.

"Can you come to Ottawa?" I wiped tears as Scott was stifled by sobs. "You can stay here with us."

"You must be Barbra." Katarina struggled to regain her composure, a forced smile through her tears.

"I'm so sorry to meet under these circumstances." I swallowed against a constricting throat and churning stomach.

"What did he do? When did he die?" She lost control and sobbed again.

"It looks like a drug overdose," I said. "He was found this morning."

"Did anyone see him yesterday?" Katarina lifted a wrinkled face of sadness.

"Scott did." My heart ached for her.

"How was he, Scott?" She shifted, as though looking for Scott.

I repositioned the computer so Scott was back on the screen. He barely looked up while struggling to answer. "Tired...and not very talkative...I didn't think he was that depressed."

"Ari has struggled with depression for years," Katarina said, her eyes closing for a moment.

We should have talked to her sooner.

"I didn't know he was depressed," Scott said.

I had tried to warn him.

"Of course you wouldn't," Katarina said. "How could you?"

"Will you come to Ottawa?" Scott asked.

"Yes. I will come to bring Ari home."

"Is there anything we can do to help?" I would have agreed to do just about anything for her in that moment.

"Look after Ari until I get there." Katarina cried as she spoke. "I'll let you know when I book a flight."

"Ari would want you to come," Scott said, tears erupting again. "He told me he loved Ottawa and hoped you would visit one day."

"He didn't leave me much choice, did he? I'll talk to you later." Katarina ended the call.

Book Two

Chapter Eighteen

KATARINA APPEARED AT the top of the same escalator in the Ottawa airport that only a week before Ellen had ridden down. My stomach twirled with instant attraction as I looked up. The lighting made it clear Katarina did indeed share her brother's good looks. Scott stood beside me and waved. A slight smile of recognition came over her face as she returned the gesture.

Katarina's hair was disheveled from the flight, making her all the more attractive as she got closer. Her resemblance to Scott was clear. Even though I had never been sexually attracted to Scott, my heart throbbed as she approached.

"Wow, she's cute." The words slipped out of my mouth and Scott flinched.

"I can't believe you just said that at a time like this." He shook his head. "Whatever you do, don't hit on her."

"Don't worry. I won't hit on your aunt." Even though she was close to my age and looked like a goddess. But no, I had enough to worry about with Ellen and whether or not I was going to have dinner with her anytime soon.

Katarina went up to Scott and hugged him, burying her face in his shoulder as though she didn't want to let go. She had started to cry and so had Scott. I moved off to the side and let them share their initial mournful encounter alone. Katarina was a bit shorter than Scott, but much taller than me and wore blue jeans with a moss green T-shirt over a toned body that rivaled Ellen's.

The last few days had been hectic as Scott and I tried to figure out what arrangements needed to be made for Ari. My parents rushed to Scott's side when they heard the sad news. Their caring and attention made me appreciate them more than ever, especially since I felt inept at knowing how to help Scott with the arrangements. My mother was happy to take over and be in control. Scott was content to let her play that mothering role. He refused to contact his adoptive parents and instead accepted my parents as his own during this difficult time.

My dad grappled with Ari's suicide and felt so bad for Scott. I was struggling too and couldn't stop thinking about my day with Ari at Black Rapids. I knew he was depressed. Why didn't I do anything that could have stopped him? How could I have been so stupid?

Scott and Katarina had stepped out of their embrace and he looked around for me. My knees wobbled as I approached.

"Hi, Katarina. I'm so sorry for your loss." We shared a brief hug that was soft and warm. I could feel tears on my cheeks and searched for a tissue when Katarina offered me a fresh one of hers.

"It's nice to meet you in person, Barbra. Ari spoke highly of you."

"Thanks so much for coming, Katarina," Scott said as he squeezed her arm.

She watched the motionless baggage carousel. "Ari wanted me to come to Ottawa to meet everyone, but I wanted him to come home instead. He got his way. Now here I am."

Katarina's hardened tone echoed with the sound of the baggage carousel clanging into action. She had come through Halifax and already gone through customs. We were able to get her suitcase and leave without any long wait. Scott had taken his car and I rode in the backseat for the drive to our place, where Mary and my parents were waiting with dinner.

My mother was watching at the front door as we pulled into the driveway. She stepped outside to meet us at the car, Mary and our dad right behind.

"Hello, Katarina. I'm Ruth, Barbra's mother." She pulled Katarina into a hug. "Scott is like a son to us. I'm so sorry for your loss."

"Thank you, Ruth." Katarina returned the hug then stepped back.

"Hey, Katarina." Mary was next in line. "I'm Mary, Barbra's sister. I'm so sorry for your loss." She embraced Katarina.

Mary's sprained arm was no longer in a sling, but she occasionally cradled it. Mary had told our parents she was staying with me because Jonathan was under a lot of stress at work and needed some time on his own. If everyone hadn't been so caught up in Ari's suicide, my mother would have figured out by now that Jonathan was responsible for her sprained arm.

"Thank you, Mary." Katarina ran a hand through her hair.

Our parents wanted Mary to go to their house when they found out Katarina would be staying with us. I knew Mary couldn't handle living with them and insisted there was plenty of room at my place, which there was. Katarina would be occupying the extra bedroom in the basement to be near Scott.

When it was my dad's turn to greet Katarina, he cried and

embraced her without saying a word. Katarina was slightly taller than my dad and she cried too.

"Katarina, this is Baxter." Scott put a hand on my dad's shoulder. "He shared a few beers with Ari and they became good buddies."

My cheeks itched with tears. My dad hardly ever cried. When he did, I cried too.

"I'm so sorry, Katarina," my dad finally said, his words barely audible. "Your brother was a good man."

"Let's get you inside now." My mother put a hand on Katarina's lower back and nudged her toward the door. "You must be hungry and exhausted."

Mary and my mother had prepared a comforting dinner of mashed potatoes, roast chicken, carrots, fresh peas, and a big lettuce salad. We were all seated at the table and ready to dig in when my phone vibrated. It was Ellen. I sent the call to voicemail.

"Barbra," my mother said, "can't you leave your phone alone for one minute?"

"Sorry." I put the cell back in my rear pocket.

"Who was calling you?" my dad asked. He'd recovered from the tears and was back to his normal self.

"Nobody," I said. "I just remembered to turn it off, that's all."

"I heard it ring," Scott said. He did that sometimes when he knew I was trying to get away with a little white lie to my parents. "Who was it?"

"It wasn't ringing. It sounds like that when I turn it off." How would I ever tell him about Ellen?

"Have some chicken, Katarina," my mother said. "Baxter, pass it to her."

"No thank you." Katarina refused the platter. "I'm a vegetarian."

My mother flinched. She believed it was an unhealthy diet lacking protein. I had tried becoming a vegetarian when I was in my twenties, but my mother made my life hell at every family meal. I eventually gave in and went back to eating meat.

"That's too bad, dear." My mother's neck was red. "Are you sure? A little bit of meat will put some color in your cheeks."

"Mother," I said. "Katarina just told you she's a vegetarian. She won't have any chicken." I was so embarrassed.

"You're right." She snapped her tongue.

Yay, my mother admitting that I was right didn't happen very often.

"Forgive me, Katarina," she said. "Can I get you something else instead of the chicken? Barbra, do you have any cheese? Or do you not eat cheese too?"

"Thank you, but I'm fine." Katarina's cheeks had some color in them now.

"You're going to be hungry."

Why couldn't my mother just let go?

"Ruth, let the poor girl eat." My dad came to the rescue. "There's lots of other food. Here Katarina, have some salad. It should be okay for a vegetarian."

"I added some sesame seeds and cashews in the salad," Mary said. "It's full of protein."

"I hope you don't have a nut allergy," my mother said.

I hoped so too because if Katarina did have a nut allergy, she could have been allergic to my mother.

"I'm okay with nuts." Katarina said. "The salad looks wonderful." She put some on her plate.

"What do you do for a living?" my mother asked.

Oh for shit's sake, why couldn't my mother just let her eat?

"I work for myself," Katarina said. "I'm a graphic artist."

"How nice," my mother said. "Maybe you can talk to Barbra here and give her some tips about working for herself. She says she's working on a business plan, but we haven't seen anything yet."

Grrr!

"Ari told me she's an architect." Katarina flashed beautiful jade eyes at me. "I'd be happy to talk to you about your business plan."

Breathe. "That'd be great." I would have welcomed my parents' air-conditioning at that moment.

The rest of the dinner was mostly light conversation, but it did confirm one important thing for me — Katarina was single.

After my parents left, Katarina got settled into her room. Mary sat in the living room with Barbie and a book. Scott and I hung out on the deck, sharing a bottle of white wine. I longed to tell him about Ellen and hoped the wine would give me courage. Ellen had left a short voicemail asking me to give her a call about dinner tomorrow night. So far I had ignored the message.

"Katarina thanked me again for letting her stay here," Scott said. "She really appreciated your parents coming over for dinner. She said Ari spoke highly of you and your family and felt I was in good hands."

"How do you think she's doing?" Could this be the right time to broach the topic of Ellen? "This must be so hard for her. It sounds like Ari was her only family."

"She said she's very tired," Scott said. "It's four hours ahead in Reykjavik so it's understandable that she'd be exhausted, even in the best of times."

"How are you doing?"

"I'm exhausted too." He sighed. "I still can't believe I just met Ari and now he's already gone. I'm glad you're here though. Thanks for everything."

"We're here for each other." I paused. "Scott, I need to tell you something."

"This sounds serious." He raised his eyebrows. "What's up? You've had enough of me and my new found family and want me to move out?"

"No." I forced a chuckle. "It's nothing like that. Ellen's back in Ottawa."

Scott winced then reached for his glass of wine. He drained it with one big swig. "Bitchellen. Fuck. I hope you told her where to go."

"Sort of. Well not exactly. She wants to have dinner with me."

"If I didn't know any better, Ethel, I'd think you're actually considering it."

Yikes. Scott had only called me Ethel once before when he was furious with me for sending a dozen roses to Ellen on what would have been our seventh anniversary. My mother used to call me Ethel when I was younger and about to get disciplined for bad behavior.

"I think she's changed," I finally said.

"You've already seen her?" His chair shook.

"We met for a coffee." Scott didn't need to know about me picking her up at the airport. "She's moved back here on her own."

"I don't want to hear about it." He stood. "I have enough problems of my own right now."

"I'm sorry. I know the timing sucks."

"It's not the timing that sucks," he said. "It's the fact you're even thinking about that bitch again that sucks. I'm going to bed."

I stayed on the deck for a while by myself. It was dark out and there were a few faint stars gracing the sky. Was Ari up there somewhere? What was I thinking in telling Scott about Ellen now that he needed me more than ever? What was Ari thinking?

Katarina had spoken briefly with Ari's lawyer in Reykjavik. Ari's wishes were to be cremated in Ottawa and have half of his ashes spread on the Rideau Canal and the other half brought back to Iceland and put out to sea with his parents.

My mother had been a big help with sorting things out with the Iceland Embassy and a local funeral home so Ari's wishes could be granted. He left Scott some money to go to Iceland for the spreading of his ashes there and he wanted Katarina to put his ashes on the Rideau Canal.

Ari hadn't been cremated yet. The funeral home was holding off until Katarina arrived and had a chance to say goodbye. Cremation was set for the next morning, right after Katarina viewed the body. Scott had asked me to go with them, but now I wasn't sure if he would want me to. Scott didn't get angry very often, but when he did he could be very cold.

He had every right to be angry with me. Would I ever learn to let go of Ellen? And now here was Katarina. Just thinking about her made me feel sweet inside. I decided not to return Ellen's call.

I looked up at the sky again and thanked Ari for bringing Katarina to Ottawa.

Chapter Nineteen

SCOTT AND KATARINA were up and gone before breakfast. They avoided me by sneaking out the side door. I hated it when Scott and I were fighting, which we rarely did, because we relied on each other for emotional support. It hurt that he left without saying anything.

Mary had reduced her work hours to sort out the next steps with Jonathan. She'd only be working half days for the week, most of the time from my house. I was sitting on the deck, sulking over the situation with Scott, when Mary stepped through the patio doors. She wore a baby blue cotton dressing gown, held a coffee, and yawned as she collapsed into a chair beside me.

"A late night or early morning?" I asked.

"Neither." She plopped her arms on the table. "I went to bed early enough but tossed and turned most of the night."

"If you couldn't sleep, why didn't you get out of bed?"

"I didn't feel like getting up." Mary let out a big sigh. "I don't know what I'm going to do about Jonathan. He wants me to come home and start a family."

"Don't even think about it." I swung around and glared toward avoiding eyes. "He's a prick and having kids isn't going to change things."

"Please try to keep your voice down." Mary patted the table. "I don't want Katarina and your whole neighborhood to hear us talking about this."

"Sorry. I just get so pissed off when I think about him. You don't have to worry about Katarina because she and Scott left early this morning." I was the one who had to worry.

"Good. She seems very nice, don't you think? I can't imagine what she must be going through right now."

"How long has Jonathan been violent? Has he always been like this?" I wasn't going to let Mary change the subject so soon, although I would have enjoyed talking about Katarina.

"No, that's what's so strange. He's always had a bit of a temper, but it's only been in the last few months that he's become violent. I know he's been under a lot of pressure at work, but..."

"Don't try to make excuses for him. What he's doing to you is outright wrong and dangerous and you've got to stop it." My jaw tightened.

"I'm trying. He says he's trying too."

"Like hell. He's trying to manipulate you to go back for more."

"I don't agree." Mary flicked a few crumbs on the table. "I decided to go off the pill."

"You what? You can't be serious?" Mary was usually the smart one who did the right thing.

"I've always wanted kids and I'm getting close to forty."

"You're further away from forty than I am and there's still lots of time for you to have kids with someone else."

"Yeah right, look at you. How many years has it been since Ellen and now you're contemplating going back to her?"

Ouch. "I'm not going back to Ellen." Or was I? "The lesbian community in Ottawa is small enough that I'd rather be friends with Ellen than have to avoid her."

"You've never gotten over her, have you?"

So what if I hadn't? I wasn't going to let myself be cross-examined by my lawyer sister who was being stupid. "What if you have kids with Jonathan? Next thing he'll be beating the kids too. Is that what you want?"

Mary started to cry.

"I'm sorry." I felt like the big sister bully who'd just won the fight. My voice softened and I touched her arm. "I'm worried about you getting hurt again."

"I'm hurting now." Mary wiped a tear. "I love him."

"I know you do." How could she? "And you're right about Ellen." It was a small concession for making her cry. "I don't know if I'll ever get over her. I told Scott last night that I saw Ellen and he's really pissed."

She sniffled. "I think it's good you told Scott and I don't blame him for being upset with you."

"Can you blame me for being upset with you? I think it'd be a good idea to tell Mom. She thinks the world of Jonathan." And I wanted to see her Jonathan world rocked.

"You know I can't. At least not until I figure out what I'm going to do."

"I don't see what there is to figure out."

"Are you willing to support me when I get disbarred?"

"You need to play his game and blackmail him too. I'm sure he won't jeopardize his career by being labeled as a wife beater."

"I've thought of that and it could work, but I want to make sure it's what I want."

"What do you mean? What else could you want?"

"For things to change and Jonathan to go back to being the way he was."

"In my mind there's no going back." I was a fine one to talk.

"I want to have a baby."

Oh for shit sake. "Then go to a clinic and have yourself artificially inseminated. Lesbians do it all the time."

"I'm not a lesbian. Jonathan's trying to change and I always pictured raising kids in our house."

"I can't believe it's still about the house."

"It's not about the house. But I don't see myself raising kids in your house."

She had that right. "I could picture you doing it in your own house. One like mine."

"I want to raise kids in a big house with a pool in the backyard."

"So that they can grow up to die from the effects of climate change?" I shouldn't have said that.

"What does that have to do with climate change?"

"A smaller house with no pool is the way to go if you care at all about the effects of global warming."

"Why do I have to be such a villain if I want a big house with a pool? I do care about climate change and I'm doing my part."

"Really. How?" She couldn't be serious.

"I always try to buy more local products and use fewer chemicals. The pool uses saltwater instead of chlorine and has a solar blanket to keep the water warm when we're not using it."

"Which is probably more than ninety percent of the time." I had to stop this. "Sorry. Let's keep our focus on you and Jonathan."

"I think I'm going to start by having dinner with him tonight and see how I feel."

"Maybe I should go with you for protection." As if I could stomach that.

"I'll be fine. I'll treat it like a first date and insist he brings me back here afterward." She stood. "I'd better head inside now and get some work done."

I needed to get some work on my business plan done too, but I couldn't concentrate. My agitation over Mary and Jonathan, as well as the situation with Scott, was really getting to me and I needed to do something to relax. The sun was shining and my car needed a wash. Perfect. I would back it out of the garage and polish the finish because it looked so brilliant when shiny. Katarina hadn't seen my Mustang yet and it would be nice to impress her.

It didn't take long to wash off the dust and buff it so the ruby red paint sparkled. I was putting the final caressing wipes on the hood when Ellen called.

"Hi." I didn't really feel like talking to Ellen.

"Hey, Bebs. I'm glad you finally picked up."

"Sorry for not calling back, but it's been busy around here." Not really for me now, but she didn't have to know.

"How are things going?" Concern in her voice.

"Okay." They were terrible at the moment because of her, and I should have just hung up.

"Can you come over for dinner tonight?"

"Aren't you working today?" Why didn't I just say no.

"I am, but I can pick up a pizza on the way home and I have a bottle of red wine that's just begging to be opened."

Maybe I could bring dessert. No. Stop that. "Sounds good, but I can't because of the situation with Scott." He'd never speak to me again.

"That's so sad. What's happening with that?"

"Ari's sister has come over from Iceland. She's staying here." And Scott wasn't talking to me at the moment.

"It must be so strange. How is she with you and Scott being gay?" She pictured Katarina as being much older.

"She's fine." She was actually a hot lesbian, but there was no way I was telling her that.

"What are you up to now?" Her voice lowered.

"I just finished polishing my car." Let her drool.

"When are you going to take me for another ride in that baby to show me what it can do?"

Never. Maybe. "I don't know."

"If you can't do dinner, what about lunch? We could meet at Black Rapids, just like the old times."

Like when she had wanted to dump me? "What time is it anyways? Isn't it too late?"

"It's only ten-thirty. There's lots of time. Will you?"

I could bike over. I hadn't gotten out for my jog so a bike ride could help de-stress me and lunch at Black Rapids would be a lot safer than dinner at Ellen's. Best to keep all options open right now.

"Okay, I'll meet you there at noon."

I made myself a ham sandwich, grabbed my water bottle, and took off on my bike. It was a lot farther than what I was used to pedaling in a hurry. I pushed on, the penance of the grueling ride easing the guilt of doing something only Ethel would do.

It took me close to an hour to get there, but I was still early and able to grab a picnic table under one of the large trees. I leaned my bike up against a maple trunk and sat on the tabletop to watch for Ellen.

"Barbra?" A familiar female voice called out from behind.

I swung around and gasped. Katarina smiled as she approached. Scott dawdled behind her.

"Hi." My heart raced. "What are you guys doing here?" How could this be happening?

"Ari said he loved this place." Katarina stood beside me. "I asked Scott to bring me here."

"Hey." Scott stayed behind Katarina. "How did you know we'd be here?"

"I didn't." Beads of sweat slithered on my forehead. "This is quite the surprise." Scott was going to find out I was meeting Ellen. Shit. Fuck. "I went for a bike ride and I'm just having a little rest, but I think I'm ready to head out now."

"We were just leaving too," Katarina said.

"Ari wants some of his ashes spread into the Rideau Canal so I'm thinking of doing it here," Scott said.

"How nice." I longed to grab my bike and run up the hill to get out of sight before Ellen showed up, but it was too late. I noticed her strolling down, shorts on and lunch bag in hand. No uniform. Yes. Maybe they wouldn't notice her. Please, please let her go the other way.

"I'll walk up with you." And try to avoid Ellen.

"I suppose you want a ride home?" Scott said. He had a bike rack on his car.

"No, that's okay, thanks." I just wanted to get him out of there.

I could have hugged Ellen when I saw her heading toward the other side of the park in search of me. She would be expecting me to be by myself. I kept in the distance with Scott and Katarina, trying to hide behind them and go unnoticed.

"I guess we'll see you at home," Scott said. We were in the parking lot and safely out of Ellen's view.

"How did it go this morning?" I didn't want to linger, but I needed to say something to acknowledge their sad task at the funeral home.

Katarina started to cry. "I will miss Ari."

I put my bike on its kickstand and hugged her. "I'm so sorry, Katarina. I'll miss him too." Scott got into the car while I held

Katarina and hoped she wouldn't feel my heart pounding against hers.

"What a nice bicycle." Katarina had eased out of the embrace and looked at my bike. "It's great you cycle places instead of driving everywhere."

"Yeah I like it." I put my helmet on and got on my bike. "I'll see you at home."

I pedaled out of the parking lot and mostly let myself glide until Scott's car passed me and was out of sight. I quickly turned around and raced back to Ellen. She was sitting by herself at a picnic table and had started to eat her lunch.

"Hey there, I was getting worried that you'd stood me up." She laughed.

"Sorry. The bike ride took longer than I thought." My heart rate was starting to steady.

"You look out of breath. Maybe you should have taken that little red pony of yours instead."

I was no longer in the mood for Ellen after just averting what could have been a disaster and still feeling Katarina's touch. If I had taken my little red pony, I'd have been caught. I'd be saddling it up right now and riding off into the sunset because Scott would never forgive me. I leaned my bike against the table and sat beside Ellen.

"Thanks for meeting me," she said. "It's been years since I've been here. The last time I was with you."

When you were getting ready to dump me. "I can't stay for long. I'm supposed to meet Scott and Katarina in an hour and it'll take me almost that to bike home."

"It's too bad I have a meeting right after lunch or I'd give you a lift."

"Thanks, but I need the exercise." Phew.

By the time I got home, I was starving because I hadn't managed to eat my sandwich. I was in the kitchen getting some juice out of the fridge when I saw Scott and Katarina pull into the driveway. The side window was open so I could hear them talking as they walked toward the door.

"Who drives that pig?" Katarina asked.

What pig?

"Bebs," Scott said. "That's her baby."

My car?

"I thought you told me she was concerned about climate change?"

I am.

"She is, I guess."

"She can't be too concerned if she drives a gas guzzling car like that."

Ouch! I rushed to my bedroom before they came inside, all sparkle gone from the ruby red that was now blood red from the wounding words.

Chapter Twenty

BESIDES HAVING SCOTT upset with me, I was now pissed at myself. I couldn't blame Ellen for my pig of a car because I'd bought it without her. I also couldn't blame Ellen for the near disaster at Black Rapids because I shouldn't have gone in the first place. Who was I to give Mary advice when she knocked on my bedroom door to tell me she was leaving for dinner with Jonathan?

"How do I look?" She came into my room and twirled to show me her skimpy sundress and sweater outfit.

"You look great." I wanted to throw up.

"Are you okay?"

"Yeah I'm fine. I'm just tired." Tired of myself.

"Why aren't you sitting outside with Scott and Katarina?"

"Oh. They're outside? I didn't know."

"How are things with Scott?" Mary sat down on the edge of my bed.

"I don't know. I think I'm going to sell my car."

"Sell your car?" She gasped. "Why? You just bought it."

"I should cut back on my expenses." And stop being such a hypocrite.

"Do you need some money to help with things?" She patted my knee.

"No, I'm okay. Thanks. Where's Jonathan taking you for dinner?"

"Our favorite restaurant in Little Italy." She hugged herself. "He should be here any minute so I'd better go. I said I'd meet him in the driveway."

"Be careful and text me if you start to feel the least bit threatened or uncomfortable."

"I'll be fine." She headed to the hall.

"What time should I expect you back?"

"No later than ten. I already told him that. Now why don't you get off your bed and sit outside with Scott and Katarina."

SCOTT AND KATARINA were sharing a dinner of East Indian takeout and both looked up when I stepped through the patio door.

"There you are," Scott said. "We were wondering if you got lost on your bike ride home."

"Hi." I smiled when Katarina's eyes met mine. "I actually got home before the two of you and was in my room."

"There's lots of food here if you haven't eaten yet," Scott said. He motioned to the spread of rice, samosa's, naan, paneer, and vegetable dishes.

"Yes, there's so much," Katarina said, "and it all tastes good."

I got myself a plate and joined them. "What did the two of you get up to this afternoon?"

"Probably the same thing you did," Scott said. "We both napped."

"How are you doing?" I looked at Katarina. Could I hug her again?

"I'm fine. It's been a long day mixed with sadness and loss, but I'm so happy that Scott and I are getting to know each other." She smiled at him.

"Me too," I said. "Scott's a good guy and I'm so glad you're here for each other."

"I really appreciate you being here too." Scott looked at me. Yes. He'd forgiven me.

"Would Mary like some food too?" Katarina asked.

"She's gone out for dinner," I said. "She's having Italian."

"Don't tell me she's with old Johnny Boy," Scott said.

"Yes." Gag. "He's taking her on a date."

"Scott told me that Mary's having trouble with her husband. It's too bad. A date won't fix things."

"Katarina has done lots of volunteering at women's shelters in San Francisco and Reykjavik," Scott said.

"That's good to know," I said. Any subject I could talk to Katarina about was good to know. Her eyes were piercing and I longed to run my fingers through her hair. I sat beside her and could feel sweet energy each time either of us leaned to reach something on the table or to stress a point. Things were looking up.

"Please feel free to talk to me if you want," Katarina said. "I handled the crisis lines a lot of the time and I know it can be scary."

Katarina was in a crisis of her own yet offering to help me. How nice was that? "Thank you. How long will you be staying in Ottawa?" I held my breath.

"I thought I'd stay for a few weeks now that I'm here and

there's nothing really to rush back for. If that's okay with you."

"You can stay here for as long as you want." Forever would be nice.

"Katarina and I can always head over to Montreal for a few days," Scott said. "Or even to Niagara Falls if you want some space."

"It's totally fine for you to stay here the entire time," I said. Katarina could be in my space all she wanted. "When are you going to spread Ari's ashes at Black Rapids?"

"Thursday," Scott said. "At least that's the plan. I hope you and your family are available."

"Of course we'll be there. Do you have any kind of ceremony planned?"

"No," Scott said. "Ari said he didn't want a big fuss."

"He just wants his ashes dumped into the canal," Katarina said. "That was Ari. He liked to keep things simple. I'm sure he thought it would be more simple if he killed himself."

"His cancer sounded pretty bad," I said. "Was his death imminent?"

"I don't know," Katarina had finished eating and pushed her empty plate to the side. "In his mind it was. I think I'll get myself another beer. Anyone else want one?"

"Sure," Scott said.

"I'm okay, thank you," I said.

Katarina took her empty plate inside, leaving Scott and me alone.

"How's it going?" I asked in a low voice.

"I'm exhausted," he whispered. "She's so different than Ari."

"In what way?" It was sexy clear for me.

"Ari was more easy going. She can be so direct sometimes and she shuts down when she doesn't want to talk about something. Just like now."

"Maybe if Ari had been more like her, his life would have been different."

"What do you mean?" Scott lifted his almost empty beer and drained the last few drops into his mouth.

"Maybe he'd have been more direct with your birth mother and you'd have grown up in Iceland. Are you planning to go back with Katarina?" It was my turn to be direct because I was dying to know.

"She wants me to. I don't know yet. Want to come with me?"

"Did you get your passport sorted out?" I needed to think.

"Of course."

"When would you go?" Iceland. Katarina. I wanted to go, but money was tight.

"I'll either go back with Katarina or leave a few days after her."

"How long would you stay?" It wasn't like I had any deadlines to get back to and if I sold my car, the money would keep me going for a while.

"I'm not sure yet." Scott stood up and collected the boxes of food. "Are you finished with everything here?"

"Yes, thanks, that was good." Scott went inside just as Katarina returned and sat back down.

She didn't say anything and I struggled for words. What could I say? I couldn't ask her anything about Ari because she'd cry. I knew what she thought of my car. I needed to pick something safe. "How are you finding the weather in Ottawa?"

"It's nice. It can be quite a bit cooler back home."

"How did you find it when you were living in San Francisco?"

"The nicer weather is the biggest thing I miss. Otherwise I love Reykjavik. San Francisco was too big."

"Could you ever see yourself moving back to San Francisco?" As in getting back together with your ex?

"No. Never. That part of my life is over."

"I see." Had Scott told her about Ellen?

"And you? Have you lived anywhere else that you would move back to again?"

"No." Ellen and I had always lived in Ottawa. I might have moved to Vancouver if she'd asked.

A text came into my phone just as Scott stepped back onto the deck. I was afraid to look in case it was Ellen, but I had to look in case it was Mary. I waited until Scott sat down before I pulled out my phone because I didn't want him to see over my shoulder. Ellen wanted to know if I had time to talk.

"It's a message from Mary," I said. "I told her to keep checking in." I responded with a no and put my phone in my lap.

"I take it that things are going okay with old Johnny Boy," Scott said.

"It sounds like it. She said the food is good." I hated lying.

"I bet," Katarina said. "Sorry, it's none of my business."

The worst thing about lying was getting caught, so when my phone rang, I had to think fast when I saw Mary's number. "Hi."

"I wanted to let you know I won't be back tonight." Her voice sounded normal and almost giddy.

"Mary, you said you would. You have to." I got up from the table and walked inside.

"Don't worry, I'll be fine. Can you feed Barbie tomorrow morning and clean her litter?"

"No, I won't." Why hadn't I seen this coming? "This was supposed to be a date, that's all."

"I know, but have you never wanted to have sex after a hot date?"

That was too much information.

"And it's not like I'm going to bring him back to your place."

"You can't spend the night with that prick." I couldn't let her.

"I wish you'd stop calling him that."

"Where is he anyway?" This was unacceptable.

"He's at the table."

"You're talking in front of him?"

"No, I'm in the washroom."

At least she still had some sense. "Stay there. I'm coming to pick you up."

Mary laughed. "Relax. I'll be fine. I'll talk to you tomorrow." She hung up.

"Fuck." I banged the counter with my fist.

"Is everything okay in there?" Scott asked.

"She's driving me crazy," I said as I stepped back onto the deck and plunked into my chair. "She's not coming home tonight. Can you believe it?"

"I guess the food really must have been good," Scott said.

"I'm not surprised," Katarina said.

"What am I going to do?"

"Be there for her when she needs you," Katarina said. "There's nothing much else you can do."

I could tell my mother. No, I'd better not. Mary would never forgive me. "I'll never be able sleep tonight."

"You have to let it go," Katarina said. "Mary is a big girl and you've done all you can right now."

"I agree," Scott said. "Sleep with your phone tonight so if Mary needs you, you'll hear it."

"I guess." I'd have rather slept with Katarina.

"I know what it's like to be a worried sister," Katarina said. "I tried so hard with Ari. I pleaded with him to stay in Reykjavik for treatments." She started to cry again. "I couldn't stop him. He wouldn't listen to me."

"I'm so sorry. You have enough to worry about right now

without getting caught up in my family drama." I put my hand on her shoulder.

We all went in to bed shortly after that, me with my phone and lustful thoughts of Katarina to avoid thinking about Mary. Or Ellen.

Chapter Twenty-one

ELLEN'S WORDS ABOUT me offering consulting services in architectural design made sense in the early morning daylight while I lingered in bed. It was a good backup plan in case I couldn't convince my dad to revive BB Construction. I needed to keep all options open, including with Ellen.

My phone had been silent all night and there were no new messages. What was I going to do about Mary? Why couldn't she just let go of the prick and move on with her life? I expected she'd pack up Barbie and return to her big house until the next time Jonathan got upset. How far could he go? I should talk to Katarina about this.

Scott had forgiven me for meeting Ellen over coffee, but would he forgive me for seeing her again? He had told me not to hit on Katarina so he shouldn't have expected me to stay away from Ellen too. It was my sex life and he wasn't going to control it. No, stop. Sex with Ellen couldn't be an option.

I really needed to talk to my dad about reviving BB Construction and convince him to work with me. He was settling into retirement quite well and his drinking seemed to be a lot less.

I remembered the times growing up when I had been held hostage by my father and some stranger as they shared beers at the end of the day. After school I had been expected to make my way to wherever my father was working and hang out near the construction site, which was often somebody's house in our neighborhood that he was doing renovations on. I would sit patiently and wait while he shared beers with the owner. It was my job to get him to stop drinking and come home. He would jump into the driver's seat of his truck and drive the two of us home. He'd always say that it was okay because we didn't have far to go. The first time he lost his license, it was only for a week. The second time it was for a year and he almost lost his business. It didn't happen again. My mother made sure of that by threatening divorce.

As soon as I turned sixteen, I got my driver's license. At first I thought it was great and I was the envy of my friends. My parents let me have free access to the family truck and car if my mother wasn't using it. I didn't even have to pay for gas. It wasn't long before I realized nothing was for free.

The price was picking up my dad and bringing him home after each bender. I especially hated those knocks on my bedroom door from my mother in the middle of the night while I was sleeping. I'd have to get out of bed, get dressed, go pick up my dad, and then try to get back to sleep. My mother could have done it herself, but she had a hard time controlling her temper and got a big speeding ticket one night that was made worse when she tried to argue with the police officer.

My mother put up with a lot from my dad, just as he put up with a lot from her. I made them put up with a lot from me too. Mary, on the other hand, had always hated controversy and was the good girl, especially when she became a lawyer and married a doctor.

My parents were enjoying their retirement. They helped keep each other in check by living on a restricted budget and yelling at each other every now and then. Could I keep my dad in check with his drinking if I talked him out of retirement? My mother would never forgive me if I didn't.

It was time to get up if I had any hopes of going for a jog. When I got outside, Katarina was just finishing up her run. She stretched those long sexy legs of hers in my driveway. I had never stretched before or after my jog until that morning.

"How was your run?" I tried to imitate her stretches.

"Great. This is a nice neighborhood. Do you run every morning?" I wished I had legs like hers.

"I try to. I don't go far, but I like to get my heart rate up." Like she was doing for me.

"That's good. I'll see you when you get back." Katarina went inside and I did a few more leg stretches before limping off.

Katarina sat on the deck by herself when I stepped out with my breakfast. My jog had been quick and shower rushed. She had a mug and empty plate in front of her and was wearing a beige T-shirt with navy cotton shorts. Her feet were bare and she wore a gold anklet around her right foot. I wanted to touch the anklet and ask her about it but decided against it.

"Is Scott still in bed?" I asked.

"Yes, I think so. He must take after Ari because I was always up before him."

"How are you doing?" Please don't let her cry because I'd have to hug her and if that happened, my lips would have to brush against her cheek.

"I'm okay. Thanks." She stared at the empty birdbath. "This

is so strange getting to know Scott and seeing him do little things that Ari does. Did."

"Like what?" I loved the sound of her voice.

"The way he moves his hands and how he wrinkles his forehead when he doesn't understand something."

"Like this?" Scott furrowed his eyebrows as he stepped out onto the deck.

Katarina laughed. "Yes, just like that."

Scott moved off the deck and got the hose. Katarina and I watched as he rinsed out and filled the birdbath.

"There," Katarina said. "That's something Ari would do. Fill the birdbath. I'm really going to miss him." Her voice shook.

"Would he do this too?" Scott flicked the hose toward us, causing a light spray of water on the deck.

"What an asshole." Katarina swayed to avoid getting wet and laughed again.

"Did you just call me an asshole?" Scott jerked back.

"Yes." She laughed. "Don't look so offended. In Iceland it's meant to be a compliment."

"A compliment?" I asked.

"We call Iceland the asshole of the world because it's like the earth is relieving itself through our volcanoes, geysers, and hot springs." She grinned at Scott. "It's a compliment for an Icelander to be called an asshole, especially kids and I think he's cute, my little nephew."

"Too funny," Scott said.

Was I her little nephew's friend and out of her league for anything more? "I haven't heard from Mary this morning. I wonder if it's too soon to check in with her."

"Of course not," Katarina said. "She needs to know you're there for her even if you don't agree with what she's doing."

"I'll start with a text." I liked Katarina's approach to things.

"I'd call her," Katarina said. "With a text, how would you know if it's her answering?"

"That's true." She was so smart.

"It wouldn't be the first time old Johnny Boy had her phone," Scott said. "I'm going in for a shower." He disappeared through the patio doors.

I dialed Mary's number and her phone rang five times before going to voicemail. "Damn, she's not answering." I threw my phone on the table.

"Try to be patient," Katarina said. "Maybe she's in the shower."

"I sure hope so." Or in the pool, floating. No. Don't panic. "I'm worried about her."

"Yes, I can imagine you would be. Next time you should have a plan so she can let you know she's okay. It's not fair for you to have to worry like this."

"That's a good idea." She was so helpful. "I never thought about a plan."

"Speaking of plans," Katarina said, "what about your business plan that your mother mentioned the other day. How is it coming along?"

"I was thinking about it this morning and things are starting to take shape." I wished.

"What is your business going to be about?" Katarina leaned forward and gave me her full attention.

"I want to focus on energy efficient housing and help in the fight against climate change." Even though I drove a gas guzzling pig.

"Nice." She held my eyes. "How do you plan to do that?"

"I want to offer architectural consulting and construction services for energy efficient renovations and new builds. My dad is a carpenter and it would be nice to work with him."

"Isn't he retired?" Katarina's eyes were such a piercing jade.

"He is, but he has a lot of experience that could help."

"What does he think about it?" She was so engaging.

"I'm planning to talk to him today." I guess I was now. "What are you and Scott up to?"

"I think we're just going to hang out and take it easy. I hope you don't mind if I park myself on your deck with a book."

"No, not at all." Shoot. Why had I just told her I was planning to talk to my dad when all I wanted to do was hang out with her?

My phone rang. "It's Mary."

"I'll give you some privacy." Katarina went inside.

"Hey," I said as I answered. "How are things?"

"Good." Her voice chirped. "I saw that you called when I was in the shower."

"I was worried about you. We should have a check in system."

"There's no need to worry about me. Things went very well last night."

"I suppose you're coming to get Barbie and moving back home."

I could hear sandals flapping against stairs. "Are you trying to get rid of me?"

"Of course not. You're going to keep staying here?" Why bother?

"If that's okay, I'd like to. I told Jonathan he'd have to win me back."

"He got lucky last night. What else does he have to do?"

"I asked him to see a counselor. He says he'll try to find one in Montreal because he doesn't want to go to one here. He's going there later this week for a conference. Did you feed Barbie?"

Shit. "I was just going to do it now."

"How is she doing?"

"Fine." She was locked in Mary's room. "Where's Jonathan?"

"He's gone to the hospital. I hope you cleaned her litter."

"Not yet. It didn't look dirty. What time are you coming back?"

"Soon because my stuff is at your place. I have to work on a few files this afternoon."

AFTER THE CALL, I got ready for a visit to my parents' house to talk to my dad about reviving BB Construction. I'd hoped my mother would be out when I got there and that my bike ride would be painless. There was no way I'd let Katarina see me drive the pig.

"I thought you went for a jog this morning." Scott was opening the windows on his car as I took my bike out of the garage.

"I did, but want to ride my bike to my parents'."

"Are you trying to impress my aunt?"

"I thought I'd leave my pig of a car at home."

Scott laughed. "You heard. I'd say you've forgiven her by the way you were ogling her this morning. Remember, she's off limits."

"Don't worry." I got on my bike and pedaled off.

My dad was sitting on a lawn chair in the shade of his backyard. The buttons were undone on his short-sleeved navy cotton shirt and he held a bottle of beer. His gas lawnmower was out and the grass was freshly cut.

"Barbra, you're just in time to sweep up."

"Sure." I leaned my bike against the back of the house and got the broom.

"I was just kidding." He laughed. "Grab a chair and sit down. What's wrong with your car?" He motioned with his bottle of beer toward my bike.

"Nothing." Everything. "I just thought I'd ride my bike for a change. Where's Mom?"

"Getting some groceries. What's going on with Mary? Why is she staying at your place?"

"I'd rather stay at my place too if I had to live with Jonathan." My dad knew I wasn't fond of the prick.

"Hey come on now. He's Mary's husband. Be nice. So what's up with them?"

"Ask Mary." I longed to tell him.

"Your mother already did, but she thinks there's something more going on. Is he cheating on her?"

"I don't know." For all I knew he could be. I quickly changed the subject. "I was hoping to talk to you about my business plan. How would you feel about reviving BB Construction and working with me?"

"Working with you? How? I'm getting too old for construction."

"You're not that old. And you have so much experience. You could help out with sales and marketing."

"What would I be selling?" He took a swig of beer.

"I want to design and build energy efficient houses. We could start with retrofitting my house to the passive house standard."

"What do you mean by passive house? You want to put solar panels on your roof? They're a waste of money, if you ask me."

"It's not about solar panels. It's about adding lots of insulation and better windows and eliminating drafts to make the house comfortable. You don't even need a furnace in a passive house."

"And what would you do? Even if you put a woodstove in your basement, you'll still need a furnace in this climate."

"No, that's the beauty of a passive house. They're building them all over Europe, especially in Germany. They work almost like a thermos because there's so much insulation."

"A thermos. You need fresh air coming into the house or else you'll be sick all the time."

My mouth was dry. "That's part of it too. There are special air exchangers for passive houses. The windows are all triple glazed and..."

"You can't be thinking of putting in triple paned windows? Do you know how much that would cost? You'd never get your money back."

"I need to change my windows anyway." I struggled to control my tone. "I'm losing a lot of heat through them."

"I'll help you put some weather-stripping on this fall."

"Barbra." My mother stepped out the back door. "I wondered who your father was talking to. Where's your car?"

"I rode my bike."

"What's wrong with your car?" She grabbed the broom and started to sweep.

"Nothing. I just wanted to go for a bike ride, that's all. I should be heading out now before I get too tired sitting here." I jumped up and grabbed my bike, almost scraping my leg with a pedal.

"Why don't you stay for supper," my mother said. "I just bought some fresh corn and Mary's coming over."

"She is?" Good, let her answer their questions about what's going on. "I can't. I already have plans." Hopefully with Scott and Katarina.

"How are Katarina and Scott doing?" my mother asked.

"They seem to be okay." I put on my helmet and mounted my bike. "See you later."

When I got home, the house was empty except for Barbie. She was flopped on the couch and didn't even look up to acknowledge me. Scott had sent a text saying he and Katarina were going to the ByWard Market for dinner and I could bike down to join them if I wanted. There was a smiley face with a tongue sticking out on the end of his text.

I stuck out my tongue and sent a text to Ellen to see if she was free for dinner.

Chapter Twenty-two

ELLEN RESPONDED TO my text right away. She suggested pizza at her place and I accepted because there wouldn't be a risk of running into Scott and Katarina. I ignored any other risks with her invitation.

"I'm so glad you could come." Ellen hugged me in the small entry of her tenth floor apartment.

"Me too." That would be the only coming I'd let myself do there that night.

"Let me show you around, although it's not much." Ellen grabbed my hand and led the way.

"It looks like you have a nice view." Her living room window and balcony faced out over the Ottawa River.

"I love it, especially at night. You'll see how beautiful it gets."

She shouldn't have been counting on that. "How are the neighbors?"

"Quiet. It's as though I'm living in this big building all by myself. I want to buy a house though, but I don't want to rush into anything."

I didn't want to rush into anything either, especially with Katarina around. "Did you own a house in Vancouver?"

"Are you kidding? Do you know how expensive it is out there? I wanted to live downtown so there was no way I could afford to buy."

What did she and Donna do with all of their money besides spend it on skimpy bathing suit trips? "I'm glad I bought when I did."

That had been one good thing I did when she dumped me. We had owned a townhouse together that was sold when we split. My parents insisted I use my half of the money to buy a place of my own instead of throwing it away in rent. My dad had helped me find my house with its 1960's character and south facing backyard that would be perfect for a passive house retrofit if only he saw it that way too.

We were standing in her bedroom now. Risky. Her bed was big and fluffy and I didn't think I could resist if she threw me on it and covered me in kisses, like she used to do. "Nice." I stepped back into the hallway, my knees shaky.

Ellen was on her best behavior. We enjoyed our pizza on the balcony and kept the conversation mostly light until she started to pry into my love life during the years she had been with Donna. She didn't need to know about my lack of a love life, but I wanted to learn about hers.

"Why did you and Donna break up?" I tried some of Katarina's directness.

Ellen paused to sip her wine then sighed. "It's a long story, but in the end I couldn't take any more. She had a lot of problems."

That was it? That was all she was going to tell me? "Did she ever hit you?" I wanted to know, especially after her comments when talking about Mary.

Ellen's eyes reddened. "What makes you say that?"

"You were so in love with her when you dropped me like a hotcake. I can only imagine it must have been something bad." It felt good until I realized Ellen had started to cry.

"If you really want to know, yes she hit me many times. My life with her was hell and I had no one to blame but myself." Tears were flowing.

"I'm sorry to hear that. I would have never hit you." Why did I have to say that too? I reached over and held her hand.

"I know, Bebs." She clutched my hand and sobbed. "You were perfect compared to Donna. How could I have been so stupid?"

Yes, how could she have been so stupid? I let her cry. The last thing I wanted to do was console her over whatever shit Donna had put her through.

"How much do I owe you for the pizza?"

"Nothing." Ellen squeezed my hand and flashed red eyes at me. "I'm just so glad you're here and that you've forgiven me."

Whoa. Who said anything about forgiving her? "Let's just say we're taking things one step at a time."

"Why don't we go sit inside," she said. "I'm finding it a bit breezy and we can have some more wine."

"I can't because I'm driving." She wasn't getting me drunk.

"Would you like a pop or some juice?"

We were inside now and I sat on one end of her couch.

"No thanks. I'm fine for now." It was seven o'clock. Scott and Katarina could have been home and sitting out on the deck.

Ellen got herself another glass of wine and sat in the middle of the couch, putting one leg under her as she faced me. "I'm so glad we've found each other again."

"Are you?" I wanted to get going.

"Of course." Ellen straightened up and took a sip of her wine. "Aren't you?"

"It's not like we just bumped into each other. If I hadn't contacted you, you'd have never called me."

"You're right." Ellen put her glass down and leaned in closer. "I'm so glad you got in touch with me after I was such a shit to you." She put her lips on mine.

A tickle rushed up my spine and caused me to kiss her back. The next thing I knew, her tongue was in my mouth and she was all over me. No. I couldn't let this happen.

I pulled away and stood. "I think I felt a text. I have to check it in case it's my friend and she needs me."

"Sure. Will you stay the night?"

No, absolutely not. "We'll see." I went over by the window to look at my phone and pretended to read a text.

"Is everything okay?" Ellen asked.

"I think so." It was time to leave.

"That's good." Ellen came up behind me, put her arms around my waist and rested her chin on my shoulder.

Her body felt nice against mine and it was tempting to take her hand and lead her into the bedroom. My head throbbed with indecision over the betrayal to Scott and myself if I let it happen. And then there was Katarina. "I'd like to take things slower."

"We can do that." Ellen kissed the back of my neck.

My knees almost gave out and I had to grab onto the handle of the patio door as I imagined Katarina's lips on my neck.

"Are you okay?"

"Sorry," I said. "I guess I didn't realize how much you were holding me up."

"We could always spend the night just hugging and nothing else."

Yeah right. "I should get going. I'm looking after Mary's cat and have to feed her."

"Oh, Mary has a cat. I didn't know that. Why are you looking after her cat? Is she out of town?"

Think fast. "No. Barbie's not feeling well so Mary wants me to keep an eye on her during the day while she's at work."

"Barbie." Ellen chuckled. "What an interesting name for a cat. What kind of cat is she?"

"Bengal." I moved to the entryway and put my sandals on.

"I'm so glad you could come tonight." Ellen put her arms around my waist.

"Me too." I leaned in and kissed Ellen goodbye, relieved that I had the strength to fight off her advances.

When I got home I was pleased to see Mary in the kitchen, opening a can of cat food. Barbie was dancing around her feet and meowing.

"When was the last time you fed her?"

"This morning." Or had I? "How was dinner?"

"Did you know they were going to gang up on me?" Mary flashed her green eyes at me. "I couldn't wait to get out of there."

"What did you expect? Did you tell them?"

"Tell them what?"

"About Jonathan and the truth about your arm."

"Of course not. I focused on the positive, like our date last night." Mary put Barbie's food bowl on the floor and silenced the annoying cat.

"I hope you didn't give them as much detail as you gave me."

"As if. Are you going out onto the deck?"

"Yes." Scott's car wasn't in the driveway so I knew it would be just the two of us. "What's your next step with Jonathan?" We sat down.

"I'm meeting him in Montreal for the weekend."

"Do you really think that's a wise thing to do? What if something happens there?"

"It won't. I'll be okay. Where were you tonight?"

"I had dinner with a friend."

Mary glared at me.

"Okay, Ellen."

"I'd hardly call her a friend." She shook her head. "I thought you were out with your friend, Scott. Or have you forgotten about him and how much he helped you get over Ellen?"

"That's not fair. And please don't say anything about this. I'm still trying to figure out what to do about her. She'd like to get back together." Or at least have sex with me.

"I'm sure it feels good to have her want you, but it won't feel good if you get sucked in and risk losing yourself again. It's not healthy."

"And going to Montreal to be with Jonathan is?"

"I'm trying to save our marriage. You don't have anything left to save with Ellen. She even took your dignity when she left."

"Well maybe I want my dignity back. She wanted me to spend tonight with her, but I was stronger than you and resisted the urge for sex after a hot date."

"I'm not going to respond to that." Mary stood up. "I have

some work to do."

She opened the patio door and stomped inside. Where were Scott and Katarina? Having fun somewhere else without me. I should have driven downtown to meet them instead of seeing Ellen. I could have been having fun too. I decided to do something productive and cut the grass.

It was getting dark by the time I switched off my electric lawnmower. I reached for my phone to see if there were any messages. There was a text from Scott checking in. I called him.

"Hey, Bebs." He yelled over loud music and his words were slurred. "What are you up to?"

"I just finished mowing our lawn."

"Guess you're too tired to bike downtown then and drive us home?"

"That's for sure." I couldn't even do it for Katarina.

"Can you pick us up then? I've had too much to drink."

"Where are you?" The thought of seeing Katarina was appealing, but the thought of her seeing me in my gas guzzling pig when I was all hot and sweaty from cutting the grass wasn't.

"We're still in the Market. Where's Mary? Could she come with you and drive my car home?"

"Maybe. I'll ask her." If she'd talk to me right now.

"You might want to bring a barf bag for my aunt. She's had a lot to drink."

"I heard that." Katarina laughed in the background. "I'm fine and don't need any barf bag."

"I'll talk to Mary and text you before we leave."

Mary was okay to come along and help out. We had both cooled off and it was as if we had never argued. Scott and Katarina were standing by his car when we pulled up. Mary got out and Scott motioned for Katarina to get in.

"Thanks, Bebs," he said. I'll ride home with Mary."

"I'm sorry about your car." Katarina settled into the passenger seat as we left.

"Please don't tell me you're about to barf."

She didn't laugh. "No, not at all." Katarina paused before continuing. "Scott told me that you heard me call your car a pig the other day. It's very nice, if that's your thing."

Awkward. "I'm thinking about selling my little piglet." What else could I say? Katarina burst out laughing. It wasn't that funny.

"Don't you have a car?" I asked.

"No, I don't need one. Reykjavik has a good bus system."

"Oh, I see." I wasn't resorting to taking the bus.

"I hope you're not selling your car because of what I said. Scott told me you love this car." She kept her hands on her knees and didn't massage the dash like Ellen had.

"I've always dreamed of having a set of wheels like this, but it doesn't really fit in with my business plan."

"How did your talk with your dad go?"

"Okay." Not really. I was getting tired.

"What did he say?"

I didn't want to talk about it. "He's going to think about it." When we hit open highway, I tramped on the gas pedal and bolted the car forward for a rush. Katarina didn't react.

"Thank you for picking us up. I thought we could take the bus, but Scott didn't want to leave his car downtown."

"That's too bad because it would have been a new experience for Scott to take the bus." And it wasn't like his car was any better on gas than mine.

"He doesn't take the bus to work? I thought he works downtown." I felt Katarina's eyes on me.

"He does, but he likes the convenience of his car." And he'd never take the bus.

"Climate change is not a convenient thing and we all have to do our part. I'll have to talk to him about this."

We drove in silence for the rest of the way, which wasn't long. Katarina thanked me again then went directly to her room in the basement. After putting my car in the garage, I went inside and picked up Barbie. She purred as my fingers caressed her soft fur. If I'd stayed with Ellen, I'd have been purring too. Headlights announced the arrival of Scott and Mary. I dropped Barbie and escaped into my room. I didn't feel like talking to anyone and it was time for this day to come to an end.

Chapter Twenty-three

EVERYONE EXCEPT MARY slept in later the next morning. She was already gone for the day by the time I crawled out of bed and headed for the shower. There would be no jog for me this morning. I had decided to take it easy on my body, especially given that my mind had been working out all night.

Katarina was complicated and would be gone soon. How could she not have liked my car? She mustn't have thought much of my business plan either. She probably didn't even like me. Why couldn't she have been some ugly old hag that didn't turn me on in the least?

If I'd spent the night with Ellen, things would have changed. Would we have been back to being Bebellen? Was that what I wanted? Bebkat had a nice ring to it. Ellen sure liked my car. Maybe she'd want to buy it. I should have seen her as an ugly old hag for what she did to me, but that lilac ponytail of hers was so sweet.

When I stepped out onto the deck to feel the temperature, a stray orange cat was eyeing the empty birdbath. I slapped my hands together and shooed it away just as Katarina strolled into the backyard in her jogging gear.

"I hope that wasn't meant for me." She came onto the deck and sat in one of the chairs.

"Didn't you see the stupid cat?" My heart fluttered. She did it to me every time.

"Barbie?" Katarina leaned back and pulled her hair into a short ponytail with both hands.

"No, not Barbie." Breathe. "She's an indoor cat." My legs were weak and I collapsed into the chair beside hers.

Katarina smiled. "Then who was the stupid cat?"

Was she flirting with me? I could feel my cheeks turning red. "I don't know. It was hunting for the cardinals. They like to hang around the bird bath."

"Scott pointed out one of your red cardinals the other day. They're beautiful."

"They are, aren't they," I said.

Katarina was still smiling as she released her hair and straightened up. "It looks like you beat me at jogging this morning."

"I've already had my shower." She didn't need to know I skipped mine.

"I found my jog a bit tough this morning. How did you find yours?"

I snickered. "It was okay because I only jogged from my bedroom to the shower."

Katarina laughed. "Maybe I should have done the same." She stood and moved toward the patio doors. "I'll go have my shower."

Could I join her?

Katarina flinched and swung around to look at me. Shit. Had I actually said the words out loud?

"I almost forgot," she said. "I think I lost my wallet in your car last night. Are you okay? You look startled or something."

Phew. I let out a breath and relaxed my shoulders. "A bug just flew into my mouth. I'll go have a look." I was off the deck before she could say anything more.

Her wallet was there, perfectly blending in with the black leather of the passenger seat. I ran my hand along the top of the seat and caressed it with my fingertips as I thought about selling my baby.

I went inside to make my breakfast and get out of the kitchen before Katarina finished her shower. I was half way through my toast when Scott stepped onto the deck, rubbing his eyes.

"Have you seen Katarina this morning?" He plopped down in a chair.

"Isn't she downstairs in the bathroom?" The image of Katarina in the shower consumed me.

Scott rubbed his temples. "She is. I'm wondering how she's doing this morning because I heard her crying last night."

His words jerked me back to reality. Her only brother had just died and here I was, lusting after her. How could I have been so insensitive? "Poor Katarina. She was just here and seemed fine. Did you talk to her?" My throat was dry.

"I tried to, but when I went to her door she pretended to be asleep. It must be so hard for her. I still can't believe he's gone. Can you try to talk to her to see how she's doing?"

"I guess." What if she started to cry and I had to hug her? Could I control myself? Thinking of Ellen might help. I needed to see Ellen again. "What's the plan for today?"

"We're going to look into options for flights to Iceland. Have you thought any more about coming with me?"

"When would you go?" My car should have already been up

for sale if I wanted to tag along.

"Probably the end of next week. Katarina wants me to go back with her."

And I wanted to go with Katarina too. "Does she know you asked me to come?"

"I told her at the bar last night."

"How did she react?" Had she been excited?

"She said that would be fine."

Just fine? "Where would we stay?" If I went with Scott, I didn't want to stay in a hotel by myself.

"With Katarina. She said the house is big enough. I could have Ari's room. I really thought I'd be going with him. I don't know if I want to go without Ari. It'll be so hard."

"I think it'll be especially difficult for Katarina once she gets home because Ari won't be there anymore. It'll be important to support her then." I could hold her hand and hug her and let her cry on my shoulder.

"So? Will you come with me?"

"For how long?" If I didn't sell my car before I left, I could always ask Mary for a small loan to pay for the trip.

"I'm thinking about two weeks. Katarina wants me to help go through Ari's things and see if I want anything."

I could handle two weeks. What I wasn't sure about was if I could handle leaving Katarina at the end of it. "Well, I've never been to Iceland, so why not?"

"Good. Do you want to come with us when we go to the travel agent?"

"I can't." I needed to get going on selling my car. Plus I wanted to see Ellen again before spending more time with Katarina. "What about the ceremony tomorrow to spread Ari's ashes. Is everything set for that?"

"Yes. We're going to do it around noon then have pizza for lunch. A picnic at Black Rapids will be Ari's Canadian funeral. He would have liked that."

"For sure." I wondered if he had planned it that way when we were at Black Rapids, telling me Katarina and I would hit it off.

It was another hot day and Ellen was more than happy to meet me for lunch. I picked her up from her office and we drove to the beach at Mooney's Bay along the Rideau River.

"I thought a lot about you last night," Ellen said. We were sitting at a picnic table in the shade, watching people on the beach. Ellen had switched out of her uniform and was wearing jogging shorts and a T-shirt.

"Me too." Although I did think about Ellen, I mostly tossed and turned, contemplating Katarina, and my situation. "I'm putting my car up for sale. Do you know anybody who might want to buy it?"

"You're selling that baby?" I could picture her eyes bulging behind those large black sporty sunglasses. "Why?"

I shrugged my shoulders, unable to tell her Katarina thought it was a gas guzzling pig and I needed money to go to Iceland. "You must think I'm crazy."

"What are you going to drive instead?" Ellen slid her sunglasses down her nose and focused her brown eyes on me.

I looked away. "I don't know yet. Some kind of hybrid that will be a better match for my business model." It sounded reasonable.

"I might know somebody who'd be interested. One of the guys I work with said he's looking for a late model used car. I'll send him a text to see if he wants to have a look at your Mustang."

I reached over and touched Ellen's ponytail while she sent her text. It made her smile. What would Katarina's little ponytail have felt like if I'd touched it? I smiled back.

"Cool." Ellen tapped my knee. "He'd like to see it. Why don't we head back and he'll take a look now?"

When we got to her office parking lot, a tall, handsome, young RCMP officer in a patrol uniform waved. He walked up to the car as we parked.

"Hey, Mike, this is my friend, Bebs."

"Nice car." He shook my hand and walked around the vehicle. "Why do you want to sell it?"

"I'm starting up a business and it doesn't really fit with my model." My head was spinning. Things were happening so fast. What if he wanted to buy it? Was that what I really wanted?

"Can I take it for a spin?" His hand was already out for the keys before I had a chance to respond.

Even though Mike was in uniform, it was my car and I was hesitant to let anyone else drive it. "Okay." I reluctantly handed over the keys.

Seeing someone drive away in my baby hurt, and I had to think of Katarina in the shower to ease the pain. Ellen and I sat on a parking barrier in some shade at the edge of the lot.

"I hope this works out for you." Ellen put a sweaty hand on my knee. "I loved it when you touched my ponytail. Can you come over tonight?"

This wasn't working. "I can't. Tomorrow is the ceremony for Ari so I need to be home tonight." I hoped she didn't ask why because I didn't have an answer.

"How's it going with Scott's aunt?" Ellen massaged my knee.

"It's going." I couldn't answer that. "Scott doesn't approve of me seeing you." I wanted to at least let her know things were complicated.

Ellen pulled her hand away. "It doesn't surprise me. He never liked me."

"Can you blame him? Mary thinks I owe it to Scott to stay away from you." She hadn't exactly said that, but I wanted Ellen to know that Scott wasn't the only one who didn't want me seeing her. "My parents don't even know that you've moved back. I'm not ready to go there with them."

"How do you feel? Can you ever forgive me?" A tear slipped out from under her sunglasses.

"There's a lot going on right now and I'm feeling a bit overwhelmed." Where was Mike with my car?

"Hopefully things will settle down next week and you'll feel less overwhelmed. Maybe we can go away for a weekend in Montreal or something."

"Sounds like a plan." I hoped to be on my way to Iceland by then.

When my shiny, ruby red chariot rolled into the parking lot and screeched to a halt, I held my breath. I hoped he wanted to buy it, but I also secretly hoped he didn't.

"I love it." Mike beamed as he stepped out. "How soon are you looking to sell?"

"Anytime." My heart sank.

"Would it be okay if I popped by your place with my girlfriend tonight to have another look? I'd like her to see it."

"Sure." I gave him my address and we arranged for a time after dinner. Ellen and I exchanged a quick hug before she went back into her office and I got into my car. I spent what could be one of the last afternoons cruising around in my baby.

MIKE AND HIS girlfriend showed up on time. I was relieved that no one else was home. Scott and Katarina had gone to a movie and Mary was at her house since Jonathan had already left for Montreal. My empty house gave me time to complete the used vehicle information package I had picked up during the afternoon. I was reluctantly ready for a sale when they showed up.

Mike's girlfriend, Jessica, loved it right away. "I can't believe you'd want to sell such a nice car." She sat in the passenger seat and caressed the front dash with her fingers. "Oh and look at the cute little pony on the steering wheel." She massaged the pony's main.

I looked at Mike and knew my car was sold. He had a big grin and was rubbing his hands together. "Can I have a look under the hood?"

"Sure. It's a four-cylinder eco-boost. Better on gas than the V-8." I wanted to sound somewhat knowledgeable with what was under the hood and prove to myself that I had at least been trying to get a more fuel-efficient vehicle.

Mike lifted the hood, glanced inside then let it drop shut. "I'll take it."

Jessica was now standing with us at the front of the car. "Aren't you going to try it out again?"

"I took it for a good enough run this afternoon. I'm sold. It looks great."

"I love the color," Jessica said. "How can you part with it?"

"It's not easy, but it just doesn't fit in with my life right now." What did?

We agreed on a price and the exchange would take place the following morning. I put my car in the garage for the last time then went inside for the night and flopped on the couch in front of the TV.

I couldn't get Katarina out of my mind. Maybe I should have tried anger. If it hadn't been for her, I wouldn't have just sold my dream car. She had been right though. The car didn't fit with my business model and wasn't the best for climate change. Still. How could she have not liked my baby?

Ellen loved my Mustang. The thought of her fingers caressing the dash still turned me on. It was good of Ellen to match me up with a buyer, but how could she have helped me rush into a sale when she loved my car?

I went to bed before Scott and Katarina came home. They must have gone out to the bars again and I was upset that I hadn't been included. They'd have to take a cab home if Scott drank too much to drive. My powerful Mustang would no longer be around to come to the rescue.

Chapter Twenty-four

SUNRISE CAME TOO soon on this Thursday morning that would begin a sad day of goodbyes. My car had sold so quickly and I wasn't ready to let it go. I rubbed dried tears from my cheeks then thought of Ari and cried again. With the turmoil of his death and meeting Katarina, I hadn't really had a chance to grieve. We'd only known Ari for two weeks, but his impact had been life changing, especially for Scott.

I heard Scott and Katarina in the kitchen. Their low monotone conversation was indicative of the mournful day ahead. I knew that their first task of the morning was to retrieve Ari, or his ashes, for the farewell ceremony at Black Rapids.

My first task of the morning was to hand over the keys to my car and let it go. I still wasn't good at letting go, as Scott and Mary could have attested to over my behavior with Ellen. To make matters worse, I would also have to begin the letting go process of Ari, and ultimately Katarina. I wanted to stay in bed.

When Mike arrived to take the car, Scott and Katarina had already gone. I managed to avoid them by lingering in the shower. It wasn't that I didn't want to see Katarina. It was more that I didn't want her to see me cry so soon in the day.

"I picked up the new plates this morning and have a copy of my insurance slips." Mike handed me a certified cheque for payment. "I'm ready to take this baby off your hands."

"He's so excited," Jessica said. She had driven Mike over. "He could hardly sleep last night."

Neither could I. "I'm glad for you." I wasn't.

"Thanks for keeping this baby so clean," Mike had removed my plates and handed them to me as he walked around the car. "It looks brand new."

What was I doing? "Here are the keys." I fought back tears. "I hope you enjoy it."

"Oh, he will," Jessica said. "We're taking it to Toronto this weekend. He wants to show it off to his brother."

"That sounds nice." I looked at the cheque. It wasn't worth showing off to anyone because I'd lost money on the car.

I ran my hand over the hood for one last time before Mike backed out of the driveway. My car was beautiful and I was glad no one was home to see me bawling as my Mustang trotted away.

The bike ride to the bank to deposit the cheque was brutal with the breeze, but it did help to get my fading heart rate up. When I got home, I checked my phone and saw there was a text from Mary. She asked if I could drive her to Ari's ceremony then on to the train station afterward. I dialed her number.

"Hey, I just saw your text. Are you working from your house?"

"Yes. So can you pick me up?"

"I don't know because it's been a while since I've given you a seat ride on my bike."

"What? Where's your car?"

"I just sold it." My voice cracked.

She gasped. "You sold your car? Why? I thought you loved it."

"It's complicated." I didn't want to discuss it. "All that to say, I don't have a car to drive you this afternoon."

"What are you going to do? Are you going to get another one?"

"Yes, eventually." After I got back from Iceland.

"Why don't you let me help you and loan you some money so you don't have to go without a car?"

"It's not a money thing," I said. "I just decided it wasn't the car for me."

"What is the car for you then?"

"I don't know yet."

"You can use mine for the weekend if you drive me to the train station."

"Are you sure?" I'd avoid letting Katarina see me driving it.

"Yes, no problem. I can pick you up on my way to Black Rapids and then you can drop me off at the train station."

I tried to focus on the positives of having dollars in the bank instead of depreciating in my car. I could use the money to buy whatever I wanted, including the trip to Iceland I was starting to look forward to. I was curious to see where Katarina lived and wouldn't let myself go anywhere near thinking about the end of the trip. Instead, I focused on immediate tasks, such as tidying up the kitchen and getting ready for the ceremony.

My mother called as I was emptying the last of the clean dishes from the dishwasher.

"How are things this morning?"

"Sad." I started to cry.

"I know, dear. How are Scott and Katarina?"

"They're getting Ari's ashes." I could hardly speak.

"Poor Ari. He was such a nice man. Your father and I will be heading to Black Rapids soon. Would you like us to pick you up?"

"Thanks, but Mary's picking me up." My voice was coming back.

"Oh, why? Where's your car?"

"I sold it this morning." Why didn't I make something up?

"You sold it? Barbra, you just bought it. You must have lost a lot of money on it."

"Not if you look at the big picture." It would have cost me more money in the long run.

"I don't think you looked at the big picture at all. You don't just buy a brand new car then turn around and sell it. I told you that you should have let your father go with you before you bought anything."

"I'll see you at Black Rapids." I hung up before she could say anything more.

The mood was somber when Mary and I arrived at Black Rapids. A picnic table by the water's edge had been set up with a burgundy tablecloth, some flowers, and the urn with Ari's ashes. Our parents' red and white cooler was on one of the benches and I could smell pizza. Mary and I were the last to arrive and we exchanged hugs and words of condolences with everyone. Scott and Katarina clung to each other and looked more like brother and sister than estranged aunt and nephew.

My dad wore a dark navy suit and burgundy tie while my mother had on a light blue floral print skirt and matching blouse. It wasn't often that my dad wore his suit and I was surprised to see him in it. The rest of us were dressed casually for a warm summer day at the waterside park.

Katarina's eyes were wet and her shoulders slouched forward. I couldn't keep my eyes off her, wanting to offer solace of any kind for her pain. Scott took the lead in the ceremony and began to speak about Ari.

"We only knew each other for two weeks, but I feel like I've known him forever." Scott struggled to control his voice. "My dad. He was a missing part of me for most of my life. And now he's gone again."

Scott wasn't able to continue speaking so my mother took over.

"He will be missed," she said, "but he'll never be gone from our thoughts."

"He was a good guy," my dad said. "It was a good thing he

did by finding you, Scott." My dad pulled a hanky from his pocket and wiped his eyes.

My voice was in no condition to speak. I just wanted to hug someone, Katarina, and cry. She looked up with her wet eyes and struggled to smile before saying a few words.

"Ari, my big brother, you were always there for me. And now that you're not here anymore, you've brought me to your son. Scott, it's just you and me now." She gave Scott a hug and they both cried.

"You have us too," my mother said. "Scott is family to us and now you're family too."

I heard a sob from my dad and that's all it took for me to burst out crying. "I'm going to miss Ari too." I went over to Scott and Katarina and joined their hug. They both welcomed me.

"He was a very nice man." Mary finally spoke, her tone business-like. "Jonathan is sorry that he couldn't be here too, but he's at a conference in Montreal."

Why did she have to bring up the prick? I pulled out of the hug to stand off to the side and fume alone. Katarina reached over and squeezed my arm, comforting me when I should have been comforting her.

Scott moved to the picnic table and picked up the urn. "I think it's time we set Ari free in the Rideau. Katarina, please do the honor."

Katarina took the ashes from Scott and we all approached the edge of the water. "Ari, may you find your peace here." Katarina placed the soluble urn on the water and we all watched it float away.

"What about a prayer?" My mother asked. "Shouldn't we say a prayer?"

"Ari wasn't religious," Katarina said. "It's not necessary."

"Well, I'd like to say something," my mother said. She leaned over the edge of the water, following Ari's ashes with her eyes, and made the sign of the cross on herself. Katarina and Scott exchanged glances. Just a little push was all that was needed for my mother to have a swim.

"God our Father, please forgive Ari for all of his sins and welcome him into Heaven." My mother finished by making the sign of the cross over the water while I cringed.

We stood in silence as Ari's urn floated out into the middle and began to sink.

"Goodbye my dear brother. I will miss you." Katarina blew a kiss to the disappearing urn.

"Let's have some pizza," Scott said. "It's what Ari would want us to do now." He moved to the picnic table and everyone followed except for Katarina. She stayed by herself at the water's edge and cried.

"The poor dear." My mother spoke in a low whisper. "Baxter, why don't you go to her? I think she could use a father figure right now."

"A father figure?" I said.

"I'm sure that's how she saw Ari, being that he was so much older," my mother said.

"I think she just needs a few minutes by herself," Scott said.

"And how are you doing dear?" My mother put a hand on Scott's arm. His body tensed then relaxed.

"I'm fine. Thanks for coming." Scott patted my mother's hand then backed away. "Help yourself to some pizza everyone."

I looked at my dad, who was watching Katarina. He had removed his suit jacket and his hands were in his pockets as he turned to look at my mother. She motioned with her chin, prompting my dad to go to Katarina and pull her into a hug to let her cry on his shoulder. He then led her to the picnic table to join our pizza gathering.

"What do you have planned for the rest of Ari's ashes when you get home?" my mother asked. "Will there be a lot of people?"

Katarina had stopped crying and was nibbling her pizza. "Ari didn't have lots of friends. He was a loner and liked to spend his time reading and watching television. So no, I don't have anything planned, but I'm glad that Scott and Barbra will be there with me."

"Barbra, you're going to Iceland with Scott and Katarina?" My mother's eyes shot to me. "Is that why you sold your car?"

"No, it's not." My teeth clenched.

"That's hard to believe because you don't have a job and need to get money from somewhere. When are you going?" My mother kept her eyes glued to me.

"We're leaving next Saturday." Scott said. "I asked her to come with me."

"How long will you be staying?" Mary's voice was shrill.

"Two weeks," Scott said. "It's a long way to go, so we might as well make the best of it and I'm going to help Katarina sort through Ari's things."

"It will be nice to have them with me." Katarina smiled at me. "Barbra has been so kind to let me stay at her place and I want to repay the favor."

Screw the car. After that smile, I would have sold just about anything to spend more time with Katarina. I looked at her and smiled back. "It's been my pleasure to have you stay with me."

"I should get going," Mary said. She paced around the picnic table, her white sandals shining against her navy capris.

"Is there anything you'd like me to bring home?" I asked. Mary had already started giving farewell hugs.

"We're good," Scott said. He gave me a hug and patted my back as my mother spoke to Mary.

"I'm so glad that you and Jonathan will be having a little holiday in Montreal," she said. "I'm sure it'll help work things out between the two of you."

If only my mother knew. I gave Katarina a hug and didn't want to let go. "I'll see you later."

"Thanks for coming." Katarina winked as she pulled away.

MARY AND I got to the train station with lots of time to spare so I went inside to join her for a coffee. She had been unusually quiet during the drive and I could tell something was bothering her. We sat beside each other on a bench, holding our disposable cups of coffee. I needed to get myself a reusable mug.

"When did you decide to go to Iceland?" Mary looked at the floor.

"Just yesterday." I studied Mary's aqua blue painted toenails that were the perfect match to her white sandals and navy capris. Why couldn't I have been more fashionable?

"I wish you weren't going." Mary shifted and crossed her legs.

There. That's what was bothering her. "Why?"

"I'm afraid that you won't want to come back." She turned to me. "And I need you here."

"I'm only going for two weeks. Why wouldn't I want to come back?" She was on to me.

"I'm getting worried about you. At first I was worried about Ellen, but I've seen the way you look at Katarina, especially today."

"What do you mean by the way I look at Katarina?" As if I had to even ask.

"Oh come on, it's so obvious that you're attracted to her. I could practically see you drooling."

"They were tears."

"It was a figure of speech. Are you sure you should go?"

"The ticket is already bought and yes, I'm sure." There was no turning back. "And what do you mean by you need me here? I thought things were on the mend with the…with Jonathan?"

"We're trying." Mary pressed her lips together, as though smoothing out her pink lipstick. "These things take time, you know."

"I hope you're feeling good about going to Montreal." She was making me nervous.

"I'm sure it'll be fine."

"I want you to keep in touch while you're there." Katarina's words of wisdom came back.

"What are you up to this weekend?" Mary's train was ready for boarding.

"I'm not sure yet." Ellen had asked me to go hiking in Gatineau Park, but I wanted to bring Katarina there.

"You should spend some time thinking long and hard about whether or not going to Iceland is the right thing for you."

The nerve. "Would you rather I get back together with Ellen?"

"Don't pull that on me. I need you around in Ottawa because I can't handle things on my own right now."

"Well then maybe you should come to Iceland with me." Would she consider it?

"Are you serious? I can't do that. I have a job, remember?" She hesitated at the door.

"I'm sure you could get a few weeks off." And she had lots of money to buy a ticket at the last minute.

"And who would look after Barbie?"

Almost everyone was on the train. She was actually considering. Was she afraid of what the weekend might bring?

"Are you sure you're okay to meet up with Jonathan in Montreal? What if something happens again?"

"It won't. Besides, it's practice to see how I'll feel about going to Paris in September. I've got to go." Mary gave me a quick hug then rushed onto the train just before they closed the door.

When I got into the driver's seat of Mary's SUV with enough seating for seven, I felt small and had to adjust everything before pulling away. I hoped it would fit in my garage. I couldn't let Katarina see me driving it and I'd only use my bike for the weekend.

Chapter Twenty-five

WE SPENT A quiet evening at home, each doing our own thing. Scott watched TV while Katarina sat outside and read. I sat outside too but played games on my computer. We had agreed to some downtime for the evening to rest up for a day of hiking in Gatineau Park on Friday.

Katarina was anxious to get out into the forest and I was anxious to spend more time with her. Ellen would have to wait. She wanted me to come over for dinner and a movie, but I kept my responses non-committal.

The park was busy enough for a Friday because the weather was nice and it was the prime holiday season. Scott drove his car, Katarina sat in the front passenger seat, and I was the kid in the back. At least that's how I felt, especially around Katarina and her fragrance-free aura of beauty.

"Ari loved it here," Scott said. "He especially liked Pink Lake with its green water."

"He told me about it," Katarina said. "He begged me to come to Ottawa, but I refused. Maybe if I'd listened to him, he'd still be here with us."

"I wish he was still here," Scott said. "I dreamt about him last night. He was standing on the deck of a small cabin cruiser that had just gone through the locks at Black Rapids. I tried calling out to him, but my voice wouldn't work. And neither did my hands or legs when I tried to get closer and wave to let him know I was there. All I could do was watch as he drifted by."

"I bet he had a smile on his face." I needed to say something because Scott's voice was shaky and I didn't want either one of them to cry. "He loved watching the boats there."

"Ari always loved boats until our parents drowned." Katarina kept looking up. "I love the trees. They're so tall."

"I bet he was imagining your parents on the ones that went through the locks." Scott glanced at Katarina. "He told me about them drowning on one of our visits to Black Rapids."

"Ari." Katarina shook her head. "He had a hard time when they disappeared. I was living in San Francisco at the time and he wanted me to move back to help find them. I did go back for three weeks, but there was nothing we could do. They were gone, swallowed by the sea."

Katarina lowered her window and stuck her head out. "In Iceland we don't have much forest so this is a real treat. It reminds me of when I visited Redwood Park in California. These trees are so tall."

"I think you've been in Iceland for too long," Scott said, "if you're comparing these little trees to the big redwoods in California."

"Maybe." Katarina chuckled. "You know what they say in Iceland? If you get lost in the forest all you have to do is stand up."

"I don't know if I like the sound of that," Scott said. "Are we going to the moon or what?"

"Shame on you," Katarina said. "Iceland is a beautiful place. We don't need a lot of trees for our beauty. Just you wait and see."

"What's your house like?" I asked, wondering if there would be enough room for Mary.

"What type of house do you think I live in?" Katarina's eyes met mine through the mirror on her door.

I grinned, shuddering at the spark. "I'm sure it's a very practical house that doesn't use a lot of energy."

"Correct." She smiled. "It has three bedrooms and is located in a convenient neighborhood in Reykjavik. There's even a bus stop right at the corner."

Three bedrooms. I'd have to share a room with Mary if she stayed with us or maybe she'd prefer a hotel. "How are the hotels at this time of year?"

"Busy. You'd never get a decent room this late in the season. But you don't have to worry about that."

We were in the parking lot for the hiking trail around Pink Lake. It had been a while since I'd been there, the last time on an utter failure of a first date with a woman who had bad breath and no sense of humor. I tried to swat the memory away with the mosquitoes that buzzed around my ears.

"Here, Bebs." Scott handed me a bottle of bug spray. "It looks like you need some."

"Those little buggers really bite." Katarina waved her hands around her head.

"Here, let me spray you." No longer the kid in the backseat. "Close your eyes." And let me touch you. "Hold your breath while I spray."

Although there were a few other cars in the parking lot, it was as though we had the trail to ourselves. The hike around the lake took about an hour and we were ready for a swim when we got back to the car.

I tried to ignore Katarina as she came out of the change room near the beach at Meech Lake. She had a brightly colored sarong wrapped around her firm waist and an open blouse over her black bikini top that gave just enough of a tease of what was underneath. My bathing suit was a navy one-piece that I had on under my clothes.

"Barbra, aren't you going to swim?" Katarina unwrapped her sarong.

"Of course. I just have to take my clothes off." I started to undo my shorts.

"In case you forgot, this isn't the nude beach." Scott wore swim trunks and carried his clothes from the change room.

"I have my suit on underneath." I rolled my eyes. Leave it to Scott to embarrass me.

Scott was the first one in the water, yelling and splashing as he dove in. Katarina followed and took forever to surface from her first dive.

"Barbra, what are you waiting for? The water is beautiful."

"She's afraid of leeches and can't swim." Scott bobbed in the water.

The water felt cold and I got some up my nose as I rushed in, but I couldn't let Katarina think I was a total geek. I swam up to them and the three of us treaded together.

"Ari would have loved this," Katarina said. "I wish he was here."

"Me too." Scott's smiling face disappeared and he moved toward the shore. "I think I've had enough for now."

Katarina and I both watched Scott as he swam back to the beach and got out of the water. "How are you doing?" I wanted to reach over and touch her, but it was taking all of my energy just to stay afloat.

"I can see why Ari wanted me to come to Canada." Katarina leaned her head back as though the lake were one big pillow. "I think I'm in a bit of shock. My life has changed so much in these last few days. I've lost Ari, but then I've found Scott. What a bittersweet lost and found. I'm so happy to have met Scott, and you, but my heart is broken. I can't believe Ari is gone." She rolled around and swam back to shore.

The rest of the afternoon felt dreary, like it was raining even though the sun was shining and the temperature was perfect. When Ellen sent me a text saying that everyone loved Mike's new car, it was as though a torrential storm had come up and completely spoiled the day. She suggested we could go shopping for a car instead of seeing a movie, if that's what I preferred for the evening. I couldn't bring myself to commit to anything. I didn't want to be by myself on a Friday evening, but I also didn't want to lose out on an opportunity to spend more time with Katarina. And then there were Mary's words of warning about my feelings for Katarina. It would do me good to see Ellen.

When we got home, Scott said he planned to meet some friends downtown and invited Katarina and I to go along. It looked like Katarina wanted to go so I declined and texted Ellen instead, letting her know I would meet her after dinner. She would have to pick me up so I wanted to make sure Scott and Katarina would be long gone by then. Ellen seemed excited. I tried to tell myself I was excited too.

I had a shower and was in my room when I heard Scott's car backing out of the driveway. The timing was good as I was almost ready for Ellen to pick me up. I had forgotten my phone on the kitchen counter so rushed out to get it. I started to write my text to Ellen while wandering over to shut and lock the patio door. I glanced up from my screen to grab the handle and was startled to see Katarina sitting on the deck. She had a book in hand and glass of wine within reach. I deleted my draft text to Ellen and replaced it with one saying I was sorry, but something had come up and I wouldn't be able to get together.

"Hey." I had gotten myself a glass of wine too and joined Katarina on the deck.

"I hope you don't mind that I decided to stay in tonight." She didn't look up from the page.

"Of course not." That was for sure. "I thought you were going with Scott."

"He wanted me to, but I'm feeling tired and think it'll be good for him to have some time on his own."

"I hope you don't mind if I hang out with you on the deck." I'd cry if she did.

"Not at all." Katarina closed her book and put it on the table. "I really appreciate all that your family has done for me. Your father is so cute."

"Ari and my dad really hit it off. You should have seen the two of them together. It was like they had been friends all of their lives. And they loved to talk about the weather." Stop rattling on.

"It must have been a big shock for Scott when he met Ari." Katarina leaned back and put her feet up on a chair, exposing that anklet again.

"It was. Ari thought I was Scott's wife when we first met."

"Ari told me." Her eyes were on mine and the corners of her mouth were slightly raised. "That's too funny."

I reached over and touched the anklet. "I noticed that you wear this all the time. It's nice."

"Thanks." She reached down and fondled it, brushing her fingers up against mine. "Ari gave it to me when I moved to San Francisco. I've worn it ever since."

My phone vibrated. Dammit. Ellen was calling. I switched it off.

"Why didn't you answer?" Katarina leaned back and picked up her book. "Don't let me stop you from doing anything."

"It was telemarketing and I never answer those calls." The telemarketing part wasn't exactly a lie because Ellen wanted me to buy into her. "I'm glad you're here, helping me to enjoy my wine." I raised my glass to her and took a sip.

Katarina eased the book down and locked her eyes on mine again. "I like you, Barbra."

Wow. "Why don't you call me Bebs?"

"No, I like Barbra." Her face was serious.

"I like you too." She was so hot.

"What do you think of casual sex?" Her voice was low.

"I don't know." Holy cow. She was so direct. I was starting to sweat.

"Have you ever had casual sex?" She didn't move.

"Sort of." Holy shit. She was so smooth. Did it count if I'd only had sex a few times with someone when things didn't work out?

She smiled. "Will you sleep with me?"

"Yes." Holy fuck. She wanted to have sex with me.

Katarina took me by the hand and led me into her room in the basement. The only lighting was the pink glow from a salt crystal lamp on the night table. We shed our clothes and climbed onto the bed, Katarina on top of me with lips and fingers exploring my body. I was twitching all over and could hardly breathe. My first orgasm erupted as soon as my fingers felt how aroused she was. My second orgasm followed Katarina's and my third left me wondering if I'd ever be able to walk again.

"Three orgasms." We were lying in each other's arms and I could see her smiling in the pink glow. "I think you must be a little slut."

I just smiled back, too afraid to speak. I was really falling for her.

Chapter Twenty-six

I SPENT THE night in Katarina's bed. Scott came home around midnight and went straight to his room. I snuck up to my bed just after dawn. Katarina and I had agreed that this would be our little secret since neither of us wanted Scott to know. Yet.

When I turned on the shower, it must have woken everyone because we all ended up in the kitchen at the same time to get our breakfast. Dark clouds were threatening rain and a strong wind tapped against the windows. We sat at the dining room table.

"How did you sleep?" Scott directed his question toward Katarina.

"I had an amazing sleep. And you?"

"I hardly slept at all. You're lucky."

"Yes, I got lucky last night." Katarina poured herself a cup of coffee.

"I had the best sleep last night too," I said. "I'd give it a three out of three."

Katarina stifled a snicker. "It's unfortunate that you didn't sleep well, Scott. Maybe you got out of the water too soon yesterday."

"I hardly think so." He was eating a bowl of cereal. "Maybe I should have stayed home last night. I was probably overtired."

"No, I think it was good that you went out last night." Katarina sipped her coffee.

"What did you get up to?" Scott looked at Katarina.

"I read for a bit then went to bed early. It was just what I needed."

Me too. No, I didn't need to be falling in love with her but what was I going to do? "I sold my car yesterday."

"You *what?*" Scott's eyes widened. "Who bought it?"

"Some guy named Mike." I couldn't let him know Mike worked with Ellen.

"What are you going to do without your car?"

"Ride my bike and take the bus until I find the right car for my business." I hoped no one noticed Mary's beast in the garage.

"Maybe you'll decide that you don't need a car after all," Katarina said. "Every little bit counts and we all have to do our part to help the fight against climate change."

"She'll need some kind of car if she wants to have her own

business," Scott said.

"You should be taking your bike or the bus to work, Scott. You need to do your part too."

"I am. I won't be commuting for now while I'm off work."

"That hardly counts," Katarina said.

My phone vibrated against the kitchen counter, where I'd left it. I jumped to grab it and send the call to voice mail because I saw it was Ellen and didn't want Scott to see. "I can't believe telemarketers would be calling already."

"You seem to get a lot of calls from telemarketers," Katarina said. "Was it the same one who called last night?"

"It might have been." Please don't go there.

"Somebody must have gotten your number," Scott said. "You should register your phone on the Do Not Call list."

My phone vibrated again and this time Scott grabbed it before I could. Fuck. I imagined Ellen was mad and wanted to talk. If Scott found out it was Ellen, it could ruin everything.

"Hello." Scott said. "Just a sec." His face had reddened. "It's Mary and she's crying."

I grabbed the phone. "Mary, what's happened?"

"I need you to pick me up." She sobbed.

"Where are you?" My heart pounded.

"I'm still in Montreal." Fear in her voice.

"Are you okay? Are you hurt?" Please let her be okay.

"Not really, but I can't go back there." She was hyperventilating.

"Try to calm down. Where are you now?" I wanted my fast car.

"I'm at the train station, but I can't go anywhere because I have no money. I just grabbed my phone and ran out of the hotel when Jonathan was in the shower."

"What did he do to you?" Fuck. I'd had enough. It was time to tell our mother.

"I'm okay." Her breathing was stabilizing. "I just had to get out of there. Can you come now? Please?"

SCOTT AND KATARINA stood in the driveway as I carefully maneuvered Mary's climate change disaster of an SUV out of my garage. Katarina didn't comment as she got in the front passenger seat. Scott jumped in the back and we were on our way. I was touched that Katarina had instantly offered to accompany me and seemed genuinely concerned. She positioned it as an opportunity to visit Montreal and Scott wanted to come too. We each packed an overnight bag and I grabbed a few things for Mary.

It took us just a little over two hours to get into downtown Montreal. Scott was driving now and I was in the back, scanning the street in front of the train station for Mary.

"There she is." Mary stood with her arms crossed and clutching her phone as she tried to get some shelter from the cool drizzle. She didn't have a jacket and wore the same navy capris, blouse, and sandals that she'd worn a few days before. I jumped out and ran up to her, pulled her into a hug, and patted the back of her head as she sobbed.

"It's okay now. We're here." I led her to the grand white chariot where Scott and Katarina were waiting.

"Thank you for coming so quickly," Mary said. "I'm sorry for screwing up your weekend."

"I wanted to visit Montreal anyway," Katarina said, "so don't apologize to me."

"I hope you don't mind that we're planning to stay the night," Scott said. "We'll get a couple of rooms and make a trip out of it."

"Yes, please do," she said. "I'll reimburse you for everything. I'm just so glad you're here."

We chose a hotel in Old Montreal and took two rooms. Mary and I shared one and Scott and Katarina shared the other. My previous night with Katarina was starting to feel like a dream while the two of us carried on as though nothing had happened. It wasn't until we were getting sorted out in our rooms, right after checking in, that Katarina opened the adjoining door between the two. Mary was taking a shower and I could see Scott lying on his bed, surfing channels.

"Your room is the mirror image of ours." Katarina walked in. "Let's see what your view is like."

I followed her toward the window, but after a few steps she swung around, grabbed me, and clamped her mouth over mine. The shower switched off and Katarina pulled away.

"I think the view is nicer in your room." She winked at me then went up to the window.

"Is it?" Wow. Who was the slut now? I sat on the bed, panting and trying to calm myself.

WE HEADED UP up Saint-Denis Street for some lunch and window-shopping. There was a slight drizzle, but everyone was okay with a walk, including Mary in her white sandals.

Mary wouldn't talk about Jonathan, other than to say he knew that she was okay and wanted a divorce. She carried on as if everything was normal, making for a pleasant afternoon that was shrouded in worry. We had a late dinner at a brasserie in Old Montreal then an early night, as we were all exhausted.

As much as I longed to share my bed with Katarina, I was happy to have some alone time with Mary so I could question her more on what had happened.

"Are you okay?" The lights were off and we were both in our beds. I could hear her sobbing.

"I'm sorry. I'm just so tired and sick of it all."

"What did he do to you this time?" My stomach felt queasy.

"Nothing really." Her sobs increased.

"Mary? What happened?" I sat up but didn't turn on the light because the room was bright enough.

"He raped me last night." She curled up into a fetal position.

While I was having the best sex of my life, my sister was being raped. "Oh, Mary, I'm so sorry." I got out of my bed and sat on the edge of hers. "Did he hurt you?" I ran my hand up and down her back.

"No. Yes. I don't know. He wouldn't stop when I asked him to. I didn't recognize him and felt so dirty afterward." Mary started to open up. "You were right. Jonathan is a prick."

Finally. "You told me things were getting better."

"They were." She sat up and blew her nose. "We went for a walk after a nice dinner, but everything changed when I let it slip that I'd told you about him hitting me. He thought I'd only said that we were arguing a lot."

Her voice strengthened as she continued. "He became silent and I could see his jaw tensing. When we got back to the room, he wanted to have sex, but I was feeling confused and guilty for telling you."

"That fucking prick. He's playing with your mind." I clutched the blankets in anger.

"When I told him I didn't want to have sex, he raped me. I wanted to leave, but he wouldn't let me. I spent the entire night planning my escape."

"Are you ready to go to the police now?"

"No." She shook her head. "I just want to move on with my life."

"I really think you should come to Iceland." I had to get her away.

"Do you think it would be okay?" She turned to me.

"Yes." It could give an excuse for me to stay in Katarina's room.

"What about Barbie? I won't leave her with Jonathan and none of my friends know."

"We could always put her in a kennel." As much as our mother loved Barbie, she was allergic and her sinuses acted up if she spent too much time around the cat. I knew my dad would never put up with it, especially since he'd be the one who'd have to clean the litter.

"No, I can't leave her in a kennel. She'd hate it and I'd be afraid that she'd stop eating."

"There might be another option." Ellen.

"What do you mean?" Mary's eyes glistened in the darkened room.

"Let me check my voicemail." I returned to my bed to reach my phone. I had been ignoring the message all day because I knew it was from Ellen.

"Bebs, this is very frustrating and I'm starting to get pissed. Are you avoiding me, or what? Call me." I didn't blame her for being angry because I knew what it felt like to be blown off when Donna started coming around.

"Was that Ellen?" Mary's feet were on the floor.

"Yes. I was thinking that maybe she could look after Barbie."

"Forget it." She crossed her arms. "I'm not going to have you sacrifice your life for mine."

"I'm not sacrificing anything." Not after my night with Katarina.

"She'll expect something in return."

"Asking her to look after Barbie is no big deal." A little pussy was just what Ellen wanted anyway.

By the time we went to sleep, Mary had agreed to let me ask Ellen. It was to be our secret.

The next morning we enjoyed a leisurely buffet brunch at the hotel. Mary seemed to be in better spirits and Katarina continued to impress me with the way she offered moral support and compassion to my sister when she had just lost her brother. I wanted to kiss her again and was hoping for an opportunity before checking out, but Scott wouldn't leave her side. His mood seemed down and it worried me because I had never known him to be depressed.

We were clearing out our rooms when I heard Scott pop into the bathroom to brush his teeth. The adjoining door was open and

I had been attentive to all activity. Katarina was standing by the window when I rushed into her arms. Our lips locked together. At least for the few seconds before the bathroom door opened and Scott re-emerged.

"Oh, you're in here. Are you ready to go?" He glanced at the newspaper on the table.

"Yes, I'm ready anytime." I faced Katarina and ran my tongue across my upper lip.

"I was just showing her the view from our room." Katarina winked.

Scott kept his focus on the newspaper. "What about Mary? Where's she at?"

"She's ready too. And what about you?" I said.

"Would I be reading the paper if I wasn't?" Scott's tone was terse.

"Are you okay?" I approached him. "You seem down this morning."

Scott let out a heavy sigh. "Sorry, I didn't sleep very well again last night."

"I hope I didn't keep you awake with my tossing and turning." Katarina was beside us.

"No." Scott moved away. "I can't believe Ari killed himself. Why would he do that when we just met? I feel like it was my fault. I must have somehow let him down."

"No, Scott." Katarina started to cry. "It wasn't your fault. It was nobody's fault. Ari was sick. It wasn't just the cancer."

"Finding me should have brought him out of his depression." Scott sat on the bed and lowered his head.

"Depression isn't that simple." Katarina sat beside Scott. "I tried for years to help him and finally realized that I had to take care of myself and make sure I didn't get depressed too. His suicide has nothing to do with you."

"I agree." I squeezed on the bed beside Katarina, putting my arm around her to touch Scott's shoulder with my fingers. "Ari was so proud of you and I don't think he wanted you to see him suffer with his cancer."

"And him committing suicide isn't supposed to make me suffer?"

"When Ari got depressed, he didn't always think things through." Katarina stood up. "Come on, let's not let Ari's problem with depression get us depressed too. I miss him so much and I wish he was here with us, but he's not and there's nothing we can do to help him now." She wiped her nose.

"Mary's the one that needs our help."

This was my opportunity. "Would it be okay if she came to Iceland with us?"

"Of course," Katarina said. "Does she want to?"

"Yes and I can't leave her alone right now."

Katarina touched my shoulder. "I'm happy that she wants to come."

"You'll have to share your room with her," Scott looked at me as he got up and grabbed his bag. "Let's go."

Scott offered to drive us up onto the Mont Royal lookout for a spectacular view of the city before heading home. The drive back to Ottawa was fairly quiet and uneventful, as everyone seemed exhausted. Except for me. I was full of adrenalin as I retreated into the theatre of my thoughts to replay my passionate moments with Katarina over and over again.

Chapter Twenty-seven

MY MOTHER STOOD in the driveway, hands on hips and ready to pounce, as we returned home from Montreal. It was late in the afternoon and the sky was grey. Her freshly dyed hair was a bit too orange and I could feel her green eyes on me.

"Don't say anything about Jonathan," Mary said as we pulled in.

"I'd say she knows something's up." I was driving, my hands tight on the wheel.

Our mother approached my door and yanked it open as soon as we stopped. "What's going on?"

"Mother, please let me get out first." I undid my seat belt then gathered my sunglasses and keys before stepping out.

"Jonathan came to our place in a panic," my mother said. "He was looking all over for Mary and of course your father and I didn't know where you were."

"That's good that you didn't know where we were," I said.

"There must have been a misunderstanding." Mary rushed to us, her breathing heavy.

Scott and Katarina kept to themselves, gathering bags out of the vehicle.

"I thought he knew I was driving back from Montreal with Barbra," Mary said.

"What were you doing in Montreal?" My mother glared at me.

"She was giving Katarina a tour." Mary answered before I could say anything.

"Mary let us borrow her vehicle to bring Katarina to Montreal for a night." I was flabbergasted that Mary still protected Jonathan, but played along.

"Why didn't you let us know you were going?" My mother's hands were still on her hips as she leaned toward me. "Your father and I are always the last to hear about everything. What if something had happened to one of us? How would we have known where you were?"

"I had my cell," I said. "You could have reached me anytime."

My mother dropped her hands to her sides and backed away. "That's not the point. We're still your parents and like to be kept informed."

"What did Jonathan say?" Mary asked.

"He was out of his mind," she said. "How could you have just left him like that?"

"I didn't just leave him. He was in the shower and I thought he knew."

"Where's Dad?" I asked.

"He's at home in case you tried to call. We didn't know what was going on." My mother's face was red and full of wrinkles.

"I'll let Jonathan know I'm okay." Mary tried to escape by following Scott and Katarina into the house.

"Let your father know too," my mother said. "He's worried."

"Okay, I'll call him." Mary went inside.

I opened my garage door, hoping she would stop with the questions. "Why don't you sit down while we finish unpacking?"

"Okay." Her breathing was heavy. "I'll grab a lawn chair and sit here for a minute in the shade."

"I should have one in here." I scanned the junk, my mind in a muddle.

"Barbra, you really need to clean this up. You take after your father. Our garage would be a disaster if it was left to him."

"I know." Yay. She was on to something else. "I wish my garage was as clean as yours." I spotted an old aluminum folding web chair that my parents had given me years before.

"What's this?" My mother grabbed the broken bamboo ski pole I had rescued from the garbage the morning Ari died. It now had a grey duct tape patch.

"I've been looking for a pair of bamboo ski poles to go with my snowshoes," I said. "I found it in someone's garbage and patched it up."

"Where's the other one?" She looked around.

"I left it there because it was missing its basket."

"You should have left this one too." She picked at the duct tape.

"No, don't." I grabbed the pole. "It's better than nothing right now."

"How big is the crack? Did you put some glue on it? A little bit of tape won't do much good if you put any weight on it."

"It'll be fine." I put the pole down and set up the chair in the shade at the front of the garage door opening. My mother sat, her hands gripping the plastic arms. "What are you planning to do when you're in Iceland?"

"Other than support Scott and Katarina, I haven't thought

any further about it." I tried to tuck away lustful thoughts of Katarina while in the presence of my mother.

"I've been looking into Iceland and it looks like quite an interesting place with all its volcanoes and hot springs." Her grip eased off the chair arms. "The scenery looks beautiful."

"Scott thinks we're going to the moon." I wished I'd had more time to research it. Then again, Katarina was the main scenery I was interested in. For me, it would be like going to Heaven. "Mary's coming with us."

My mother jumped up, hands flinging to her hips. "Mary? Why? Especially since she's going to Paris in September."

"I don't know." Let Mary explain. "She decided this weekend."

"Barbra, tell me what's going on with Jonathan. Now." Her green eyes glared at me.

"He's beating Mary." There. I said it. There was no turning back.

She staggered backward. "What? Not Jonathan. I don't believe you."

"How could you say that?" He really had her fooled. "No wonder Mary doesn't want to tell you."

My mother dropped back down into her chair, her shoulders slumping. "It can't be true."

"Well it is true and Mary has bruises to prove it." My jaw was so tight.

"Her arm." My mother straightened, gripping the lawn chair again. "I knew something wasn't right." She paused, her breathing heavy. "I figured it was something bad, but I never would've figured Jonathan for that."

I squeezed my mother's stiff shoulder. "I'm afraid for Mary and that's why I want her to come to Iceland with me."

My mother almost knocked her chair over as she jumped up again and paced in the opening of my garage door. "What happened this weekend?"

"Mary finally decided she's had enough, that's all. We drove to Montreal to pick her up and stayed the night to show Katarina a bit of the city."

"Something must have happened. How long has this been going on?" Her hands were in fists.

"I don't know," I said. "I only found out a few weeks ago."

Her head shook back and forth. "Your father and I thought it was strange when he came looking for Mary this afternoon. He was as polite as usual, but seemed stressed. If only I'd have known." Glaring green eyes burned into me again. "Why didn't you tell us, especially your father?"

"Mary didn't want me to." I plopped down on the lawn chair. "She didn't want to worry you."

"We've been worried out of our minds." I braced at her raised voice. "What's happening with the two of you? You don't have a job and now she won't have a husband. What are we going to do?"

"Nothing." I jumped up. "Mary and I have each other and we'll figure things out."

"In Iceland?" My mother teetered.

"Maybe." I heard a car door slam. Jonathan barreled up the driveway.

"Where is she?" His face was red and his mustache distorted over his little mouth.

"Get out of my yard before I call the police." I waved a fist.

Jonathan scowled then stopped when he noticed my mother. Her lips were pursed so tight it looked as if she were going to whistle. Her students had called it her ruthless whistle face when she was about to lose it. I had always wanted to crawl into a corner and hide when she put on that face, but not now. No way. I wanted to see Jonathan suffer the full force of the ruthless whistle face and even wished I had a couple of pompoms to cheer her on. What could I use? I saw the dangling leather strap on the handle grip of my grey duct tape decorated bamboo ski pole. I grabbed the strap and twirled the pole in a circular motion at my feet.

The twirling caught my mother's attention and she practically ripped the pole out of my hand. "You dirty bastard." She pointed the tip at him. "I trusted you with my daughter. Get out of here and I don't want to ever see you again."

"Ruth, wait please." His hands were out in front, palms raised. "It's all a big misunderstanding."

"Get out of here now!" My mother whacked the pole on the side of my garage.

"I just want to talk to Mary for a minute." Jonathan continued to plead with my mother, but he didn't know the ruthless whistle face and that it was a waste of time if that face showed up.

My mother whacked the pavement with the pole. "Barbra, call the police."

"Mom, wait." Mary put one foot out onto the driveway, clutching the screen door. "I need my purse."

"There you are." Jonathan started toward Mary.

My mother walloped the pole against the garage again. "Don't get any closer to her. Barbra, get your sister inside."

"What about my purse?" Mary clung to the door as Scott and Katarina scooted around her to step outside.

"Get her purse and give it to Barbra." My mother's eyes hadn't left Jonathan.

"No, give it to me instead." Scott stepped forward.

"I just want to talk to Mary." Jonathan's voice shook.

"Get her purse." My mother wagged the pole at him.

Jonathan slowly turned around and trudged to his car. Scott started to follow.

"No, wait, Scott." This time Katarina stepped forward. "Let's get in the house and he can leave the purse on the driveway. Hurry."

I ushered my mother to the door while everyone rushed inside then yelled at the prick. "Leave her purse on the driveway!"

My mother pushed me aside then stuck her head out the door. "Leave her purse then go on and get the hell out of here!"

"Ruth, step back and let's close all the doors." Katarina was now in control. "We should have called the police."

"No, don't." Mary was crying and biting her nails. "I'm so sorry everyone. I've ruined everything."

"It's not your fault," Katarina said. We were in the living room now, trying to peek through the window to watch Jonathan.

"I have my finger by my speed dial for 9-1-1," Scott said. "If he has anything other than Mary's purse in his hand, I'll hit it."

"Good," Katarina said. "I'm not feeling comfortable with this. Let's move away from the windows."

"You're scaring me," Mary said.

"You should be scared," Katarina said.

I was frightened. I was also proud of the way Katarina took control from my mother and was keeping us safe. "Katarina's right. Jonathan is out of control and we need to protect ourselves."

We watched as he traipsed up the driveway and put Mary's purse on the front seat of her vehicle. He ambled back to his car, shoulders hunched, and sped away. We stayed in the house, watching Mary's vehicle and waiting to make sure he didn't return before Scott ventured out to get the purse.

Afterward, my mother sat on the couch talking with Mary. Scott had popped downstairs and I snuck Katarina into my bedroom for a quick embrace. I was shaking.

"I'm so sorry you had to be part of this. " I fell into the hug, her soft embrace filling me with reassurance.

"Don't apologize." She spoke into my hair. "Besides, I owed your family one for all you've done for Ari."

"Thank you for stepping in and helping to keep us safe." I kissed welcoming lips.

"Barbra, where did you go?" We both jumped back as my mother called out. "I'm ready to leave."

When we got back to the living room, my ski pole was leaning against the same wall it had been on the morning Ari died. It would have to go back into the garage.

"Your father's going to be very upset when I tell him what happened." My mother stood by the door. "He wanted to come with me, but I made him stay at home. It's a good thing because there's no telling what he would've done when Jonathan showed up."

My mother liked to talk as though my dad could be tough, but I knew he would have let her handle the situation. I also figured he might cry when my mother filled him in.

Mary went to her room as soon as our mother left. Katarina picked up the bamboo ski pole and examined it.

"Your mother forgot her weapon." Katarina chuckled. "She got lucky and it really seemed to work."

"I couldn't believe her," Scott said. "She held that broken pole like a master swordsman." He put one hand behind his back and challenged Katarina with an imaginary sword. She laughed and raised the ski pole. Scott backed off.

Who would have thought my broken duct-taped bamboo ski pole could have come in so handy? I reached for the pole. "I'll put it back in the garage. It's supposed to go with my new snowshoes."

"Oh," Katarina said. "I thought it was meant for the garbage."

"It was in the garbage," Scott said. "Someone else's garbage. Bebs is a garbage picker and pack rat."

"I am not." I held the pole to my chest.

"I think it's good if you can keep things out of the landfill," Katarina said. "And bamboo is good too. It's good for the environment and it brings you luck."

Would it fit in my suitcase? I was going to need all the luck I could get over in Iceland to win Katarina's heart and keep it forever.

Chapter Twenty-eight

BARBIE WAS THE center of attention as the four of us sat in the living room after dinner, the TV on a nature show for a bit of relaxing distraction. It had started to drizzle and gotten darker earlier than normal. I wasn't looking forward to talking with Ellen, but I knew I had to answer her call. Barbie depended on me convincing Ellen to look after her.

I slipped into my bedroom. "Hey." My best defense was to let on everything was okay between us.

"Why are you avoiding me?" Ellen's tone was harsh.

"I'm sorry. Things have been crazy around here." I spoke in a low voice.

"Like all weekend too? I thought the ceremony was on Thursday."

"It's Mary." I needed to calm her down and find a way to ask about Barbie.

"Mary?" Ellen dragged out the word.

"Yes. She was the one being abused and didn't want anyone to know."

"I thought you said she was still with Jonathan." Her tone softened.

"He's a prick. I need to get her away from him."

"Wow, I never would've thought Jonathan would be like that. Is she okay? Did he hurt her?"

"Physically she's okay." I sat on the edge of the bed and wondered what to pack.

"Where is she now?" Adrenalin rang in her words.

"She's staying with me." My feet jiggled against the floor.

"Did she lay a charge?"

"No. She doesn't want the police involved."

"Oh, Bebs, be careful. Do you want me to come over and stay with you?"

"Thanks, but I'm okay. It's a full house here now with Mary, Scott, and his aunt." Police officer or not, there was no place for her at my house.

"Let me know if there's anything I can do." Ellen sounded sincere. I reminded myself of Donna.

"Well, actually there is something." Perfect timing. "I don't know if I mentioned it, but Mary has a cute little Bengal cat."

Mary had come into my room and was sitting beside me on the bed. She must have suspected I was talking to Ellen. That was a good thing because I didn't want Scott to know and she'd be my cover if he heard me talking.

"I always wanted a Bengal cat, but they're so expensive." Ellen's tone lightened. "It must so be cute."

"I was wondering if you'd be able to look after her for a few weeks?"

"Is Mary going somewhere?"

"Yes, she's coming to Iceland with us." I held my breath, fearing for a minute that Ellen would ask to come too.

"What? You're going to Iceland? Why?"

"I want to support Scott during the ceremony for his dad over there and spend a few weeks romping around Reykjavik." A lot of which I hoped would be done in Katarina's bed.

"You're so lucky." I could hear Ellen's tongue as she spoke. "I've always wanted to go to Iceland. I wish I could go too."

"All that to say, we have a little pussy that needs looking after while we're gone and I was hoping you could take care of her." I was desperate and figured a bit of flirting couldn't hurt. Mary squirmed and wagged a finger at me.

"What's her name?" Ellen bit and I thought of Donna to brush off any feelings of guilt.

"Barbie. She's a little doll and loves to be petted."

"Like someone I know?" Ellen snickered.

Enough. "So you'll do it?"

"Sure, why not? When are you going?"

"We're leaving this Saturday. I could drop Barbie off on Friday night."

"That'd be great. We could do dinner again."

"Thanks, but I'll be too busy." I planned to spend every last minute with Katarina. "Barbie's an indoor cat and should adjust well to your apartment, especially the view."

Mary shook her head when I hung up. "I hate the word pussy. Why did you have to go there?"

"Did you want to put Barbie in a kennel? I was desperate and used everything I could think of."

"I never would've agreed to this if I'd known the levels you'd stoop to with her. You're not going to her apartment by yourself on Friday. I won't let you."

"I won't be alone. I'll have your little pussy with me."

"Stop that." Mary stomped out of my room and into hers.

Scott and Katarina had gone to bed by the time I got back into the living room. I wanted to go downstairs and crawl into bed with Katarina, but that couldn't happen. Not with Scott home. But then again, my laundry room was in the basement.

I gathered up a few dirty clothes and made my way down. It was dark now and Katarina's door was closed, but her light was on. I resisted the urge to open it and went into the laundry room. I was putting soap in the machine when I felt Katarina's arms wrap around my waist and her lips on my neck.

"Have you ever had laundry room sex?" She whispered in my ear.

I maneuvered myself around, so aroused. "Not here." Not ever, really. "What about Scott? He might hear."

"Start the washing machine." She kissed me while I turned it on then slid her hand into my pants.

The noise of the water filling the machine and then the clothes swishing around covered the sound of our heavy breathing and orgasmic moans that lasted throughout the spinning cycle.

By the time I got back upstairs to my bedroom, it was late and I was exhausted. Sleep came easily and the morning arrived too soon. It was pouring and a jog was out of the question until I saw Katarina lacing up for a run in the rain.

"Now that's dedication," I said. "I wasn't planning to run this morning, but you're inspiring me."

Katarina did a few stretches by the side door. "I usually don't run in heavy rain so don't feel bad about not getting out this morning. I just need a little bit of fresh air and won't be long."

"I'll put the coffee on." I watched as she stepped out the door and trotted down the driveway before starting off on her jog. What was she thinking? What was she feeling? I didn't know what I was thinking, but I did know how in love I was starting to feel.

We spent a large part of the day finalizing details for our trip to Iceland. Mary was able to get a ticket on the same flight as us and was beginning to seem excited about our trip. She wanted to get some clothes from her place and make sure she had everything she needed. Jonathan was in surgery for the afternoon so we accompanied Mary to the mansion. It had stopped raining, but the sky was still a heavy grey. Scott, Katarina, and I were outside by the pool while Mary gathered things in her room.

"I can't believe two people would live in a big house like this." Katarina shook her head. "It's no wonder things weren't right here."

"I could live in a big house like this if I had the right sugar-daddy," Scott said. The three of us stood by the edge of the pool and the water looked a bit dirty.

"Even the mermaid at the bottom of this pool is ugly," Katarina said.

"Here, here." I raised my right fist in a cheer, but resisted the urge to spit in the water. Scott laughed.

"What's that all about?" Katarina asked.

"Bebs hates the bitch at the bottom of the pool."

"It's a long story that has to do with an ex of mine and her new girlfriend," I said.

"Let's not go there," Scott said.

"Okay, I'm ready to go." Mary had joined us. "I have everything I need and can't wait to get out of here."

"I hope you grabbed some warm clothes because the weather will be cooler in Reykjavik," Katarina said.

"I hope it's not too cold," Scott said.

"There won't be snow, if that's what you mean," Katarina said. "Long sleeves and a jacket will be fine. You might even get lucky and wear T-shirts and shorts."

When we got home, I started going through my clothes. It was easier to pick an outfit that just required shorts and a T-shirt, but when it came to long sleeves and jackets, I wasn't sure how much to pack. It was a good excuse to invite Katarina into my bedroom.

"What should I pack?"

"Bring lots of clean underwear." Katarina sat on the edge of my bed, her voice low.

"Clean underwear? Are there issues with the drinking water?"

She rolled her head back and laughed. "No, not at all." She leaned over and whispered. "We'll only have two weeks left and I plan to keep you wet much of the time."

Only two weeks left. My heart dropped. She had really meant it when she asked for casual sex. I tried to joke back. "Who's the little slut now?"

I spoke the words louder than I should have and Scott heard. I heard him get up from the living room. "What are you guys talking about in there?"

Think fast. "I was just telling her about the slut at the bottom of Mary's pool."

"Oh Donna," Scott said. "I thought we weren't going to go there."

"What slut in my pool?" Mary appeared at my bedroom door.

"It's nothing," I said. "I was talking about the mermaid at the bottom. Don't you think she looks like a slut?" I hadn't told Mary about naming the mermaid Donna, only Scott.

"Who's Donna?" Mary asked.

"The name I gave to the ugly mermaid in the bottom of your pool," I said.

"Ugly mermaid?" Mary said. "Where did that come from?"

"It's my fault," Katarina said. "I thought it looked ugly. The whole pool looks ugly if you look at it through a climate change lens. Don't you have public pools here?"

Mary's eyes reddened. "I suppose the two of you are going to gang up on me now."

"I won't let them." Scott stood beside Mary and put an arm over her shoulders. "They can say what they like, but in the end they're just hairy leg, Birkenstock wearing lesbians."

Katarina grabbed one of my pillows and threw it at Scott. "I don't even own a pair of Birkenstocks."

Scott caught the pillow and laughed. "Stop picking on Mary then."

My phone rang. "It's my mother. Hi."

"How are things over there? How's Mary?"

"Fine and fine. For some reason, it seems like everyone is in my room."

"Oh great. Why don't you put me on speaker phone so I can tell everybody our news at the same time."

"Okay. My mother has some news to tell us and wants to be on speaker." Scott and Mary joined us on the bed.

"Hi, everyone," my mother said. "Can you hear me?"

"Yep, no problem hearing you," I said. "So what's up?"

"Your father and I just booked a trip to Iceland. We're coming with you."

"What?" Mary and I spoke in unison. Scott and Katarina looked at each other and smirked.

"There won't be enough room," I said. This couldn't be happening.

"What do you mean there won't be enough room?" my mother asked.

"Katarina's house only has three bedrooms and probably only one bathroom."

My mother laughed. "Oh we're not staying with you. We've booked ourselves into a hotel."

"How did you manage to do that?" I struggled to control the shriek in my voice.

"There was a last minute cancellation while we were at the travel agent. Can you believe our luck?"

No, I couldn't believe it. And I could forget about needing extra pairs of clean underwear.

Chapter Twenty-nine

GETTING ORGANIZED FOR our trip was the focus for the rest of the week. Katarina didn't seem to mind hanging out around my house, reading, and having sex with me whenever we could manage to sneak some private time. We hadn't yet managed to spend another night together, but it was Friday and we had made a pact that she would spend her last night in Ottawa with me in my bed.

Scott had been particularly quiet and withdrawn over the last few days while Mary appeared somewhat gleeful. If ever there had been a time when I felt bipolar, this had been the week. One moment I'd be giddy with the prospect of visiting Reykjavik and spending more time with Katarina. The next I'd be in tears as I thought about leaving her at the end of the trip. It didn't help that my parents kept popping over to my house unannounced and either wanting to show us their new luggage or get Katarina's validation for clothes they were packing.

I was having my coffee and toast out on the deck by myself when Scott joined me. He looked as if he'd hardly slept and his hand trembled as he sipped his coffee. He'd had quite a bit of wine the night before.

"How are you doing?" I was concerned.

"I'm all packed and ready to go." He looked at the dry birdbath, but didn't move.

"You don't look like you're ready," I said. "What's wrong?"

Scott sighed and put his head in his hands. "I really don't want to go. I know I should, but the prospect of seeing where Ari lived and going through the remnants of his life is so depressing."

"Oh, Scott, I know it's going to be hard without Ari around." I could relate to his sadness and my stomach churned because it was going to be unbearable when Katarina was gone. Scott and I really needed each other now and I had to make sure he didn't bail on the trip at the last minute.

"Try to look at this as an opportunity to find out about yourself and your heritage," I said. "I know it has to be hard for you, but think of Katarina. Ari wanted you to be there for her."

"He was never there for me." Scott flung his head up. "All those years of having to tolerate my adoptive father with his religious rants and then his outright hatred for who I was. Where was Ari then?"

I reached over and touched his arm. "You have every right to be angry, but don't take it out on Ari. He would've come sooner if he'd known about you. What if he hadn't come at all? There'd be no Katarina and who knows what you'll discover in Iceland."

"I guess you're right." He sighed.

"I know I'm right. You have to focus on the positive. It'll help get you through this." I couldn't think of any positives for me at the end of the two weeks in Reykjavik.

Scott looked at the birdbath. "I'm so glad you're coming. I need to add some water for those poor birds before I take my shower."

I wasn't alone on the deck for long when Katarina popped her head out the patio door and brightened my mood. She had just finished her jog and was sexy sweaty with a small towel slung over her shoulders.

"I thought maybe you were still in bed." She used the towel to wipe her face then sat beside me.

"No," I said. "There's too much to do today. I've already gone for my jog and I'm just finishing my breakfast."

"Good for you." She reached over and rubbed my knee, but yanked her hand back when my parents materialized from around the side of the house into my backyard.

"Hi, girls." My father carried a box with a few grocery items in it.

"What's up?" Shit. I just wanted some alone time with Katarina.

"It's good to see that you're up already," my mother said. "I was afraid you might still be in bed." My parents stood on the grass and looked up at us.

"Would you like some coffee?" Katarina asked.

"No thank you," my mother said. "We just wanted to drop off some food we won't get around to eating before we leave. We thought you might be able to use it up today."

"You're not leaving until Sunday though." I got off the deck and stood beside them. "Why don't you keep it for yourself?"

"We have all of our meals planned out before we go and this is extra food," she said. "We thought we'd bring it here to see if you could use anything before getting rid of it."

"That's nice of you." Katarina had joined us on the lawn. "I'm looking forward to having you over for a dinner at my place, especially after everything your family has done for me."

"Oh thank you," my mother said. "It's been such a pleasure to have both you and Ari enter our lives. I never would've expected to visit Iceland in my lifetime and I'm so excited."

"Here, Barbra." My dad handed me the box. "I have to get back to mow the lawn."

"Where's Mary?" my mother asked. "She couldn't still be in bed, could she?"

"No," I said. "She had to go into the office this morning."

"I'm so glad you're getting her away from here. Who's looking after Barbie?" My mother held her hand over her eyebrows to shade her face from the sun.

"She's staying in a kennel."

"Oh, which one?" My mother wouldn't let up.

"I'm not sure," I said.

"Come on, Ruth, let's go."

When Katarina and I went into the kitchen with the box of food, we were only able to share a short necking session before Scott turned off the shower. I didn't want to let her go, but she pulled away as soon as we heard the bathroom door open. It was clear she still didn't want him to know about us. I took her arm and led her down the hall.

"I could use some help with my packing." I thought I'd try luring her into my bedroom for a few extra kisses.

Katarina laughed then turned serious. "Why don't you have someone in your life?"

"I don't know." We were now standing in my room, arms wrapped around each other, and I was rubbing my lips over her salty skin. "What about you?"

"I like being on my own." Katarina ran her fingers through my hair. "When I left Julie and San Francisco, I swore I'd never let myself get hooked into a relationship again."

"What happened?" Her touch felt so good.

"I thought we had it all. I gave up my life in Reykjavik for her and believed we'd be together forever, lesbian bed death or not. But I don't know. Something happened inside me and I just had to get out. She had started to drink and smoke a lot. I don't think either one of us was happy in the end. I like the freedom of being single. Like now." She kissed me. "And what about you? I don't think you like being single."

"Not really." How could she like being single and especially now? "I thought I had the right person once, but she dumped me for someone else. Now she wants me back."

Katarina leaned away to look at me. "And how do you feel

about that?"

"I don't know. I'm still mad at her and Scott would never forgive me." And I just found the love of my life.

"What does he have to do with your love life?"

"He helped me out a lot when she dumped me. I was pretty messed up." Like I knew I was going to be again in two weeks.

"I think you're ready to move on." Katarina gave me a lingering kiss on the lips. "What's her name?"

"Ellen. She actually dumped me for that ugly mermaid at the bottom of Mary's pool."

Katarina laughed. "How could anyone dump you for an ugly mermaid?"

"That's what I thought." My throat tightened and I had to fight off tears. "Do you want to meet my ex?"

"Where?" Katarina's eyes focused on mine.

"At her place. I have to bring Barbie there later today. Ellen's going to be looking after Barbie for Mary."

"Cool. Does she know about me?"

"Yes, but only that you're Scott's aunt from Iceland. She thinks you're much older."

"Are you trying to make her jealous?" Katarina kissed me again.

"Sort of." Katarina was the one I hoped to make jealous.

Mary seemed relieved to not have to go to Ellen's and she gladly gave me all the instructions and supplies for Barbie's stay. It was shortly after dinner when Katarina and I were on our way up to Ellen's apartment, arms full of Barbie and her stuff.

Ellen's jaw dropped when I introduced her to Katarina. We were standing in her small entryway and Barbie was anxious to get out of her cage. After an uncomfortable pause, she invited us in. Katarina kicked off her shoes and let Barbie out of her cage.

"Where would you like the litter box?" I asked. Katarina had followed Barbie into the living room.

Ellen's eyes were wide as she whispered to me. "I can't believe she's Scott's aunt. Shouldn't she be much older?"

"She's hot, eh?" I couldn't help myself.

"Wow, is she ever. You can just leave it here for now."

Katarina stood in front of Ellen's patio doors, Barbie in her arms, admiring the view as Ellen and I approached. "It's beautiful up here. You must really like it."

Ellen edged up beside me. "I love it, especially at night. It's too bad I didn't get to meet you sooner. You could have come over for dinner with Bebs the other night."

"Barbra knew I wasn't available." Katarina handed Barbie to Ellen then looked at me. "Okay, babe."

"It's Bebs," Ellen said.

"No, it's Barbra." Katarina put a hand on my arm. "Let's go because there's still lots to do for our trip."

Ellen's jaw had dropped again. There was a slight awkwardness as we said goodbye with a quick hug and kiss. Katarina waited in the hallway and was quiet after that. She had called me babe. What did that mean? We were driving home when she finally spoke.

"Why do you let people call you Bebs?"

"I don't know. What's wrong with Bebs?"

"It sounds derogatory. Kind of like babe and I think it's insulting. And what about the name for Mary's cat? It's pretty close to Barbra, except for the last two letters. Why did she pick that name?"

"Because she loved her Barbie doll when she was little and thought it was cute to name her cat after it." It had seemed reasonable to me.

"It sounds too close to your name. And it's almost as if people are making fun of you by calling you Bebs. When I first heard Scott call you Bebs, I thought you were his fag hag."

"It's just a nickname." Where was this going?

"You deserve better." We were in my driveway and Katrina started to undo her seat belt.

"Why did you call me babe in front of Ellen?"

She stopped and looked at the front dash. "Because it made me angry when she called you Bebs and I wanted to make her jealous. Besides, it sounds like everyone's calling you babe anyway." She got out of the vehicle and stormed inside.

A text from Ellen pinged as I stepped into my kitchen. She asked if there was something I wasn't telling her. I ignored her text and sent one of my own thanking her again for looking after Barbie. The rest of the evening was frustrating and long. Scott didn't seem to want to go to bed and Katarina hardly said a word. I finally gave up and went to my room.

With the mood Katarina had been in, I wasn't sure she'd even want to spend the night with me. I finally fell asleep and it wasn't until long after midnight when I awoke to feel Katarina spooned up against me. She was in a deep sleep, and gone by morning.

MY STOMACH STILL twirled at the sight of Katarina. I

couldn't believe that only two weeks before I had been looking at her in the arrivals section of the airport. Now here we were, in the departures on our way to Iceland. She sat with Scott, across from Mary and I as we waited to board our flight. My life had changed so much in the past two weeks. How could the next fourteen days in Reykjavik ever top that?

Book Three

Chapter Thirty

THE LANDING AT Keflavik International Airport was smooth and uneventful as we flew in over water then barren land to touch down in Iceland. The bilingual announcements sounded so foreign to my Canadian ears because there was no French—only English and Icelandic.

It had been close to twelve hours since we'd left my house for the night flight that landed at five-thirty in the morning Iceland time. Going through customs and the forty-five minute bus ride into Reykjavik made for a long journey. We were all exhausted and needed some sleep when we finally arrived at Katarina's house.

In the bright sunlight of a clear morning, we stood in front of a modest, updated bungalow with an attached garage and bright white stucco. I was pleasantly surprised, as I'd been expecting an outdated house like mine that needed repair.

"Welcome to my home," Katarina said. She unlocked the door and led us into a sparkling entryway with ceramic tiles and a metal shoe rack containing a pair of work boots that likely belonged to Ari.

"We made it," Scott said.

Katarina started to cry as soon as she noticed the boots. "I'm sorry. I wanted to call out to Ari and let him know I'm home. It's as though I keep forgetting he's gone."

Scott picked up the work boots and held them as though they were his and in the way. We were huddled together beside our luggage and I couldn't get around my suitcase fast enough to console Katarina. "There's no need to apologize. We're here for you."

Katarina sobbed while Scott and Mary moved out of the entryway and into the house. I could hear Mary admiring the place.

"I want you to sleep in my room." Katarina whispered. "I don't want to be by myself."

"How should we tell Scott and Mary?" I knew this would have been hard on Scott too and didn't want to upset him anymore.

"We won't." Katarina wiped tears then pulled her suitcase into the house. I followed.

"Your place is beautiful," Mary said. "Thank you so much for letting me stay here."

"I'm glad that you are here," Katarina said. "I really appreciate you and your family coming to Reykjavik to be with me. Let me show you the rest of the place and your rooms so you can rest."

The house was tastefully decorated and immaculate. It smelt of lemon and eucalyptus. The kitchen was modern with cork flooring, updated maple cupboards, and new appliances. The living room was traditional and modern with bamboo flooring, white painted radiator heaters, and an antique buffet.

I hadn't been sure what to expect, especially after hearing Ari's story about his boxes of stuff that led to the letter about Scott. Katarina explained that it had been a four-bedroom bungalow. When she moved back from San Francisco, one of the bedrooms had been converted into an en suite bath for her.

Ari's room hadn't been emptied yet, but Katarina had changed the bed and moved some of his things out of the room in anticipation of Scott returning with her. I doubted she had planned on a house full of guests, yet she was prepared. Scott stayed in his room as we moved on to the spare room for Mary. It was neatly done up with a white duvet on the queen-sized bed.

"This is nice," Mary said. It had been years since we'd slept together and I could see her bracing herself for what she must have thought would be inevitable. "I'll put my suitcase in the far corner and take that side of the bed if it's okay."

"You can sleep on whichever side you like," Katarina said. "I'll show Barbra her room now."

"I thought she'd be sleeping in here with me." Mary looked at me then Katarina. "Where are you going to sleep?"

"I'll sleep on the couch. It's big enough."

"No you won't," Mary said. "You can't. I feel like I'm taking your bed by being here. There's lots of room for Barbra in here with me."

"Barbra has done so much for me by letting me stay at her place that I won't make her sleep with her sister when she can be in my bed."

"Barbra?" Mary's green eyes were on me.

"I'll go wherever Katarina wants me to."

"Then it's settled," Katarina said.

When Katarina led me into her bedroom, it just felt right. Her neatly made bed with its fluffy white duvet and sky blue accent pillows was so inviting.

"I'm sorry I didn't change the sheets, but I wasn't expecting to have company in my bed." She turned on a lamp and acted as if we weren't lovers alone in a bedroom.

"Which side would you like me to take?" I almost had to jump up to sit on the edge.

"It doesn't matter because I expect us to be in the middle anyway." Katarina got me a towel and put it on the bed. Feel free to borrow any of my sweaters if you like. It can get chilly in the morning and I don't want you to be cold."

I slid off the bed and put my arms around her. "Thanks. You must be tired and this has to be so hard for you."

"I feel numb inside." She dropped her head to my shoulder. "He's everywhere. How could he have done this to me?"

"I'm here for you." Her back was full of knots.

"It was like a dream in Ottawa, as if I was on a vacation. But now that I'm home, it's more like a nightmare. I don't know what I'm going to do without Ari."

"He knew he was going to die," I said. "He told me. I'm sure he did this for you and not to you. I think he wanted you to come to Ottawa to meet us."

"I know he wanted me to come to Ottawa. He was so excited the day he met you and Scott. He begged me to jump on the next plane. I was too stubborn. And stupid. Why didn't I go? He'd still be here."

"You don't know that," I said. "He was in pain and suffering. I think he held on for as long as he could."

"I'm so glad you are here." Katarina gave me a hug and kiss then left to check on Scott.

I was just finishing up when Mary came into the room, already in her pajamas and housecoat, and looked around. "Nice room and your own bathroom too. You're lucky."

"Isn't it nice?" I was by the bed and had put on a heavy sweatshirt and sweat pants. I didn't plan on wearing pajamas to bed.

"You're sleeping with her, aren't you?" Mary's lips were puckered.

"What makes you say that?" I sat on the bed.

"I saw the way you practically jumped over my suitcase to hug her when she started to cry. And now this?" Mary motioned around the room. "What could you possibly be thinking?"

"That I'm falling in love with her." There was no sense in trying to deny it. Mary was on to me.

"Oh, Barbra." Mary came over to the bed and sat beside me.

"This can't be happening. And here I was so worried about you seeing Ellen. I was almost sick to my stomach for leaving Barbie with her because I was so afraid of what it could lead to. Does Scott know?"

"No and please don't tell him."

"Why not? Why are you hiding this?"

"It's complicated."

"Does she feel the same way about you?"

When I didn't answer, Mary sighed. "Oh, Barbra. What are you going to do?"

"Enjoy the next two weeks as much as I can." What else could I do?

"And after that?" Mary folded her arms.

"I don't want to think about it. I just want to live for the moment and enjoy our trip."

"Maybe I should do the same." Mary dropped her arms. "I wonder if Katarina knows any good looking men that might be interested in a Canadian fling."

Was that all I was to Katarina? And Mary? What was she thinking? We all went for a nap shortly afterward. Katarina put a pillow and a few blankets on the couch to make it look like her bed, but as soon as everyone's door closed, she cuddled up against me.

A few hours later I awoke to an empty bed and dark room. There was movement in the kitchen and when I checked the time, it was almost noon. I hadn't planned to nap so long and opened up the room darkening blind as soon as I got out of bed.

Katarina's bedroom window overlooked the backyard, which was private and well landscaped with a variety of bushes and trees. There was a large ground-level deck off the dining room and I was horrified to see Katarina in the arms of another woman at the far edge of it. They were both in jogging gear and must have run together. The woman was slightly taller than Katarina, but gangly and had short dark brown hair.

Freshly showered and wearing a borrowed Icelandic sweater from Katarina's closet, I peeked out the window again and saw them sharing an intimate conversation, but no longer in each other's arms. I dropped the blind and ventured into the kitchen where Scott and Mary were sitting at the table, studying a map of Reykjavik.

Scott rolled his eyes when he noticed the sweater. "I hope you're not into her pants too."

"She told me I could borrow one of her sweaters if I wanted."

I forced a smile, poured myself a coffee, and sat at the table.

"We're trying to decide where we should venture out to today," Mary said, a giddy edge to her voice.

"Who's that in the backyard with Katarina?" I couldn't think about anything else.

"I thought she was out for her jog." Mary went to the window. "I can't see her from here."

"A friend of hers was supposed to drop off some food for us," Scott said. "Where were they?"

"On the back deck." It was a struggle to keep it together.

"What were they doing?" Mary asked. "It must be cold sitting outside."

"They were in each other's arms." My voice cracked.

The front door burst open and we could hear voices. I could also feel Mary's eyes on me. Katarina led the woman into the kitchen.

"I hope everyone had a nice nap," Katarina said. "I'd like you to meet my good friend, Vagna Orrisdottir."

Scott was the first to stand and offer his hand. "Hi, I'm Scott."

"Oh my gosh, you look so much like Ari." She smiled then pulled him into a hug. "I am so sorry for your loss." She spoke with a strong accent and I guessed that she was older than Katarina, probably around fifty. Her dark brown hair was obviously a dye job because there were no signs of grey.

Mary was the next one to be introduced and when it was my turn, I gave a cardboard hug. "It's nice to meet you, Vulga."

Katarina laughed. "It's Vagna. She was kind enough to bring us some milk and bread and fresh fruit. I hope everyone helped themselves and had enough to eat."

"Bebs sure had no problem helping herself," Scott said. "Isn't that your sweater she's wearing?"

"I noticed and it looks better on her than on me. I think she should keep it." Katarina patted my arm.

"I must be going," Vagna said. "I look forward to spending time with all of you." She hugged Katarina and said something to her in Icelandic before leaving.

"Why don't I take everyone for a drive around Reykjavik today?" Katarina looked at the map. "We can use Ari's vehicle, which is parked in the garage."

"Is it okay for you to drive it?" Mary asked. "The insurance might not be valid anymore."

"It's okay," Katarina said. "Just before he left for Canada, Ari insisted on putting it in my name." Her eyes glazed over. "I wanted him to sell it instead, but he wouldn't hear of it. The more I think about things, the more it seems like he had this planned. Ari could be good at planning when he wanted to be."

"Ari made sure I was prepared to drive here when we were organizing to come back together," Scott said. "It's been awhile, but I can drive a standard."

"That's perfect," Katarina said. "You can have a Reykjavik driving lesson. The keys are by the door. Feel free to get it out of the garage while I have my shower."

"I can't wait," Mary said. "It looks like such a beautiful city."

"It is and I love it here." Katarina motioned for me to follow as she left the kitchen.

"Hey you, why the long face?" She pulled me into a hug as soon as I got into her room.

My mouth was dry. "I saw you and Vagna out in the yard. I don't want to be in the way."

"You aren't in the way." She kissed me. "I want you to have fun while you're here and not worry about anything else. Let's just live for the moment before it disappears. Okay?"

I kissed her back and forced a smile. "Okay."

Chapter Thirty-one

SCOTT CAREFULLY BACKED a shiny black, older model Land Rover out of the garage. He only stalled it once. Katarina was finishing up with her shower and my mood had improved since our kiss. I was looking forward to her tour of Reykjavik, but I was shocked it would be in an SUV after she had called my car a pig. She was full of surprises.

"This is nice." Scott got out of the vehicle and stood back to admire it. "Mary should feel right at home in it."

"Perfect," Mary said. "I've always wanted to take my car somewhere out of the city where I could try out the four-wheel drive. I hope Katarina takes us off the beaten path in this."

"If you want adventure, you've come to the right place." Katarina joined us. She had glowing skin and damp hair with a bright smile that helped to warm me in the cool breeze.

"By the shape it's in," Scott said, "it doesn't look like it's had much off-roading. It must have been Ari's baby."

"It was." Katarina stepped forward, spread her right hand on the hood, and looked at the driver's seat as though she could see Ari sitting behind the wheel. "He was so proud of his Land Rover. He bought it right after the economic crash in two-thousand and eight and for a steal. He paid cash and often referred to it as his trophy for beating the financial disaster. I called it his beast because it certainly isn't a trophy for climate change. I feel guilty every time I drive it, but sometimes it has been a necessary evil."

"Like today," Scott said. "We'll be evil and take it for a spin."

"For Ari," Mary said. "He was such a nice man and deserves to be honored, especially in his trophy."

"Yes, let's do that." Katarina lifted her hand off the hood and ran fingers over her lips. "We can stop by Old Harbour and see if my friend, Karles, is there. He has a fishing boat that he charters out for tourists. I'd like him to take us out to sea with Ari's ashes."

"What day are you thinking for that?" Mary asked.

"I would like to do it this week," Katarina said. "Perhaps Wednesday. I want it to be a very small ceremony because Ari didn't like being around lots of people."

"Maybe we shouldn't have all come," Mary said.

"No, not at all. I am so glad you are here." Katarina flashed her beautiful blue eyes at me. "Ari would have wanted you here."

"Once Ruth and Baxter get here," Scott said, "we'll be a big enough group from Canada. Who else will be there?"

"Only a few close friends. You've already met Vagna and there's our good friend, Loki. I will also invite Ari's ex-wife, Anja, and her daughter Inga. Although Anja and Ari divorced years ago, they had become friends again over the last few years after her husband died. And then there's Karles. I want us to be on his boat. Ari liked to spend time with Karles. I think he saw him as a son he never had. Or never knew he had."

Of course Vagna would have to be there. I hoped whoever this Loki person was would take care of her because I had no plans to share Katarina during the next two weeks.

"Let's first head to *Hallgrimskirkja*," Katarina said, "otherwise known as Hallgrim's Church. It's the tallest building in Reykjavik and I want to bring you up into the tower for a view of the city so you can get your bearings and have a small taste of what you're in for."

Katarina drove us there and I enjoyed the view from the seat behind her. She handled the vehicle and the traffic as though she could drive that Land Rover through anything. I was impressed but still wondering how she could have called my car a pig.

The large church was very distinctive and could be seen from almost anywhere in Reykjavik. I felt so small as we stood at the entrance of the massive concrete building with its tall steeple and impressive architecture of clear lines and jagged edges that fanned out at the base of the front.

"This church took years to build," Katarina said, "and was designed to represent the Icelandic landscape where lava has cooled into basalt rock."

"It looks more like a rocket ship to me." Scott's hands were in his pockets and his shoulders hunched forward in the cool breeze.

"This is amazing." Mary's head was almost at a ninety-degree angle to her body as she looked up at the steeple. "I read that it took over thirty years to build."

"That's correct," Katarina said. "Let's hope the organist is practicing because there is a huge pipe organ that sounds beautiful."

I was happy to get inside and out of the cool breeze. The interior was simple and modern with a massive white ceiling and acoustics that made voices angelic. Katarina took care of our entrance fee for the lift to access the tower since we hadn't yet mastered the Icelandic Krona.

The view of the city from the steeple was spectacular. I hadn't realized how beautiful Reykjavik was with its vibrant rooftops and clean streets. Scott and Mary stood up front and pointed out landmarks while Katarina and I viewed from behind. The organist started to play just as I felt Katarina's hand discreetly slide up the back of my sweater and massage my spine, making me feel closer to Heaven than ever before.

Katarina then brought us to Old Harbour and the fishing boat of her friend, Karles. He was inside the small cabin and rushed out to greet Katarina as soon as he saw her approaching. He jumped off the boat and the two of them embraced, speaking in Icelandic to each other. It had been the first time I'd heard Katarina speak Icelandic and it was as though she had suddenly become someone else. Her dialect and tone were so foreign that I couldn't even begin to think about pronouncing some of the words she used.

Mary and I stayed back as Katarina introduced Scott to Karles. He was around our age and would have been a perfect model for a tourism brochure advertising the services of his boat. He had a slim muscular build and a tightly cropped, light brown beard.

"He's cute," Mary whispered. "He doesn't have a wedding band. I wonder if he's single."

"I thought you were joking about having a fling. Remember that our parents will be arriving this evening and you won't have time."

"You can't be expecting me to babysit them while you're off having your fling with Katarina."

"Barbra and Mary, come and meet Karles," Katarina said.

Mary's face lit up as she shook hands with him. "I'm pleased to meet you, Karles. You have a nice boat."

"I am happy to meet you too." Karles carefully pronounced his words. "It will be nice for you to ride on my boat this week."

Mary touched the back of his right hand with her left before letting go. Scott glanced at me with wide eyes.

"Oh look, there's Vagna and Loki." Katarina waved and smiled. "I asked them to join us for lunch. Karles, I hope you can join us too."

Vagna marched up to Katarina and gave her a big hug that wasn't necessary because they'd just hugged in the morning. She approached me for a hug, but I put my hand out instead.

"It is nice to see you again, Mary."

"I'm Barbra."

"Oh yes, that is right." Vagna smirked as she gave my hand a weak shake. "You are the one that's Scott's friend."

"And she's my friend too." Katarina came up from behind and put an arm around me, squeezing my shoulder before letting go to touch the arm of her other friend. "Loki, I'd like you to meet Barbra. She's been very helpful over the last few weeks."

Loki turned to us and took my hand, smiling at me. "I am happy to meet you." He was a handsome, tall, blond fortyish man who set off my gaydar.

"And this is her sister, Mary." Scott ushered Mary toward Loki, trying to regain his attention. I hadn't seen such a smile on Scott's face since before Ari died.

We settled on a small restaurant not too far from Karles's boat. It was packed and the Icelandic chatter kept reminding me that I was now on Katarina's turf. It had been so much simpler in Ottawa when it was just Katarina. Now, as I watched her banter with Vagna and Loki in Icelandic, things were no longer simple. Mary sat close to Karles and seemed to be comfortably enjoying herself. Scott strived to remain the center of attention by struggling to pronounce a few Icelandic words on the menu and making everyone laugh.

After lunch, Katarina took us for a drive around Reykjavik to point out some of the tourist attractions and shopping districts. The streets were modern and driving didn't look much different than in Ottawa. It wasn't long before Scott was comfortably behind the wheel and driving us back to Katarina's. We stopped at a grocery store along the way and followed Katarina through the aisles, picking out food for the next few days. The selection was abundant and again, it could have been any large grocery store in Ottawa, with the exception of a few things like Icelandic signage and dried sheep head in the meat section.

Katarina prepared pasta for dinner and I worked on a lettuce salad. Scott had gone to his room for a short nap while Mary was in her room, e-mailing with Ellen to check in on Barbie. I hadn't even looked at my e-mail or thought at all about Ellen.

"How long have you known Vagna?" I was cutting tomatoes and Katarina grating Parmesan cheese.

"It's been about five years now. Thank you for helping with the salad."

"My pleasure. I thought she was a lifelong friend, or something."

"Nope. She moved down from up north and we got together then."

They were a couple? "Are you still together?"

Katarina embraced me from behind and nibbled at my neck. "In what sense?"

"As in sleeping with her." I too had stopped what I was doing but couldn't bring myself to turn around and face her.

"No, because I'm sleeping with you now." She rested her head against my back.

"And after I'm gone?" Please say no.

"Will you sleep with Ellen then?" She tensed.

"Should I?" I didn't want to think about what it would be like after I left.

"If that's what you want." Her voice was calm.

My voice shook. "No, that's not what I want."

Katarina turned me around and pulled me into her chest. She stroked the back of my head and held on tight, but she didn't answer my question about Vagna.

Dinner conversation between Katarina and me was reserved. Mary and Scott, however, chatted non-stop about their day and couldn't seem to get enough information about Loki and Karles, who were both single. Katarina only had good things to say about them and confirmed that Loki was gay. I wanted to ask if Vagna was his fag hag, but decided against it. She was a hag as far as I was concerned. I was determined to keep that hag away from Katarina while I was there, even if it meant I had to get up extra early to jog with them.

We were relaxing in the living room, watching a televised nature documentary that only Katarina could understand, when the home phone rang.

"Welcome to Iceland," Katarina said. My parents had arrived. "I hope you had a good flight."

Katarina had to pull the phone away from her ear as my mother giddily described their flight and bus ride into Reykjavik.

"I hope you can come here for dinner tomorrow night," Katarina said.

"Yes, thank you. We'd love to." My mother's response echoed in the room.

"That's great. I'll let you talk to one of your daughters now."

I motioned for Mary to take the phone. Katarina gave the handset to Mary, who wandered into the kitchen as she started telling about our day.

"I have to meet with one of my work clients tomorrow

morning," Katarina said. "Otherwise I'd have invited them for lunch."

"It's too bad you have to work this week," Scott said. "I thought you'd be able to get more time off."

"I wish, but since I work for myself, I don't get paid if I don't work."

"Where's your office?" I hadn't noticed a set-up in her house.

"I rent space downtown. I tried to work from here when I first started, but it was too distracting. That's how I met Vagna. She works for herself too as a technical writer and has the office next to mine."

So much for getting up early to jog because Vagna would be all over Katarina at the office.

It was still light out when everyone went to bed so Katarina didn't need to fumble in the dark to find her way to me. She stripped naked before crawling into bed.

"I've been waiting for this all day." She wrapped herself around my nude body. "I hope you're in the mood for some sex."

"Most certainly." I rolled on top of her with every intention of making sure she'd be too tired to even look at Vagna the next day.

Chapter Thirty-two

THE NEXT MORNING, Katarina was up and gone before I had a chance to kiss her goodbye. Mary and Scott were finishing their breakfast when I strolled into the kitchen.

"I can't believe you're just getting up now," Mary said. "The morning's half over."

I headed to the coffee machine. "There must be something in this Icelandic air."

"Or maybe there's something in that Icelandic sweater you keep wearing," Scott said.

"What's everyone up to?" I asked in an effort to divert attention from me.

"I'm taking Mom and Dad to Old Harbour." Mary put on her jacket. "Want to come?"

"Are you going?" I looked at Scott as he brought his dishes to the sink.

"No, I want to start sorting through some of Ari's things."

It was settled. I stayed with Scott. Mary could handle our parents on her own and I suspected she was on a mission to bump into Karles anyway. Katarina had left a bus schedule and some tickets for us. She was so considerate, and I hoped she'd be home early.

Scott started in Ari's closet and I sat on the bed to offer moral support. "Don't get too far back into that closet."

He chuckled. "There's no need to worry about that, especially after meeting Loki. I wonder if I could get lucky with Loki?"

"Not you too." I hoped to keep Scott's mood jovial. "Why do you think Mary's dragging our parents to Old Harbour?"

"I'd hardly say she's dragging them." He began removing boxes from the shelf and placing them on the bed. When he opened them, they were all empty except for some product packaging. "Now why would he have kept these?"

"Maybe for warranty or insurance purposes," I said. "Here's the box for the radio beside his bed. And here's another box for a camera. I wonder where he kept his pictures?"

"I noticed some photo albums on his bookshelf," Scott said. "This feels kind of creepy. It's like I'm invading his privacy."

"Why don't you wait for Katarina to go through it with you?"

I got off the bed to grab some of the photo albums.

"She said she preferred it if I go through his room without her. I think she's finding this really hard." Scott sat beside me and grabbed one of the albums. "I wonder what he looked like when he was my age?"

"Just like you." I had already opened an album and found some older pictures of Ari. In one of them he wore a red flannel shirt that still hung in his closet.

"Let me see." Scott leaned against me and we flipped through the pages.

We spent the next hour browsing the albums and seeing Ari's life through pictures. In some of the photos, including his wedding pictures, Ari had a beard. Even with the beard, the resemblance to Scott was remarkable.

"It's like he's my doppelgänger," Scott said. "I don't know if I like this."

"Why not? It's so obvious he was your birth father."

"I don't want people to see Ari when they look at me. Sometimes I think Katarina looks at me as though I'm a replacement for him, but I'm not."

"But you're his son and should be proud. And you should be grateful that he wasn't some hideous beast. At least this way, you might have a chance of getting lucky with Loki." I jabbed an elbow into his side and he chuckled.

We continued flipping back and forth through the albums. In one of the photos, Ari was about sixteen and holding a baby, Katarina I imagined. The picture was followed by a progression of photos of him carrying her at different toddler ages. There were some pictures with a couple, probably their parents, but most were of just Ari and Katarina.

In one family picture, Katarina was about fourteen and leaning against Ari as though he was protecting her from them. They were lined up on a dock and in front of a fishing boat that was likely their father's. In another, it must have been just before she left for San Francisco, her hair was cropped short and Ari had his arm casually slung over her shoulder.

"Life is so strange," Scott said. "You live and then you die and leave behind your stuff and old photo albums for someone else to go through and get rid of." He leaned back and sighed.

"Let's put the pictures away for now and focus on the clothes," I said. "Instead of getting rid of everything, you should pick out a few things for yourself."

"I don't want to wear a dead person's clothes." Scott moved

in front of the closet and folded his arms.

"You're making this too negative." I went beside him and rummaged through the hangers. "Look at this beautiful Icelandic sweater. I'm sure it'd fit you perfectly and you should be proud to wear it."

"You sure seem to love Katarina's sweater." He tugged at my shoulder.

"It's so warm." I pulled the sweater off the hanger. "Here, try it on. You can wear it to the ceremony on Wednesday to honor Ari and your Icelandic heritage."

"And what's your excuse for wearing Katarina's sweater?" Scott slipped it over his head.

"It keeps me warm," I said. "There, it looks great on you. Try wearing it for a while and see what you think."

Scott looked in the mirror and shrugged his shoulders. "I guess it's not too bad."

"Think of Ari's spirit being in it. I'm sure it'll make you feel warm, especially when we get out on the cold water."

"I hope so because I can't believe how cold that wind can be." Scott rubbed his hands up and down the sleeves. "You know, you're right, Bebs. I shouldn't just get rid of everything. Katarina told me to take whatever I wanted from Ari's things."

"I think it's great that you're here to help her with this."

"I'm glad you're here too and that you stayed back to help me."

The front door opened and my heart skipped a beat as Katarina called out. "Is anyone home?"

"Hey there." I resisted the urge to run out and greet her with a hug. "Scott and I are in here."

"Good. I was hoping you'd be home because I decided to take the rest of the day off." Katarina came into the room, took one look at Scott and her face crumpled with tears.

"I'm sorry." Scott tugged at the sweater, struggling to pull it over his head.

"No, don't." Katarina went up to him and clutched the sweater with both hands. "I let myself forget that he was gone, but then when I saw you in his sweater…" She buried her head in Scott's shoulder and sobbed.

Scott patted the back of her head and comforted her like I imagined Ari would have done. I sat on the bed.

Katarina finally let go of Scott and went to the closet. "Ari cleaned up a lot of his stuff before he left for Canada. He only kept the clothes that he liked and wore often, except for the sweater. I bought it for him as a Christmas gift a few years ago and he hardly wore it. I thought he didn't have the heart to get rid of it, but now it's as though he left it for you, Scott."

We spent the next half hour boxing up the rest of his clothes and some of his personal items, mostly in silence to avoid more tears. We then headed to Old Harbour for a beer and to see if we could meet up with Mary and my parents.

The wind off the water was bitter and I imagined Scott would have been happy he'd kept the sweater on. It didn't take us long to spot my parents in their matching orange jackets. Along with Mary, they hovered around the empty slip for Karles's boat as though they didn't know what else to do.

"There you are." My mother noticed us approaching and directed her comments toward me. "Your father and I couldn't understand why you weren't with Mary this morning and wanting to see as much of the city as possible while you have the opportunity."

"Barbra was very good to stay back and help Scott this morning." Katarina gave each of my parents a welcoming hug. "It's nice to see you again."

"It's so beautiful down here," my mother said. "What's that fancy big building over there?"

"That's *Harpa*." Katarina didn't have to turn around to know which building my mother was referring to. The modern design was spectacular, a unique structure made of geometric shaped glass over a large steel framework. I drooled at the architecture while Katarina continued. "Harpa is Reykjavik's concert hall and conference center. I'll have to show you the inside because it's quite remarkable."

"Our own personal tour guide," my mother said. "How special is that?"

"Well, you are special people for coming all the way to Iceland for Ari's ceremony. I really appreciate you being here." Katarina squeezed my arm.

The sky was a dark grey and threatening rain so we made our way to one of the restaurants for some warm local cuisine. Mostly everyone ate fresh fish of some sort, with me choosing to follow Katarina and stick to a vegetarian salad option. The fish and chips smelled good and I was relieved when my mother offered me some of her fries.

After eating we headed over to Harpa and entered the magnificent and massive modern glass structure with its high ceilings, open staircases, and glass-railed walkways. Despite all of its beauty, Harpa wasn't a building for the vertically challenged, like my dad and I were. We stayed on the main level while the rest followed Katarina up the stairs for a tour.

"So who's this Karles guy?" We sat on stools at a small table near the window and my dad gripped a coffee.

"He was a friend of Ari's. Why?" As if I had to ask.

"Mary sure talked a lot about him so I was just wondering. How's your sister doing anyway? Has she heard from Jonathan?"

"Not that I'm aware of." And if she had, I hoped she hadn't responded. Although he may have figured it out on his own, we didn't want him to know where we were.

"What did he do to her?" My dad's hands trembled as he raised his cup.

"He hit her a few times and was just outright miserable." No need to go into any more detail.

My dad gasped. "Why didn't you tell me?" His voice shook and his eyes reddened. "Don't you know that you can come to me no matter what?"

"I do and I really wanted to tell you," I said, "but Mary didn't want me to." I loved my dad and couldn't imagine moving away from him to stay in Iceland. I started to cry because I didn't want to think about leaving Katarina either.

He put a hand on my shoulder. "It's okay. I know you were looking after your sister. What's important is now we know. You were right not to like him."

After Harpa, we all headed back to Katarina's. Vagna would be joining us for dinner and she was preparing an Icelandic dish for everyone to try. Katarina gave my parents a tour of her house then parked them in the living room with Scott and Mary while we prepared the rest of the meal.

"So I heard you are named after Barbra Streisand." Katarina rinsed lettuce for the salad. "It seems that your mother and Mary are fans. They told me all about her concert in Ottawa, but it doesn't sound like you went with them to see your namesake."

"Nope. I heard too much of her music growing up and always hated being named after her."

"So that's why you let people call you Bebs. Your mother told me that your middle name is Ethel. It's an approved Icelandic name and I think it sounds nice. Maybe I should call you Ethel instead of Barbra."

"No, please don't. My mother always called me Ethel when she was mad at me. I prefer Bebs."

"You prefer Bebs over Barbra?" Katarina put her hands on

her hips and looked at me.

"With my close friends, yes." I was about to sneak a kiss when the door opened and Vagna burst inside. Katarina rushed over and helped her carry a large covered pan into the kitchen.

My mother was thrilled to hear that Vagna had brought over a traditional Icelandic dish with meat because the rest of the meal consisted of mashed potatoes, turnip, and salad. We were all seated at the table, our plates served up with the potatoes and turnip, when Katarina asked Vagna to introduce the meat dish.

"You haven't experienced Iceland until you've tried *svið*."

"It sounds interesting." My mother leaned into the table in hungry anticipation, but recoiled as soon as Vagna removed the lid.

"This is a very traditional Icelandic dish," Vagna said. "Sheep heads are cut in half, singed to remove the fur, and then boiled. I hope you enjoy them." Six portions stared up from the pan, eyes, mouths, and noses still intact.

"Ruth, as you believe in the importance of having meat at every meal, I asked Vagna to prepare her special traditional sheep's head dish for a treat since I only cook vegetarian." Katarina smiled. "It will put some color in your cheeks."

My mother was speechless and her neck was red. Thankfully I had noticed the dried sheep heads in the supermarket the day before.

"Here you go." Vagna took one of the half heads and plopped it on my mother's plate. "The best meat is in the cheek and it is very tender and tasty. The eyeball is considered a delicacy."

My mother stared at her plate. "Barbra, have you tried this yet?"

"No. I've been eating vegetarian."

"Well I think you should give it a try." The redness had now gone up into my mother's ears.

"Sorry, but I'm not eating meat these days." I wasn't going to eat that.

My dad pushed his plate forward. "Here, give one to me and I'll take a bite out of its cheek."

Scott tried to refuse when Vagna dropped one onto his plate, but she insisted. "This is part of your heritage so you must taste it."

Vagna took one for herself then left the rest of us to decide on our own. Mary looked at me and shook her head with a horrified look of disgust.

Vagna was the first one to dig in, pulling out the eyeball and shoving it in her mouth. "Mmm. This is so tasty."

My dad was the next to try with a speck of meat he cut from the cheek. "It's not so bad if you can get past the head on your plate."

"It must have been a Viking dish," my mother said. "She picked at the meat for awhile then had to excuse herself from the table, saying she wasn't feeling well.

Scott nibbled his in silence while Vagna wolfed hers down and my dad ate a few more morsels. As much as I hated seeing my parents vulnerable to others, when Katarina winked at me, I smiled back. It felt good to see my mother finally pay for every snide comment she'd ever made about being vegetarian. And I was proud of Katarina.

Chapter Thirty-three

THE NEXT DAY Katarina had arranged for Loki to take us on a tour outside Reykjavik. Scott cheered at the prospect of spending more time with Loki while I sulked because Katarina had to work and wouldn't be joining us until dinner.

Scott drove Ari's Land Rover and Loki sat up front with him, leading the way. Loki was a geologist and had taken the day off to be our tour guide on the popular Golden Circle drive. It was the route for a day trip out of Reykjavik that Katarina wanted us to experience to get a better perspective of and appreciation for the varied landscapes in Iceland.

The morning was fresh and sunny with no clouds in sight. My parents insisted on sitting in the two pop-up seats in the rear of the vehicle so Mary and I could be directly behind Scott and Loki. Our eyes were feasting on the scenery and I could hear the constant click of my mother's camera as we started out. I didn't feel like talking and Mary was quiet too. Scott and Loki, however, bantered with each other.

"I understand that there are elves in Iceland," Scott said. "Should we be on the lookout for them?"

Loki snickered. "They're very hard to spot because they like to hide. And don't worry, they won't attack you."

"Should I be worried about something attacking me in Iceland?" Scott asked. "Do you have any bears here?"

"Do you want to be attacked by a bear?" Loki grinned.

"No, I don't really care for beards," Scott said.

Loki's head flung back in laughter. "That's good to know."

Scott giggled. I was pleased to see him laughing and having fun again. Loki seemed to be his perfect match and they could have even passed for brothers.

Our first stop was in *Þingvellir* National Park. We got out of the vehicle and looked at Loki to guide us. My parents wanted to visit the washroom first so Loki pointed the way and Mary went with them. My mother claimed that her stomach was still a bit unsettled from dinner the night before and made it clear to me she wasn't interested in tasting any more traditional food.

"So how long have you known Katarina?" Scott asked Loki. We were waiting by the vehicle.

Loki smiled. "For most of my life. We went to school together and even dated a few times when we were in our teens. Luckily we both figured out around the same time that we were gay. After that, we became the best of friends."

"And Ari? Was he a friend of yours too?" Scott's hands were in his pockets, jiggling keys.

"You look so much like him it's eerie." Loki flashed a smile at Scott, their eyes meeting and I felt forgotten. "He was very protective of Katarina and always wanted the best for her. He used to get mad at me when I'd tease her about being a dyke and checking out other women. But yes, I considered him a friend at times."

"And at other times?" Scott's soft tone was barely audible against the whirring wind.

Loki stepped back and looked down, his hiking boots kicking against gravel. "He felt like a father-in-law, especially during the last few months when he knew he was dying." He took a deep breath, his voice shaking. "Before he left for Canada, he came to see me and said he was worried about Katarina and how she would be after he was gone. He wanted to make sure that I would be here for her."

"Did you think about coming to Canada with her?" I asked, hoping to change the mood before he burst out crying.

Loki dug a tissue out of his pocket and wiped his eyes. "Yes, I really wanted to go with her, but she can be stubborn. Vagna offered to go too." He grinned. "I think she even had her bags packed, but Katarina didn't want Vagna there with her. In the end, she decided to go on her own."

"It's too bad," Scott said. "I would have loved to have shown you around Ottawa."

No it wasn't. If Vagna and Loki had come to Ottawa with Katarina, I'd have been standing in Ottawa instead of Iceland, back to being Bebellen. I shuddered.

"Barbra, you look frozen." My mother's shrill voice rang out against the wind. Her bright orange jacket was done up to her neck and she had her hood on as she approached. "Didn't you bring a jacket? I don't think that sweater will be warm enough in this wind."

"I'll be fine." At least that's what I kept telling myself.

Loki toured us around the world heritage site of Iceland's first law making parliament with its archaeological features and landscapes of earlier times. He also pointed out geological characteristics of the volcanic area, including fissures and cliffs indicating inter-continental drifting.

After an hour, we were anxious to get back in the vehicle and continue on our way to *Geysir*, one of Iceland's famous hot springs.

"Katarina called me an asshole when I sprayed some water on her in our backyard," Scott said. We were standing in front of Geysir, waiting for it to erupt. "From what I understood, we're all looking at an asshole of the earth."

"That's right." Loki chuckled. "We have lots of assholes in Iceland."

"We do in Canada too. I work with some of them." Scott and Loki laughed and playfully tapped each other.

Steam started to drift up from the dark blue circular pulsating pool of water. It looked like the top of a cauldron of liquid about to reach its boiling point. We were gathered around the edge in anticipation of its eruption, but nothing prepared us for the massive greenish bubble of water that seeped up from the ground and exploded, sending white sprays of steaming water into the sky. The pulsating pool had emptied itself, revealing a small crater before the water rushed back in.

"Holy moly." My mother jumped to avoid being sprayed. "The water is boiling. Stand back everyone before you get burned."

Loki laughed as we all stumbled around in the excitement of the aftermath. "It's amazing, isn't it?"

"Let's watch it again," Mary stood beside our parents, bundled up in her navy jacket with a matching silk scarf around her neck. The three of them huddled together as they waited for another eruption.

I walked over and my parents shifted so I could be in the middle with Mary. Just like the old days. I felt lucky to have my family.

After watching a few more gushes from Geysir, we continued on to the majestic waterfalls at *Gullfoss*. We had lunch before making our way over to see the falls.

"I highly recommend the lamb soup," Loki said. "It's very tasty and the warm broth will help to keep away the chills by the falls."

"No offence," my dad said, "but I'll pass on the lamb. I'm more of a beef eater myself and don't like to look at the cow when I'm eating it."

"Vagna made her sheep's head dish for dinner last night," Scott said. "She forced some of us to eat it."

"I see." Loki laughed.

"We Canadians aren't used to that kind of food," my mother said.

Loki winked at Scott then looked at my mother. "You don't eat lamb?"

"We do," she said, "but not with it staring back at us. We don't like to look at our animals when we eat them. I guess you could say we aren't from the Vikings." She chuckled.

"What about pig roasts?" Scott said. "We Canadians like our pig roasts."

"Oh, I don't care for pig roasts." My mother straightened up. "They're barbaric, in my opinion. I didn't mean to imply that Icelanders are barbaric. You're tougher, that's all."

"I don't mind a good pig roast once in a while," my dad said.

"Why don't we just order," I said.

"Yes." Scott perused his menu. "I'm glad Vagna's not here to tell me what to order. She was bossy last night with the sheep's head."

Loki laughed. "Vagna can be bossy sometimes. She likes to get her way and usually does."

Even with Katarina? I didn't want to think about it.

I wasn't enjoying the day as much as everyone else seemed to be because I longed for Katarina. I was starting to feel exhausted and just wanted to climb into bed to sleep the day away until she came home. Forget about living for the moment during this once in a lifetime experience of touring Iceland's spectacular scenery with my family.

After a leisurely lunch, we headed to the walkway and platforms by the edge of the falls. My dad wanted to wait up in the parking lot, but my mother insisted he make the trek so we could get a family picture. The wind was strong and sprays of water hit my face as I looked out over the spectacular falls. I longed for Katarina to be by my side.

"Let's get a family picture," my mother said. "Barbra get your father and come over beside us. One of the guys can take the picture."

"You're too close to the edge," my dad said as he stood a safe distance away from the rope barrier. "Come on up over here."

"We have to get the falls in the picture." My mother motioned with her arm. "You need to come over here."

"I'm not jumping the fence," he said.

Scott and Loki giggled as my dad slowly approached.

"Of course we won't cross the safety lines," my mother said. "It's too dangerous. Now maybe Scott can take a picture of us."

"I'll take the picture." Loki approached my mother. "Scott needs to be in the photo."

"We'll take a picture with Scott," my mother said, "but first I want a family one with just the four of us."

I didn't want my picture taken and especially wasn't in the mood for a photo shoot. "Let's just do one. Scott's part of our family, you said so yourself, and I think it's time we start to think about heading back." I wanted to make sure we got home in time for a dinner that included Katarina.

"Barbra, get over here." My mother positioned Mary and my dad for a view of the falls. "This'll only take a minute."

We ended up taking more than a few pictures and Scott got some nice ones with his arm around Loki.

On the drive back to Reykjavik, Loki texted Katarina and we organized to meet for dinner. Mary insisted we go to Old Harbour to see if Karles could join us too. My parents were okay with that as long as we ate at the same restaurant where they enjoyed their meal the day before.

Karles was able to join us and Vagna was there too. She sat on one side of Katarina and I made sure I was on the other. Katarina slipped her hand on my knee when I sat down. Mary parked herself beside Karles while Scott and Loki were still stuck together. My parents also sat beside each other, making everyone a couple except Vagna.

"It's so nice that everyone could meet us for dinner." Mary shared a menu with Karles as she spoke. "What a perfect way to end a great day in Iceland."

"Let's have a toast to Loki for being such a good tour guide." Scott raised his glass toward Loki.

"It was my pleasure," Loki said. "I love getting out on the land and it was a fun crowd. A toast to the tourists." He raised his glass toward Scott.

"Perhaps we should have a toast to Ari," Vagna said. "After all, he is the reason you are here in Iceland."

"Yes of course," my mother said. "Let's make a toast to Ari to thank him for coming into our lives and introducing us to this beautiful country."

The mood turned sombre as we talked about Ari's cancer. Loki and Karles did most of the talking, and Katarina remained fairly quiet. She had pulled her hand away and her breathing was heavy. Vagna must have noticed too because before I could do anything, she had her arm around Katarina's shoulders.

"I think melanoma has to be the worst type of cancer," I said.

I slid my hand on Katrina's leg, rubbing it.

"All cancer that anyone dies from is the worst kind of cancer," Vagna said. She pulled Katarina closer to her.

"Yes, you're right." Katarina shifted back toward me. "The message that Ari liked to give about his cancer was to get screened and not ignore unusual spots or pains. He waited too long before going to the doctor."

"He was mad at himself," Karles said. "He kept telling me to get checked."

"He could have been a spokesperson for cancer," my mother said.

"He never would have done that," Loki said. "He was too private."

"It must have been hard for him to come to Ottawa," Scott said. "He was by himself and at the mercy of strangers."

"Yes he was," Katarina said. "I'm so happy that you people were the strangers he met up with." She squeezed my hand.

"Here, here," Loki said. "Now let's order and eat."

After dinner we brought my parents back to their hotel then Loki came back to our place so he could take Scott out to experience the Reykjavik nightlife. Mary settled into her room as soon as Scott and Loki left, leaving Katarina and I to share a hot bath in her oversized tub. The taps were on the side, making it comfortable for two.

"I missed you today." I pushed bubbles around her with my toes.

"Really?" Her head rested on an inflatable pillow. "Even with all of your family and Scott on the tour? Didn't you find things beautiful?"

"I did, but I missed not being able to share the beauty with you. For me, Iceland is you."

"And what about Ari? Don't you think of him too when you think of Iceland?"

"Of course I do, but it's different with you."

"Yes, I guess it is. Tomorrow is going to be a difficult day. I'm glad you're here with me tonight. Let's just enjoy this time together and forget about everything else for now, okay?"

"Okay." I wasn't okay, but I was happy to be in the moment with Katarina.

Chapter Thirty-four

THE ALARM CLOCK blared to announce the arrival of morning. I stared into the grey light of the room as Katarina lay pressed up beside me, twitching awake. After our intimate bubble bath the night before, we had climbed into bed and Katarina fell asleep almost instantaneously. Her breathing had been even and heavy for most of the night.

Katarina flung her arm up to shut off the alarm then let out a loud sigh.

"Good morning," I said.

She folded an arm across her forehead and stared at the ceiling. "The first minute of every morning is always the most painful." Her voice shook and she sniffed. "It's like I forget about Ari when I'm sleeping, but my first thought is a cruel reminder that he is gone."

I rolled over and wrapped an arm around her, mustering all of my strength to keep my voice steady. "I wish I could say something to help ease your pain, but I don't have any words to replace the time you'll need to heal."

Katarina cried on my shoulder before getting out of bed to head to the shower. Everyone was finishing breakfast by the time I got to the kitchen. Scott and I wore our Icelandic sweaters while Mary had on a navy fleece jacket. Katarina was dressed in black, her slimming pants and tailored sweater fitting for her sombre mood.

"Did you take your pill yet?" Mary looked at me. Our mother had given each of us medication to avoid seasickness on the boat.

"I took mine." Scott had been out late with Loki and it wasn't until the early hours of the morning when I heard him sneaking in. Thankfully he didn't have to pass by the couch that Katarina was supposed to be sleeping on before going to his room.

"I imagine you needed one of the pills before you even took it," I said. "How were the clubs?"

"They were great. Loki took me to three different ones and the people were so friendly. I can't believe how many people he knows here."

"Reykjavik is small enough, especially in the gay community." Katarina regained her spirits as she tidied up around the kitchen. "Barbra, what can I get you for breakfast?"

"She not only gets to sleep in your bed," Scott said, "but also gets her breakfast made by you."

"Hey, I made your breakfast too." Katarina was quick to respond. "There is oatmeal left and I have pumpkin seeds and strawberry skyr too. I can put some on your oatmeal if you'd like."

"That sounds great," I said. "You're the perfect hostess." Perfect in so many ways.

"You'll need to hurry with your breakfast," Mary said. "We have to leave soon because everyone'll be waiting for us."

After wolfing down my garnished oatmeal and gulping my coffee, I brushed my teeth and rushed out to the driveway where I was the last one to the vehicle. We picked up my parents then made our way to Old Harbour. A few people were already on Karles's boat.

I helped my father get onto the vessel while the others jumped aboard. Katarina cradled Ari's ashes as she carried them into the small cabin where a tiny table had been decorated with a white lace cloth and some flowers. She rested the urn on the table then hugged Karles, Loki, and finally Vagna, who didn't seem to want to let go.

"Here comes Anja and Inga," Karles said. "Once they are here, we can head out."

The two women wore matching wool ponchos as they hurried toward the boat. Katarina hugged each in turn when they boarded and spoke in Icelandic. I loved hearing her speak Icelandic and wished I could have understood what she was saying. Anja started crying as soon as she noticed Scott and spoke in Icelandic before she grabbed onto his sweater and pulled him into a tight hug. She buried her head in his chest and sobbed. Inga awkwardly stood in the background, watching her mother while Vagna yapped away in Icelandic to her. When Anja released Scott, she saw me and immediately approached, speaking in Icelandic.

Katarina laughed then said something back to her. "She thinks you're Scott's wife."

"I always thought they might as well be married." My mother spoke the words as though it should have been a no-brainer.

"I'm very glad they're not." Katarina surprised even me with her quick response. She put a hand on my shoulder and massaged it with her fingertips as she spoke in Icelandic to introduce me to Anja.

"You good for Katarina," Anja said. "Ari be happy." She

smiled and gave me a firm hug.

I could feel all eyes on me, especially Vagna's and noticed Loki whispering something to Scott, who then nodded his head and frowned. I looked at Mary. Her eyes were bulging. I suspected that Karles had translated for her. Our mother had shuffled to be beside Mary.

It wasn't long after finishing with introductions that Karles took the boat out to sea. Reykjavik was still in the distance, but we had moved far enough from land to remind me that I hadn't taken my pill to prevent seasickness. Things felt as if they were spinning as I looked at my mother's puckered mouth, Scott's frown, Mary's wide eyes, and Vagna's glare. The rest of the mourners became blurry as they focused on the sad task of saying goodbye to Ari. My dad wiped away tears and Katarina held my hand as we stared at the bobbing water.

When we had left the harbor, portions of the sky were blue and the sun was peaking out, making the water on the surface sparkle for a peaceful resting place. By the time we got farther from land, all blue sky had disappeared. The water was grey and choppy for a cold and dark burial at sea.

My stomach had gone from being unsettled to outright sick. The strong smell of fish churned my stomach and the squawking sea gulls flitting about were like jack hammers on my head. I was going to puke. I let go of Katarina's hand, rushed to the side of the boat and dropped to my knees. I made it just in time to vomit into the sea and watch bits of oatmeal and pumpkin seeds bounce on the waves before barfing again.

We all wore lifejackets and someone grabbed onto the back of mine as I knelt hunched over the side. Karles shoved a bucket in front of me as we made our way to a bench near the middle of the deck. "It is too dangerous by the edge," he said. "I do not want you falling off the boat, especially with the water this rough."

"I'll stay with her." Mary sat beside me.

"Barbra, didn't you take the pill that I left you?" My mother stood with her hands on her hips until the boat hit a big wave and sent her flying into my dad.

I threw up into the bucket until my stomach was empty then continued with dry heaves. It was one of the worst feelings I'd ever had. I missed the entire ceremony for Ari and had to leave Katarina at the mercy of Vagna.

Mary stayed with me for most of the ceremony but joined the others to bid her farewell to Ari. My mother took over during that short time and her disapproving silence was no comfort as she sat on the bench beside me.

Worse than feeling the sickest I'd ever been, I felt awful for letting Katarina down when she needed me the most. I just wanted to be by myself, under the covers in my bed back home in Ottawa. I felt pathetic when Katarina eventually came and sat beside me. She put her arm over my hunched shoulders and pulled me close. I felt gross with vomit splatters on my sweater and a mouth that was dry and raw.

"Here, have a drink." She held a water bottle while I sipped.

"I'm so sorry. I feel like such an idiot." I slumped and put my hands over my face.

"About what?" Katarina took my hands from my face and had me straighten up.

"I wanted to be here for you and I let you down." I couldn't look at her.

She touched my chin and eased my face to hers. "I appreciate all that you've done for me and I'm really going to miss you."

A big wave knocked into the boat and I almost fell off the bench, but she caught me and held on. I was shivering and the splash of water along with the wind made the trip back almost unbearable, even with Katarina at my side. I could have moved into the cabin for the rest of the ride, but I couldn't even stand up. How was I ever going to survive without her?

When we got back to the harbor, everyone wanted to go for something to eat. I just wanted to go home and get into bed. Loki drove me back to Katarina's while the rest of them went to one of the restaurants for an early dinner. I took a warm shower then crawled into bed and watched the room spin until I fell asleep.

"Hey." Katarina was sitting on the side of the bed, rubbing my forehead. "How are you feeling?"

"Like shit." I could barely open my eyes and couldn't force a smile. "How long have I slept?"

"I've been home for an hour now. I thought I'd check on you to make sure you're okay."

"Where's everyone else?" I tried to lift my head but decided I wasn't ready.

"They've all gone to a bar. I'd had enough and just wanted to come home."

"What did you tell Anja about me, us?" What was I in for?

"I told her that we were lovers." Katarina lay down beside me. "I couldn't have her thinking you were Scott's wife."

"Really? You told her that we were lovers?" I struggled to

prop my head up and looked at her.

"Well not exactly in those words." Katarina moved her eyes from the ceiling to mine. "But she got the drift."

"And so did everyone else," I said. "How's Scott with it?"

"Why are you so worried about what Scott thinks? It's your sex life, not his."

"He could tell I was attracted to you and told me not to hit on you." Fearing that my breath was bad, I tried to speak out of the side of my mouth.

"You didn't hit on me." Her voice was so soft. "I was the one who seduced you. And am I ever glad that I did. Besides, he's probably having sex himself with Loki."

"And what about my mother? Did she say anything?"

"You're almost forty years old. Why are worried about what your mother thinks?"

"I don't know. She looked furious with me."

"So what if she is? She'll get over it. No parent wants to think of their daughter having sex, let alone casual sex with another woman. And look at your sister. She's just out of a rotten marriage and it's so obvious she wants to sleep with Karles."

"She already knows about us." I cringed.

"Everybody does now," Katarina said.

"Mary figured it out the first night we got here. She's afraid I'm going to get hurt."

"She should think about herself and how she's going to hurt Karles." Katarina sat up, fluffing a pillow behind her back. "I can tell that he's really taken with her. He is shy but a very nice man, and I don't want to see him hurt. His heart will be broken once all of you leave."

"And yours?" Mine will be too.

"I knew right from the start this couldn't go anywhere. It's nice it's turned into whatever it is that we have, but it cannot be anything more because we live too far apart."

"What about Vagna?" My head hurt. "Have you slept with her?"

Katrina rubbed her knees. "Yes, but that's over now. We're just friends."

"I saw the two of you on the deck the first morning. It didn't look very over to me." My mouth was so dry.

"She would like to sleep with me again, but I don't see her that way anymore." Her words were firm. "I love her as a friend, but not as a lover and I like being single."

"Will you have casual sex with her after I'm gone?"

"What about you?" She folded her arms. "Will you have sex with Ellen when you get back to Ottawa?"

"Do you think I should?" The room was starting to spin again.

"You need to take more control of your life." She scrambled off the bed. "You worry too much about what other people think. How you manage your sex life is no one else's business but yours. I'm going to tidy up in the kitchen a bit before I come to bed. Can I get you anything to eat or drink?"

"No, thanks. I think I need some more sleep."

Katarina closed the door when she left the room.

Chapter Thirty-five

THE NEXT DAY Katarina and Scott had an appointment to meet with Ari's lawyer for the reading of his will. Scott had been requested to attend and we were all wondering what it could mean.

For the rest of us, it was a shopping day. We took a shuttle to a local mall in search of souvenirs and a light lunch then returned to the city centre to explore the many boutiques there. The plan was to meet up with Scott and Katarina for dinner at the end of the day.

My dad had bought himself a souvenir Viking helmet and wore it in the restaurant as we waited for them to join us. My mother had her camera out and was taking a picture when Scott and Katarina arrived. They laughed when they saw my dad, the Viking from Ottawa. Thankfully Vagna wasn't with them and I suspected Mary was disappointed that Karles wasn't either. Katarina hadn't spoken much that morning and I was eager to sit beside her and check her mood.

"I saved the chair beside me for you." I motioned her over.

She smiled and kissed me on the cheek before sitting down. How could she have thought of this as just casual? Scott sat on the other side of her.

"How did it go?" My mother asked.

"It went very well," Katarina said. "And I can see that your souvenir shopping went well. Did you get a helmet too?"

My mother laughed. "No. I preferred a nice sweater. I can't believe all of the shops you have here."

My parents hadn't said a thing to me about Katarina. They acted as if nothing had been said about us being lovers. Mary had told me that our mother was very upset, but she wasn't going to let it ruin the trip. I suspected Katarina talked to Scott about us because he seemed fine and eager to tell me something. He motioned for me to lean back behind Katarina so we could talk privately.

"I'm rich," he whispered. "Ari left me a bunch of money."

"What about her?" I pointed to Katarina.

"She got lots too."

"Barbra, what are you two talking about?" My mother had her teacher voice. "If you have something to say, I think you should share it with everyone."

I straightened up. "Scott wanted to know where dad got his helmet."

My mother's ears turned red. "Barbra, that's not funny."

"I thought it was." Katarina chuckled as she picked up a menu. "So, Bebs, have you decided what to order?"

My heart thumped. She had called me Bebs. What did that mean?

After dinner, my parents were eager to go back to their hotel. They were meeting up with Mary early the next morning for a day trip to see some of the glaciers and volcanoes to the south of Reykjavik. They had wanted me to go too, but I insisted on staying back with Scott and Katarina, who was taking the day off work to go through more of Ari's things.

Katarina poured us each a glass of wine when we got back to her place. Loki was going to pop by and take Scott out for a nightcap at one of the bars downtown. He had to work late and felt bad about missing dinner and wanted to make it up. Karles had taken out an overnight fishing expedition and wouldn't be back until later the next day, so Mary looked a bit forlorn. I had hoped Vagna was on the overnight fishing trip too, but when Katarina's phone rang, I cringed. Katarina took the call in the kitchen.

I longed to ask Scott more about the will, but I wasn't sure if he wanted to discuss it around Mary. He lowered his voice as soon as Katarina left the room and I realized she was the one he didn't want to discuss it around.

"He left me enough money to live off of for quite some time, but there's a caveat. I have to stay in Iceland for at least a year."

"What?" This couldn't be true.

"He left his half of the house to Katarina, but with the stipulation she let me live with her for the year."

Katarina returned and sat beside me on the couch. "Vagna wanted to pop by for a quick visit to see how today went, but I told her not to bother."

I was stunned. Not only was I going to lose Katarina at the end of next week, but now also Scott.

"That's good," Mary said. "I think we all need a quiet night."

"Speak for yourself," Scott said. "I'm looking forward to heading out with Loki. He wants to show me his place."

"I suppose you won't be back tonight," Katarina said.

"He has to work tomorrow so I can't keep him up too late. I'll bring my key with me though in case you're in bed when I get home."

"I usually don't sleep in," Katarina said.

When Loki arrived, Katarina got up with Scott and followed him outside. I hadn't said a word the whole time and felt numb.

"Are you okay?" Mary asked. "You look like you're still seasick."

"Shell-shocked is more like it," I said. "It's going to be hard enough leaving Katarina, but now Scott too? I don't know if I can handle it."

"Yes, you can." Mary moved beside me. "We need you in Ottawa. Mom and Dad are getting older, and I don't even want to think about the situation with Jonathan."

Could I really have stayed in Iceland with Scott and Katarina? No, Mary was right. I was needed in Ottawa. Besides, Katarina didn't want me to stay.

"I haven't thought about him much since we got here," Mary continued. "I don't want to think about him because it makes me sick. I just want to have fun for the rest of our trip. Ellen wants me to Skype with her. Why don't you join the call and say hi? I'm sure she'd be happy."

I couldn't go back to Ellen or imagine wanting anyone else ever again after Katarina. I would need a friend though. "Okay."

When Katarina came back into the living room, Ellen was on Mary's computer screen, cuddling Barbie. "Wow, Iceland seems like such a neat place."

"It is." Katarina squeezed in beside me. "Maybe you will visit one day."

"Really? Thanks for the offer. That'd be great."

Katarina backed out of the screen and raised her eyebrows to me. She hadn't meant for Ellen to take her suggestion as an invitation.

"I don't know why they call it Iceland," Mary said. "It gives the impression of a cold barren country, but it's not. The scenery is beautiful and the people are so warm."

"It was named by the Vikings," Katarina said. "Wait until you see some of our glaciers and volcanoes tomorrow. We are a land of fire and ice."

"I wish I was there," Ellen said. "I'd love to see the glaciers and volcanoes. I hope you take lots of pictures, Bebs. I'll have you over for dinner when you get back and you can show them to me."

Katarina got up and went into the kitchen. I wanted to follow, but I couldn't just leave like that. I sat there with a forced smile but didn't say anything.

"I'll make sure we get lots of pictures," Mary said. "It was nice chatting with you and my little Barbie. Thanks again for looking after her."

"I'm really enjoying having her. I might just have to get a little Bengal of my own when you get back." Ellen kissed the top of Barbie's head before we disconnected.

I found Katarina at the kitchen sink, tidying up a few dishes. I put my arms around her and rested my head on her back. She continued washing the dishes.

"You called me Bebs at the restaurant tonight. I thought you liked Barbra."

"I did, but now I prefer Bebs." Her voice was soft.

"Why?" Could she be falling for me too?

Her tone changed. "I didn't like the sound of Barbra when your mother kept repeating it tonight. It was like she was scolding you."

"Why did you get up and leave when Ellen mentioned having me over for dinner?"

"There was no need for me to be part of that conversation. I'm really tired and ready for bed. You can stay up longer if you'd like and have another glass of wine."

"No, I'll go with you."

Katarina stayed on her side of the bed until after I'd fallen asleep. At one point I awoke to feel her body wrapped around mine then the next thing it was morning and she was gone.

When I got up, Scott and Katarina were discussing Ari's will while sipping coffee at the kitchen table. Mary had already left for the day.

"It will be good for you to stay here and learn more about your Icelandic heritage."

"Are you sure you're okay with me living with you for a year?" Scott asked.

"Yes because now it won't be so lonely for me."

"But it'll be lonely for me." I put a few slices of bread in the toaster then leaned against the counter with my arms folded.

"You have your family," Katarina said. "Scott is the only family I have left and it will be nice to have him here."

"You can use my car until you get a new one of your own." Scott's face beamed with excitement over this sudden change for him. "And you can come back and visit once you get your business up and running."

He hadn't asked me to stay. "Thanks." I poured a coffee and

prepared my toast. Just as I sat down, the two of them stood up.

"I'd like to start in the garage," Katarina said. "Ari had all kinds of tools that we need to deal with."

How was I ever going to survive after all this? Iceland really was the place of fire and ice as my emotions fluctuated between hot and cold.

Katarina and Scott were sorting through Ari's large toolbox as I entered the garage. I just stood back and watched. An outsider.

"Maybe you'll want to try mechanics while you're here," Katarina said.

"I don't think so," Scott wiped his hands on a rag. "Maybe Karles can use the tools. He looks like the mechanic type."

"That's a good idea," Katarina said. "Ari was always fixing some engine or other with him. I think he'd have been happy to know his tools went to Karles."

"Hey, look, some bamboo ski poles for Bebs." Scott picked up two pairs that still had the tags on them.

"Yes, for sure." Katarina smiled as she took a pair from Scott and handed them to me. "I want you to have these and you can think of me when you use them."

"Where did you get these?" Scott examined them.

"I got them as a gift when I bought my bamboo flooring. The company was promoting the use of bamboo for more than just flooring. I gave a pair to Ari, but neither one of us ever used them."

"Brand new," Scott said. "Can you believe your luck?"

"Thanks." I gripped the handles and leaned on the poles.

Scott and Katarina spent the rest of the day focused on cleaning out most of Ari's things in the garage. I stayed with them the entire time, clutching my new poles in hopeless angst.

Chapter Thirty-six

WE STOOD IN the tidied garage when Mary returned with our parents from their day trip on the South Coast. Karles drove a high vehicle with monster tires that they had to climb down from.

"Barbra, you missed an amazing day," my mother said as she stepped off the stool Karles had placed by his truck. "When are you ever going to get another opportunity like this to see the glaciers and volcanoes."

Katarina stepped forward. "As a matter of fact, she will be getting a personalized tour on Sunday because Loki is going to take us there."

"Well, we'll be gone by then," my mother said. "I can't believe we only have one day left."

"We stopped by to see if anyone wanted to join us at the Old Harbour for dinner," Mary said. "Karles offered to take us on an evening boat ride afterward."

"You can't expect me to get back on that boat." Even I was surprised at how fast I blurted the words.

"Barbra." My mother glared at me. "I'm sure it'll be okay if you take your pill this time. You should be grateful that Karles was nice enough to offer."

"Thank you, but we already have plans," Katarina said.

"I hope you enjoy yourselves then," Mary said. "We won't hold you up and I'll see you later."

"I need to use the bathroom before we go," my dad said.

"What did you do all day?" My mother looked around the garage.

"We cleaned up Ari's things," Katarina said. "Karles, now that you're here, we were wondering if you'd like to have Ari's tools. It seems that Scott doesn't have an interest in mechanics."

Karles's face lit up as he followed Katarina to the large red toolbox on wheels. "Are you sure you want to give them to me?" He picked up a big wrench and fondled it.

"Yes" Katarina said. "Ari would have wanted you to have them."

"I have many memories of him with these tools. I will take good care of them."

"I know you will," she said.

"I am really going to miss him." Karles hugged Katarina.

"Thank you so much for this. I will have to come back later for them."

My mother noticed my ski poles leaning against the wall and went over for a closer look. "These still have the tags on them."

"They were Ari's but he never used them," Scott said. "We gave them to Bebs so she won't have to look for a pair on garbage day anymore."

"I hope she will think of Iceland whenever she uses them." Katarina picked up the poles.

My mother reached to take them from her. "These are perfect. Baxter and I can share them out at the Blue Lagoon tomorrow."

"You won't need any walking poles there." Katarina held onto them.

"We want to explore the volcanic landscape around the place." My mother tugged on the poles, but Katarina held firm.

"I want them to match mine so Bebs can think of me when she's snowshoeing in Gatineau Park."

My mother would not let go and finally pulled them out of Katarina's grasp, leaning on them as she studied their shiny shafts. "They are nice, aren't they? They'll be perfect souvenirs for Barbra's time in Iceland."

"Yes, they will be." Katarina snatched them back then looked at me. "They are special, like Bebs, and I wouldn't want them to get broken."

"Okay, let's go." My dad had returned. "We'll see you tomorrow."

Katarina, Scott, and I got ready to be picked up by Loki for dinner downtown. I was pleased that Katarina had kept my poles from my mother, but more so because she had referred to me as being special. I wasn't pleased, however, when Vagna met us at the restaurant.

"Why did she have to come?" I whispered to Scott as Katarina and Loki got up to greet her. They spoke Icelandic and we stayed seated.

"Loki told me she invited herself. You're invading her territory."

"She's invading my territory right now and I don't like it. There isn't even room for her at the table."

"She can squeeze in beside you." Scott laughed.

"Hello, Barbra." Vagna sat down, taking Katarina's spot.

"Hi. That's Katarina's chair."

"She's getting another one and can put it here beside me." Vagna tapped the side of her left leg.

"Here you go, Vagna" Katarina said. "You can have this chair as I was sitting beside Bebs."

Yes!

Vagna slowly got up and switched chairs. "Of course you want to sit beside Barbra because she'll be gone next week."

"But I won't be," Scott said.

"And I'm so glad." Loki nudged up against him.

"I hope Loki is feeling like he got lucky because I am." Scott laughed.

"Am I going to have to put up with this for the next year?" Katarina said.

"I imagine that you will." Vagna leaned into the table and looked over at me. "And it is a good thing I will be here to help you."

Bitch. How could Katarina have put up with her? The rest of the evening was tolerable, especially since Katarina kept touching me, but not as fun as it would have been had Vagna not been there. I was still conscious of my stomach and stuck to drinking glacial water. We went to a few bars and all danced together, but it wasn't until Katarina toppled over that we realized she was drunk.

"Are you okay?" I was on my knees before Vagna had a chance to react.

"Oops. I think I fell." She tried to get up, but dropped back to the floor. "Scotty, where are you? I need some help to get up."

Scott and Loki each grabbed one of her hands and pulled her up. Vagna sank her claws into Katarina as I was standing up. I forced my arm around Katarina's waist and pulled her to me. "Let's get you home."

"I can't take a bus because I feel like I've just been hit by one." Katarina started to laugh. "How am I going to get home?"

"I will drive you." Vagna breathed down the back of my neck as she spoke to Katarina.

"It's okay because Scott and Loki will take us." My teeth were clenched.

"Fine then." Vagna conceded. "Take care of her. I have never seen Katarina like this before."

Katarina passed out in Loki's vehicle on the way home and they had to carry her to bed. It was late and Mary wasn't back yet. Scott sat down with me in the living room while Loki used the washroom.

"I couldn't wait to get away from that vulgar woman."

"She was annoying tonight," Scott said.

"She's totally jealous." Loki had come back and sat beside Scott. "She can be very possessive of Katarina and doesn't want to see her get hurt when you leave."

"Katarina made it clear right from the start that this is just casual," I said. "If anybody's going to get hurt..." I started to cry.

"I knew this would happen." Scott stood up and put a hand on my shoulder. "Why do you think I told you she was off limits when she first came to Ottawa?" He massaged my shoulder. "Ari told me he thought the two of you would make a good match but Katarina would never commit. He said that she had been scarred after San Francisco and had broken a lot of hearts."

"Including Vagna's," Loki said.

"But I love her," I said.

Scott tightened his grip on my shoulder. "Have you told her?"

"No."

"Well, I think you should," Loki said. "You have nothing to lose, and I think it's time she moves on from whatever happened in San Francisco."

"She'd never move to Ottawa," Scott said. "And Bebs can't move here. Her family would never let her go."

"Well, then maybe they should all move here," Loki said.

"You're discussing me as though I'm a child. None of it matters anyway if Katarina sees me as nothing more than a fling. I'm going to bed."

I went into Katarina's bedroom and closed the door. I sat down on the edge of the bed and watched her sleep. What was I going to do? Even though she was passed out drunk, I still wanted to crawl in bed beside her. I sat there for a long time after I heard Scott and Loki leave, long enough to realize that Mary wouldn't be home. When Katarina heaved, I sprang into action and got her to the bathroom just in time to avoid a mess.

Chapter Thirty-seven

MARY CAME HOME early the next morning to prepare for a day at the Blue Lagoon geothermal spa with our parents and Karles. I hardly slept at all, but Katarina had fallen into a deep sleep and was still in bed when Mary arrived. I sat at the kitchen table, drinking coffee and mulling the fact that a week had already gone by.

"Have you given any more thought to coming with us today?" Mary poured herself a cup of coffee and sat down.

"I want to stay here." I heard movement from the bedroom.

Mary leaned toward me and lowered her voice. "You look like hell and I think a day away from her would do you good."

"And where were you all night?" I didn't appreciate being berated.

"Where do you think?" Mary waited for me to respond then continued when I didn't. "At least I'm being realistic with Karles and enjoying the moment instead of stressing over something I know could never happen."

"But you don't love him," I said.

"Don't love who?" Katarina lumbered into the kitchen and grabbed onto a chair before sitting down. She wore a white bathrobe.

Mary looked at me to respond, but when I said nothing she answered. "We were talking about Jonathan."

"That bastard," Katarina said. "I hoped you'd forget all about him while you're here and just enjoy your trip."

"That's what I'm trying to do. Now, if you'll excuse me, I'm going to shower and change." Mary went to her room.

"I am so sorry, Bebs." Katarina put her elbows on the table and dropped her head into her hands. "I hate drunks. I couldn't even look at myself in the mirror this morning."

I touched her shoulder. "You've had a rough time lately and there's no need to apologize."

"You were my guardian angel last night. Thanks." She kept her head in her hands. "I'm afraid that I won't be much of a hostess today. Just make yourself comfortable."

"You're up." Scott came into the kitchen and put a hand on Katarina's other shoulder. He was still wearing his jacket.

I hadn't heard him come in. "Where's Loki?"

"Unfortunately he has to work this weekend to make up for the time he took off." Scott slung his coat on the back of a chair, poured himself a coffee, and joined us. "He's going to pick me up after lunch and take me to one of the spas."

"Sounds like fun," Katarina said. "It looks like things are going well with Loki."

"He's amazing." Scott's face lit up. "Why didn't you tell me you had such a sexy friend?"

"I didn't want to see either of you get your heart broken when you had to leave. I'm happy for the two of you with the way things worked out."

"And you?" Scott glanced at me, but his question was meant for Katarina. "How do you feel about the way things have worked out with Bebs?"

"I'm enjoying my time with her very much." She stared at the table and smiled. "We'll both have some wonderful memories once she leaves."

I got up and poured the rest of my coffee down the sink. "I think I'll head for my shower now."

Mary was gone by the time I showered and dressed. Scott was still in the kitchen with Katarina, but she got up and left to get dressed when I returned. I sat at the table.

"It's good to hear that things are going very well with Loki." Could it be love? "It's nice to see you so happy."

Scott smiled. "If it wasn't for him, I couldn't picture staying here for a year."

"Not even for the money?" I found that hard to believe.

"I want to be happy too. Loki makes me happy and I like being around him."

"Are you falling in love with him?" Dare I ask?

"I don't know about that, but I love the sex with him. His penis is so perfect that I'd like to take a picture of it to include in my photo album of natural wonders in Iceland."

"Ew, I don't want to hear about his penis. What does he think about you staying here?"

"He's happy."

"How come he's single?" It couldn't all be good.

"It's a recent thing." Scott became serious. "We haven't talked about his ex much. I gather it's still a sensitive topic."

"That's too bad." I didn't like the sound of that. "So there's only sex and no commitment?"

"We just met." Scott stood. "It's way too soon to think about commitment."

"You said that you couldn't see yourself staying here for a year if it wasn't for Loki. How do you define that?"

"I don't. I'm living for the moment and I'm having lots of fun right now. Ari should have spent more of his life living for the moment because now he's dead and there aren't any more moments."

"I think he did live for the moment, especially when he met your birth mother."

"He lived most of his life for that one moment. What a waste. I sure hope you don't get caught up in another vortex like that once you get home."

"Home will never be the same again. I'll miss you."

"I'll miss you too, but I have the sense you'll miss my aunt a lot more than me. I think the timing is good for me to stay here because Mary can move into my room. You have to admit that things would have been crowded with the three of us there."

"I don't know if I can handle living with Mary full-time."

"Your house will be too quiet to live in by yourself. If it's not Mary then you should think about getting another housemate."

"What about all of your stuff?" I didn't want another housemate.

"I'll come back next month to get rid of most of it and bring the rest back here with me, if that's okay. I'll keep paying my rent until then."

"So you're really going to do this." How was I going to survive? "It sounds like you're starting a new life."

"It's more that I'm starting the life that belongs to me, but I never had until now."

"I hope you don't forget about me," I said.

"Of course I won't." He moved away. "I'm going to have a nap before Loki comes because I didn't get much sleep last night."

Katarina must have gone back to bed after her shower, so I sat alone in the kitchen for almost two hours thinking about the barren life I was going to have when I got back to Ottawa. I couldn't imagine any waterfalls, geysers, or hot springs to take off the harsh edge. Not even Ellen. All I could think of was the dark, rocky, and lifeless volcanic landscape that I'd be seeing on the way out to the airport as I left Scott and Katarina behind.

When Katarina finally reappeared, her face had more color and she was dressed for the day in jeans and a heavy purple knit sweater. She poured herself the last cup of coffee and sat down. "Has Scott left already?"

"No, he's gone for a nap. How are you feeling?"

"Better. I won't be doing that again any time soon. It's not worth it." She folded her arms as though she were chilly. "How are you feeling?"

I hadn't been expecting her to ask me that and all of a sudden found myself choking up.

She moved her chair closer to mine and put a hand on my knee. "What's wrong?"

I shook my head, looking for words. "I'm such a wuss. I've gone and fallen in love with you."

Katarina pulled her hand back. "We can't let that happen."

"It's too late." I stared into my lap, afraid to meet her eyes. "I can't imagine life without you now."

"It hasn't been long enough for that." Her tone was matter-of-fact.

"It has for me. Love doesn't come around very often, but when it does, it does."

"You hardly even know anything about me and what my life has been like."

"It doesn't matter. I have gotten to know you as a person and that's all that counts."

"Maybe it's lust." Her tone turned sympathetic. "I know for me the sex has been great, some of the best I've ever had in my life."

"For me too." I didn't want her sympathy. "Just looking at you sets me on fire. But it goes much deeper than that. I feel like you're my other half."

"You need to feel whole on your own." Her chair shook. "I don't want to ever again feel half of someone else."

"I do feel whole when I'm with you. I want to share my life with you."

"How could something like that work?" Her tone bit with sarcasm. "Are you willing to leave your family to move here?"

"I don't know. We could figure something out." She could move to Ottawa.

"I'm not interested in a long distance relationship. I just thought we could have some fun to get through this awful sad time. I needed a distraction to help with the pain over Ari."

"That's all I was? A distraction?" This couldn't be true.

"No, of course not." Her tone softened. "I didn't mean for it to sound like that, but I did say right from the start it was about casual sex. I thought you understood."

"I thought I could handle it, but I can't. I was attracted to you the moment I saw you. And the chemistry we have. Don't you feel it too?" How could I get her to understand?

"Barbra, I've just lost my only brother. Why can't we enjoy the rest of your time here and live for the moment? I can't deal with anything more right now."

That was it? I was Barbra again? This conversation wasn't working and I had to think fast to come up with some way to salvage what was left. I put a hand on her knee.

"I don't want to pressure you. Let's just have fun and not worry about tomorrow."

"Are you sure?" Katarina pulled her knee away. "If not, then maybe you should think about leaving tomorrow with your parents."

No! How could she even suggest it? The back of my throat constricted and I could hardly speak. "Are you trying to get rid of me?"

"No, not at all." She reached for my hand. "I want you to stay, but I want you to be happy."

"I am happy when I'm with you." It was the thought of leaving her that was the problem.

Katarina cradled my hand, her fingers so soft and soothing. "I like the way you are very caring and committed to your family. And to Scott."

"Maybe I should be committed for letting myself fall for you." I was able to force a smile as I tried to joke and pretend things were back to normal between us.

"You're very special, Bebs. I wouldn't dream of taking you away from your family." She brought my hand to her lips and covered it with kisses.

It wasn't long after that when Loki arrived to get Scott. Once they were gone, Katarina and I took the bus downtown to spend the afternoon relaxing at a café and browsing some of the shops. She wanted to take me to one of the thermally heated pools, but after my bad experience at sea, I wasn't interested in having anything to do with water. We picked up a few groceries then headed back to the house for a quiet dinner and evening. At least that's what we called it as all references to romance were avoided, even if we did feed each other before sharing a long hot bath that was followed by multiple orgasms.

Chapter Thirty-eight

KATARINA AND I were up early the next morning, rushing about to get ready for a day trip to tour Iceland's southwest with Scott and Loki when my parents stopped by on their way to the airport. They were with Mary and Karles.

"I can't believe our week is over already," my mother said. "If I'd have known it was going to be this much fun, I'd have tried to book something for two weeks."

"A week was good enough," my dad said. "It's time to get back to cut the grass. I'll do yours too so it's not out of hand when you get back."

"Thanks." An overgrown lawn was the least of my worries as we stood in Katarina's driveway. The air was crisp and the sky hadn't yet decided on blue or grey when Scott and Loki pulled up.

"I thought Scott was still in bed," my mother said. "I didn't expect that he'd be up and out already. Is he just getting home?"

"Loki is taking us on a tour to see some volcanoes and glaciers," Katarina said.

"Are you on your way?" Scott walked up to my parents.

My mother pulled Scott into a tight embrace. "Now you take care of yourself. We're going to miss you and I know that Barbra's going to be lonely without you. In the end, it's a good thing the two of you aren't married." She wiped a tear. "I wouldn't want to see her staying here too."

"Thanks for everything you've done." Scott hugged her. "I know Ari would have been touched that you and Baxter came to Iceland."

"Yes, he would have been." Katarina hugged my mother. "It was so nice to meet you, and thank you again for everything that you've done for us."

"It's too bad Iceland is so far away," my mother said. "I don't imagine we'll ever be back so we may never see each other again, unless you come to Ottawa."

"I guess this will be it then because I don't think I'll ever be back to Ottawa." Katarina hugged my dad. "Take care of yourself, Baxter."

I heard my dad sniffle and felt a tear trickling down my cheek.

"Take care too." My dad squeezed her. "And make sure our two girls get safely back to us next week."

"I will." Katarina let go of my dad and stood beside Scott.

I went into my dad's arms and tried not to cry on his shoulder. "I'll see you next week."

He hugged me tighter. "Be careful. I love you."

"I love you too." My mother had put her arms around me and joined the hug with my dad. "I'll be happy when you're back at home, safe and sound."

When my parents left with Mary and Karles, Katarina hugged me, running her hands up and down my back. "I can see how much they love you. That is something very special that you are lucky to have."

"Yes, you are lucky," Scott said. "Despite their many idiosyncrasies, their love for you has always been obvious to me."

I wiped another tear. Scott was right. I was lucky.

"I wish I could have said the same about my parents." Katarina moved toward the house. "Shall we get our things and head out?" She disappeared inside before any of us had a chance to respond.

"What was that about?" Scott asked.

"She had a crappy relationship with her folks," Loki said. "Ari was more of a parent to her than they ever were."

"We were wondering," Scott said. "We had a look at some of Ari's photo albums and she almost looked afraid of her parents."

"They were very strict and traditional," Loki said. "I'm sure you've figured out by now that Katarina isn't very traditional. She's more of a free spirit."

"She can have some pretty strong views," Scott said.

"Yes, she can," Loki said. "When she gets something in her head, it's impossible to change her mind."

"Do you think so?" I hoped not. "What about her views on climate change? Ari's Land Rover isn't exactly an endorsement for fighting against climate change. She drives it as though she's been behind the wheel many times before. I don't get it."

"She hasn't always driven his Rover," Loki said. "She used to call it his gas guzzling pig and hated it. When Ari got sick, she put her views aside to drive him to every medical appointment and sat with him through all of his treatments. She's very dedicated and committed to those close to her and I love her for it."

There was movement at the door and Katarina stepped out. "Is everyone finished in the house?"

We piled into Loki's vehicle, another tall gas-guzzling SUV equipped with huge tires for driving off-road through the rough terrain for a long day of sightseeing. My Mustang hadn't been that bad after all.

Scott sat up front with Loki while Katarina and I were comfortably seated just behind. The start of the drive took us through some of the same scenic terrain we had passed on our tour of the Golden Circle, but we would be visiting other spectacular sights in this country of seemingly endless awe-inspiring landforms.

"Our first stop will be the Seljalandsfoss Waterfalls," Loki said. We had been driving for quite awhile and were ready for a break.

"I brought our bamboo ski poles." Katarina spoke to me in a quiet voice. "They will be handy and I want us to get a picture with them. And then I want you to send me a picture of you using yours in Gatineau Park."

"I won't have anyone to take my picture," I said.

"Maybe Ellen will take it."

"Did I just hear you say Ellen?" Scott swung around.

"I meant Mary. You have big ears."

"If I thought Bebs was going back to Ellen, I'd go crazy."

"You must really hate this Ellen."

"She almost destroyed Bebs." Scott glared at me in his mirror. "You wouldn't do that, would you? Go back to her?"

"There's no going back," I said. "I do have to move on with my life though, especially since you won't be there anymore."

"You make it sound like it's the end of the world," Scott said. "I'll be back next month and then who knows in a year from now."

"You're going to love it here," Loki said. "How could you not with views like this?" He stopped the vehicle and pointed to the most beautiful waterfalls in the distance. "The neatest thing about *Seljalandsfoss* Waterfalls is that you can walk behind it."

"We'll bring our poles," Katarina said. "The rocks behind can get slippery."

We got out and made our way to the base of the waterfalls. Scott and Loki wandered off to one side when Katarina noticed that the lighting was perfect for a picture of the two of us with our poles. There were a number of other tourists around and she approached a woman around our age that we could hear speaking English.

"Excuse me, would you be able to take a picture of us?"

Katarina asked.

"Sure." The woman reached for Katarina's camera. "Oh, look here come your husbands. I can wait and get them in the picture too."

"That would be nice to get a picture with them," Katarina said. "But while we're waiting, could you please take a picture of me with my wife?"

The woman twitched and her face turned red, but she quickly regained her composure and smiled. "Sorry, I shouldn't have assumed."

She snapped a few pictures of Katarina and me before Scott and Loki returned for a group shot.

"Why did you refer to me as your wife?" The four of us were standing together and still admiring the waterfalls after our photographer had gone.

"Because I hate it when people assume that everyone is heterosexual," Katarina said. "I find it insulting."

"You're not in San Francisco anymore," Loki said. "Give the poor tourists a break."

"Are you kidding?" Katarina leaned on her poles and glared at him. "They're visiting my country and shouldn't be making assumptions about me."

"I knew that would get her going." Loki laughed. "Scott and I decided it's too wet to go behind the falls today. Go ahead if you two want to."

"Bebs won't like the stairs," Scott said.

"She'll be fine," Katarina said. "I'll be with her and we have our poles."

"There's a lot of mist from the falls," Loki said. "You're going to get wet."

Katarina led the way to the bottleneck of tourists on the small staircase at the edge of the falls. I could feel water spray on my face then a gust of wind made it rain. The small steps were slippery and when we got up to the next level of the path around the falls, my vertigo kicked in and I couldn't continue. I stepped to the side and leaned on my poles.

"Are you okay?" Katarina put a hand on my arm.

"Sorry, but this is as far as I can go," I said. "Go ahead if you'd like."

"I won't leave you," Katarina said. "We'll turn around and go back together."

My knees shook and my arms trembled as I gripped the stair railing with one hand and grasped my poles with the other to fight against the oncoming flow of eager tourists trying to get by me. I could feel Katarina's hold on the back of my jacket and let out a large breath when I finally got to the bottom.

"Thanks for coming back with me," I said. "I don't know if I could have managed it on my own."

"Sure you could have," Katarina said.

"I'll wait here if you'd like to go," I said.

"No, that's okay," Katarina said. "I've been there before and I prefer to be with you."

I put my arms around her and held my poles against her back. "I want to be with you too."

"Sorry to interrupt," Loki said, "but we should get going because we have lots of driving left to do today."

The next stop was at a visitor center at the base of a volcano. We were standing in the parking lot when Loki began commentating. "This peaceful looking little ice cap that you see in the distance is one of the smaller in Iceland, but it brought the world to its knees in 2010 when the underlying volcano called *Eyjafjallajökull* erupted and closed European airspace for six days."

"One of my colleagues missed out on a trip to Paris because of it," Scott said. "Was he ever pissed."

"Iceland may be a small country," Katarina said, "but our volcanoes can cause big problems for the rest of the world."

"Yes," Loki said, "and the problems could be a lot worse than grounded flights. Some experts say it could result in global financial disaster and famine."

"You're scaring me," Scott said. "How could that happen?"

"A huge eruption would release a cloud of ash to ground flights again," Loki said, "There would be noxious gases that some predict could block incoming solar radiation and cause crop failures across Europe."

"It sounds like you're fortunate to be going back to Ottawa." Scott looked at me.

"You can't live your life in fear," Katarina said. "The world is full of threats, the biggest of which is climate change."

"Your volcanoes sound a lot worse than climate change," Scott said. "Even pronouncing the name of this one is scary."

Loki laughed. "It's easy for Icelanders. Eyjafjallajökull. I'd be more afraid of terrorism if I lived in Ottawa."

Volcanoes, climate change, or terrorism didn't top my list of fears. Saying goodbye to Katarina did. I couldn't think of anything worse than that. We spent the next few hours touring the visitor center, watching a video of the erupting volcano, and seeing photos of the ash-covered farm following the eruption.

"It's hard to believe that everything was so completely covered in ash," Scott said. "Bebs could have used her snowshoes to walk on it, but look at things now. It's all been cleaned up and the area looks more fertile than ever." We were back in the parking lot.

"I think we got off lucky this time," Katarina said. "The next time might not end as nice."

"If anything, this shows me the power of man against nature," Scott said. "If you ask me, we spend way too much time worrying about things like climate change."

"Excuse me?" Katarina folded her arms. "What are you trying to say?"

"Scott, you don't want to go there." Loki shook his head and smirked.

"I don't want to feel guilty every time I take out Ari's vehicle. I've never been a bus person and don't plan to start now."

"You could always get a bicycle," Katarina said. "There's no need to drive everywhere and besides, I was thinking of selling that pig."

"Good," Scott said. "I'll buy it from you because I'm going to need something to drive while I'm here. I won't crush under pressure, like Bebs did with her car."

"I don't want to be part of this." My jaw clenched. Scott's words were a harsh reminder that I wouldn't even have my car when I got back to Ottawa.

"So you don't give a shit about the planet then?" Katarina didn't move.

"Of course I do," Scott said. "We have to live too. We can't just avoid things because we're afraid of consequences that may never happen. You just said so yourself."

"There's a big difference between living in fear and living responsibly," she said.

"I don't break the law," Scott said, "and I try to live a healthy lifestyle. That, in my mind, is living responsibly."

"Yes, you are right." Katarina dropped her arms. "I'm glad I don't have a criminal moving in with me for the next year."

"Okay, enough of this," Loki said. "Let's go for a ride alongside the glacier."

We drove over volcanic terrain around the edge of the glacier as Loki took us to places that the tour buses couldn't go. When we got back onto the road, we drove to another feast for our eyes at the Skogafoss Waterfalls. It had started to rain, but I didn't care when I stepped down from the vehicle. The rain-mixed mist from the falls felt refreshing against my face.

"We can take the stairs up alongside to the top." Loki almost had to shout to be heard over the sound of the falls.

"How steep are they?" I wasn't going anywhere near them.

"They're steep enough," Katarina said. "It's okay if you'd rather not go."

"Go ahead without me then. I can stay here by myself."

"I know you can," Katarina said, "but Scott and Loki can go on without us."

We walked to the base of the waterfalls and watched as Scott and Loki started up the stairs. There were lots of other tourists flitting about with their cameras and speaking in a variety of languages. We managed to find a comfortable spot and sat on the ground, grateful for our rain pants.

"I can't believe how beautiful your country is," I said. "There are so many waterfalls and they're all just so stunning."

"I think you are stunning." Katarina put a hand on mine. "I want to thank you for helping to make these last few weeks special and much less painful than what I expected. I will never forget you."

"I don't want to —"

"Shhh." Katarina put her fingers against my lips. "Let's just enjoy the moment."

How could she be so immune to my breaking heart? I stood up. "I need a coffee."

Our next stop was for a walk along the black sand beaches near the community of Vik. The sky was grey and the wind blowing off the water was quite cold, but at least it wasn't raining. Scott and Loki stuck close together as they walked to the far end of the beach. Katarina put an arm around me when she noticed I was shivering.

"We can go sit in the restaurant if you're too cold," she said.

"I'm fine," I said. "It's stunning here too, but in a different way. Everywhere I look the scenery is just so beautiful."

"Hopefully we'll see some puffins," she said. "If you keep your eyes up near the cliffs, you might get lucky and see them."

"This is so amazing." My teeth chattered. "I know you've probably been here many times before, but I hope you're enjoying this even half as much as I am."

"I am loving this," Katarina said. "And yes, I've been here many times before, but never like this with you."

Could she be coming around? Could there be hope for us after all? "You have to be feeling it too. The chemistry. It's so strong."

Katarina stopped to look at me. "Yes, I do feel a strong attraction to you. I wouldn't have asked you to sleep with me if I hadn't. But it can never be anything more. I won't let it."

"Why not? I don't understand." There had to be a way.

"Because my life is in Reykjavik and yours is in Ottawa. When your parents said goodbye to you this morning..." She paused to swallow and take a deep breath before continuing. "You are lucky to have that relationship with them."

"We can't just let this end." I tugged at her sleeve. "We have to figure something out."

"We must let this end." Katarina pulled back and kicked at the black sand. "I will never agree to anything else because I won't keep you away from your family and I will never leave Iceland again."

"But why?" What could I say to convince her?

"All those years of flying back and forth between San Francisco and Reykjavik make me shudder. I won't do it again. It's just not appropriate with climate change."

"Why are you so afraid of climate change and not of the volcanoes?" My life depended on winning this debate.

"There's nothing I can do about the volcanoes, but I can do my part to fight climate change. My carbon footprint on this earth is already too big."

"It's like you're giving up your life for climate change. There has to be a compromise."

"It's not about giving up my life. It's about making sacrifices. We all have to make sacrifices if we're going to beat climate change and the easiest things to give up are personal wants rather than needs."

"But I need you." This wasn't working.

"No, no you don't." Katarina took my face in her hands. "You are a very special woman who is going to do great things to fight climate change when you start your business and make houses more energy efficient in Ottawa. I am proud of you. Now let's find the guys and go for dinner."

We had a quiet dinner then made the long drive back to Reykjavik. The day had been overwhelming with magnificent scenery and mixed emotions that brought on restless sleep soon after we got home.

Chapter Thirty-nine

KATARINA SNUCK OUT of bed early again the next morning, having already showered and dressed before I noticed she was up. She looked impressive in her business attire of black wool pants, a mauve pullover sweater, and a grey blazer. I watched in awe as she gathered her computer and work files before realizing I was awake.

"Hey." She sat on the edge of the bed and kissed my forehead. "Sorry, I didn't mean to wake you."

"I'm glad you did." I sat up and propped my pillow behind my back. "It's too bad you have to work today. Any chance of getting off early?"

"Maybe. I have to do a few things this morning to get ready for an off-site meeting tomorrow. I'm doing some work for one of the geothermal power stations. It's an interesting place and I could organize a tour for us if you'd like to come along?"

"Yes, I'd love to." I was keen to know more about the professional side of Katarina.

"Perfect. I'll be in my meeting for an hour or so while we're there, but there's a lounge where you can wait. Perhaps you could work on your business plan while I'm in my meeting. It will be good to start preparing for when you get home."

"Sounds good." The only planning I wanted to do was find a way to convince Katarina to keep things going between us.

She left for work shortly afterward. I took advantage of the geothermal-heated water with a long hot shower then made my way to the kitchen. I thought I was by myself and was stunned to see Mary sitting at the table, sipping coffee and reading e-mail on her laptop.

"This is a surprise," I said. "Where's Loverboy?"

"Excuse me?" She raised her eyes. "As if you're one to talk. I was afraid to come home last night in case I interrupted another long bath or something."

"You actually slept here? Did you have a fight?"

"Of course not. Karles had to take a group out fishing early this morning so he thought it best I sleep here."

"I was expecting that since our parents have left, I wouldn't see you until we leave on Saturday."

"Is that what you were hoping? So you could have the place

to yourself with Katarina?" She closed her computer and crossed her arms.

"It's not as if she's here anyway." I poured myself a coffee and sat down.

"Is she off running around with Vagna?"

"You can be cruel sometimes." I had forgotten about Vagna and that she'd probably be all over Katarina.

"I'm just giving you a reality check since we'll be getting back to reality soon. Mom and Dad sent me an e-mail to say they made it home okay and that they're looking forward to us getting home too. They're worried about you and afraid you'll end up staying here. I gave them my word that I wouldn't let it happen."

Mary wasn't going to control my life, even if staying wasn't an option.

"Ellen sent me a long e-mail with some cute photos of Barbie," she said. "I miss my cute little putty tat. Where's Scott?"

"I imagine he spent the night at Loki's. Who knows though, he could be in his room because I thought for sure you'd be with Karles."

"Well, you thought wrong. How's Scott doing anyway? He must be overwhelmed with everything that's happened since he met Ari. And then to have Loki thrown into the mix too."

"I've never seen him so happy." I was jealous. "He says he's coming back next month to get his things in order. He wants Loki to come with him too."

"What about Katarina? Will she come too?"

"I wish. She says she'll never leave Iceland again because of climate change."

"That doesn't make sense. She didn't seem to mind the hot weather when she was in Ottawa."

"It's not about the weather." How could she still not get climate change? "It's about her carbon footprint. Flying is hard on the environment and bad for climate change. She's trying to reduce her footprint."

"So she's just going to bury herself in Iceland and let life go by because she doesn't want to fly anymore? Has she asked you to stay?"

"No." I dropped my head. "She doesn't want to take me away from my family."

"You mean you'd actually consider moving here? Barbra, we need you back in Ottawa. You can't even think about it. That's what I told Karles when he asked me to stay."

"He wants you to stay? Already? You just met." Maybe our parents could move here too.

"I know. I'm not interested in staying any longer. My life's a mess right now and I just wanted to have some fun. He's starting to plead with me so I think it's a good thing that we're not together today."

"Is there any possibility your fling with Karles could lead to something more?" I crossed my fingers.

"Of course not. He's a fishing boat owner in Iceland. I'm a lawyer from Ottawa. I could never settle with him. We don't have anything in common except for the good sex and that never lasts anyway."

"You sound like a snob. Like you're too good for him." I'd much rather see her with him than another prick.

"I'm a realist. I could never see Karles in Ottawa. He'd be like Ari, watching the boats at Black Rapids and seeing his life go by on each one."

"Have you had any contact with Jonathan?" She better not have.

"No. I want these two weeks to myself. He knows that."

"What are you going to do when you get back to Ottawa?" Move into my basement?

"I've been in contact with a family lawyer and the divorce proceedings will start as soon as I get back. I'll have to move out of the house because I can't afford it on my own and I won't stay there with him."

"I'm glad to hear that. You can move into Scott's room if you want."

"I was hoping to stay with you, but I don't want to be in the basement. What's wrong with the room beside yours?"

"I thought the basement would give us more space." And I was going to need lots of space to get my life back in order, if that was at all possible. "You'll have to stay in the room upstairs for awhile anyway until Scott comes back and moves his stuff out of his room."

"It's going to be so strange without Scott around."

"Tell me about it." I tried to block it out.

We spent the rest of the morning doing our own thing. Mary turned back to her computer and stayed at the kitchen table. I did some laundry and house cleaning. I washed the sheets on Katarina's bed and polished her big tub in anticipation of another shared bath. I was back in the kitchen, fixing some lunch when I heard Katarina come in the front door. My stomach twirled.

"Oh, Mary's here too." Katarina washed her hands. "I'm starving."

"Good," I said, "because I just finished making a big salad and I'm cooking a couple of grilled cheese sandwiches. I'll put one on for you too."

"Perfect." Katarina sat at the table. "This is so nice to come home to."

"Please don't do this." Mary's green eyes glared at Katarina. "It's going to be hard enough for Barbra to leave you as it is without you making her feel like she could be your wife."

"You're right." Katarina straightened. "I'm sorry."

"There's no need to apologize." I glared at Mary. She was out of line.

"And you?" Her green eyes turned to me. "Stop acting like you're her wife. Do you know that she spent the morning doing laundry and housecleaning?"

"Mary, enough," I said. "We've been staying here for a week now so it's the least I can do. Maybe you should think about doing some of your own laundry. I'd suggest washing your sheets too except that you've hardly slept here enough to get them dirty."

The smoke alarm screamed as I grabbed the spatula and flipped the grilled cheese toast. "Damn, they're burnt. Shit. Fuck."

Katarina jumped to silence the alarm then came to the stove and put a hand on my shoulder. "Here, let me finish. It's my fault. I don't mind eating a burnt one."

"I can eat a burnt one too," Mary said. "I'm sorry."

We split the two burnt sandwiches between the three of us and shared the salad for a light and reserved lunch of strained conversation. It wasn't until Scott came home that the dialogue picked up.

"It smells like something was burning in here," Scott said.

"Have you had lunch yet?" Katarina asked.

"Yes, I had lunch with Loki. I made it for him because the poor guy had to get up and go to work while I stayed in bed. He dropped me off on his way back to the office. I could get used to being a wife."

Don't go there.

Mary stood up. "If you'll excuse me, I have to shower and change before Karles picks me up. He's going to take me out on the boat again tonight. I love watching the puffins." She left the kitchen.

"It seems like things are pretty tight with the two of them," Scott whispered. "What do you think?"

"It sounds like they're having a good time together," I said, "but I don't think they have much in common for anything more."

"His boat's not big enough?" Scott asked.

"Something like that," I said.

"His boat is plenty big enough and Karles would never hit her." Katarina looked at me. "I was pleased to see her standing up for you because you have done so much for her."

"What did I miss?" Scott asked.

"I haven't done that much," I said.

"Are you kidding?" Katarina said. "You're very caring and committed to your family. Ari told me he could see that in you. In just the short time I've known you, there's been all kinds of things. You let Mary move in with you. You raced off to Montreal to pick her up. You brought her to Iceland. You found a place for her cat to stay. The list goes on."

"So where is Barbie staying?" Scott asked.

"She's my sister," I said. "Anyone would do that for family."

"Not everyone," Katarina said.

"Excuse me," Scott said. "Am I invisible or what?"

"No, you're not," Katarina said. "Let's talk about you now. We need to get you working instead of this thing of sleeping in and getting up to make lunch for Loki."

"I feel like I'm on holiday," Scott said. "Besides, I have to get things sorted with my job back in Ottawa first."

"Are you going to quit?" I hoped not.

"I'm going to ask for an extended leave of absence for now. I don't want to rush into anything."

"That sounds good," Katarina said, "but I don't think you should waste any time in getting back to work here."

"Where am I going to find a job here? I don't speak Icelandic and I'm not a citizen. No one will hire me."

"I will hire you," Katarina said. "I have too much work as it is, but now I've fallen even further behind. I could use some help."

"I'm not a graphic artist," Scott said. "I'm a policy analyst. I analyze policy ideas and then write about them."

"Perfect. That's exactly what I need. I'm always being asked to take on more work than graphic design and it will be a real asset to have someone who can write good English. Vagna has been helping out, but her English isn't always the best."

"How could this work?" Scott said. "I really don't know anything about what you do."

"You can come with us tomorrow," she said. "I have a meeting at one of the geothermal plants and Bebs is coming along for a tour. I can also show you what I've done on their website right now if you'd like."

"Sure," Scott said.

I envied Scott for this opportunity to work with Katarina. We spent the next hour looking at various websites Katarina had helped design. It didn't surprise me that she was in high demand because her work was very professional and impressive.

We headed into town afterward and met up with Loki for dinner at one of the pubs. It wasn't a late night because we had to be up and out early the next morning for Katarina's meeting at the geothermal plant.

Chapter Forty

THE RIDE OUT to the geothermal plant gave me time to relax and hang on to the moment as much as possible since things were getting closer to coming to an end. We took Ari's vehicle instead of the bus, mostly at Scott's insistence. He drove and Katarina sat up front with him, talking about her work and the role he could play. I occupied the backseat and stared at the barren landscape.

The geothermal plant was in the middle of a lava field. There wasn't much vegetation around and the steam from the building was visible from quite a distance. A balding blond man of around forty was waiting for us when we got to the main entrance. He wore a navy suit with a white shirt and red tie that gave him an air of authority.

"Hello, Lyngar. Good to see you." Katarina smiled as she shook his hand.

"Nice to see you too," he said. "And these must be your Canadian visitors."

Katarina introduced us. His spicy aftershave lingered on my hand after we shook. I was impressed that she was meeting with senior management and the ease with which she handled the introductions. We entered the building and I was lead to a comfortable chair in a small lounge before the others made their way to the conference room.

I sank back into the chair with a renewed feeling that Katarina was out of my league. I was an unemployed architect. She was an established business owner providing professional expertise to senior management at one of Iceland's leading geothermal power plants. And now she would also have a staff member with Scott. How would I ever come up with a business that could compare? I couldn't even convince my dad to work for me.

I spent the next two hours going over possible scenarios of what my business model could entail. Katarina would be asking and I wanted to demonstrate professional competence in my response. I had to avoid all thoughts of leaving her and get into the mindset of starting my business back in Ottawa. It was what I'd wanted to do most of my life—build energy efficient houses.

I wrote down some goals and targets. My first goal would be to put all of my life into the business. I couldn't picture myself having any other kind of existence right now so that seemed feasible. I would target homeowners by offering architectural consulting services for major renovations. My second goal would be to get enough clients to start generating a good reputation and profit within the first year. I would then save enough money to buy a piece of property to design and build a passive house. It would be my ultimate goal. Katarina would be impressed.

Scott came out of the meeting ahead of Katarina and joined me in the lounge. "You should have seen her in there. You'd think she was an engineer and knew every nut and bolt in this place. I'll never be able to keep up."

"This sounds like a great opportunity for you." I said. "I wish I had even half her drive to put into my business plan."

"What about your life plan?" He leaned back in his chair. "Next week at this time you'll be back in Ottawa. How are you going to manage?"

"You're going to make me cry and I don't want to embarrass Katarina or myself."

"I'm worried about you," he said.

"Me too. You'll keep in touch, won't you?"

"Of course I will. It's really not that far and I'll probably be back a few more times during the year."

"Katarina won't like that because your carbon footprint will be too big. I'm sure she'll have you taking the bus to work and avoiding driving when possible."

"She's not going to control my life." His back straightened. "I may be living in her house, but I'm fulfilling Ari's wishes, not hers. There has to be balance with climate change and carbon footprints. Climate change mitigation is about reducing your carbon footprint. Eliminating it all together would mean we'd have to stop living. It's really about balance. Mitigation balance."

"Sorry to keep you waiting so long." Katarina studied her phone as she strolled into the lounge. "Lyngar can take us on a tour now."

Lyngar was an industrial engineer who had worked his way up to one of the director positions. He had an in-depth knowledge of the machinery and seemed very pleased to be giving us a tour.

"I'll start by showing you one of the first turbines in the plant then take you to see some of our more recent additions." He led us out of the office area and into the guts of the building with its intimidating machinery and complex network of pipes. How could anyone ever understand how it all worked together? How did Katarina do it?

"Our energy comes from renewable resources and we try to

reduce waste as much as possible," Lyngar said. "We consider ourselves to be one of the most advanced plants in maximizing the geothermal benefits while minimizing the amount of greenhouse gases released into the atmosphere."

"Most homes in Iceland are heated by hot water that is generated through our geothermal plants," Katarina said.

"It sounds a lot cheaper and cleaner than heating homes in Canada," Scott said.

"I guess there wouldn't be much need for energy efficient housing here," I said.

"That's not true," Katarina said. "Just because we have these renewable resources available to us, it doesn't mean we should waste them."

"Where does all the energy come from?" Scott asked.

"From the centre of the earth," Lyngar said. "We are lucky in that magma oozes up from the earth's core and provides perfect conditions for our renewable geothermal energy."

"The plant uses salt water and steam to produce the electricity," Katarina said. "Wells are drilled deep into the ground to access the hot steam and there is a large filtration system to remove the salt so it doesn't corrode the pipes."

"It sounds pretty complicated," I said.

"It's not really," Lyngar said. "We produce energy from pressurized steam by injecting it into turbines which spin to produce electricity. It's as simple as that."

It didn't sound simple to me. Life never was. We toured the rest of the plant then thanked Lyngar before heading back to Reykjavik. Scott and Katarina would be returning the following week with a draft information report for their review.

MARY SAT AT the table with her computer when Scott and I entered the kitchen for a late lunch. We had dropped Katarina off at her office where she planned to spend the rest of the afternoon working on the draft report.

"I didn't expect to see you here," I said. "If you'd have been home sooner, maybe you could've come with us to see the geothermal plant that Scott's going to have to become an expert on."

"Tell me about it," Scott said. "I'll never be able to keep up with her. I feel like I need a nap and if you hadn't been with us, I'm sure she'd have made me go to the office too."

"Jonathan's cut off my access to all of our bank accounts." Mary slammed her laptop closed. "I have no money."

"He can't do that." My teeth clenched. "It's your money too."

"He can and he did," Mary said. "He insisted on being the main account holder and I went along with it."

"What about your salary?" Scott said. "Your pay must get deposited into an account that belongs to you."

"It does, but Jonathan has access to it and he's cleared it out. Since I haven't been working a lot lately, there's nothing much going in anyway."

"I should've figured the miserable prick would do something like that," I said. "I hope you've been in contact with your lawyer and she can put a stop to this."

"She's working on it," Mary said. "I didn't think Jonathan would try to ruin my trip."

Surprise. Surprise.

"Don't let him," Scott said. "I'm sure Bebs can help you out, especially with all the money she just got from her car."

"Of course I can, but she can't let him get away with this." Why did he have to mention my car? "How much does Karles know about your situation with Jonathan?"

"He knows that we've just split and there's a lot of things to work out. I didn't go into all the gory details, but I did want him to know that I can't bear to get into another relationship now."

"And he's okay with that?" I asked. "He's going to be okay when we leave in a few days?" How could he be?

"He has to be all right with it because there's no other option," Mary said as she stood. "Let's not waste any more time on this. We should be out doing stuff before our trip is over."

The three of us ventured downtown for the rest of the afternoon. We studied some local street art then hung out at one of the cafés. I was feeling better about things after establishing some goals and targets for my business. Katarina had motivated me. Her suggestion that I work on my plan and then seeing her in action at the geothermal plant was just the impetus I needed to keep me going.

She worked late that evening and long hours the next day, leaving me to entertain myself. Scott, Mary, and I hung out together in Reykjavik for the day then each went our separate way in the evening to spend the night with our lovers. Katarina had asked me about my business plan and appeared pleased to hear about my goals and targets. She encouraged me to start working on an action plan and filled me with ideas. It was as though she were becoming my partner in business too. I shuddered as the end of my Iceland vacation crept closer.

Chapter Forty-one

KATARINA TOOK FRIDAY off work so we could spend my last full day in Iceland together. She insisted we visit the Blue Lagoon spa for a day of relaxation. Scott, Loki, Mary, and Karles also came along for the couple's day. Vagna hadn't been invited.

Scott drove and Katarina wanted us to sit in the back pull-down seats. She held my hand and massaged it with her thumb for the entire drive through the barren moss-covered rocky landscape on the way to the spa. The grey sky had patches of blue where clouds swirled from the gusts of wind. The weather was perfect for my Icelandic sweater that I now couldn't seem to go without, but I'd have to put it away for a few months when I got back to Ottawa.

My spirits were surprisingly upbeat, given that I was now down to counting hours left in Iceland. Mary seemed to be enjoying herself, despite the fact that she'd soon be back to reality too. Her lawyer had managed to get her access to enough money to set up on her own back in Ottawa. She would stay at my place and we had already talked about converting my third bedroom into an en suite bath for her.

The parking lot was full when we arrived at the Blue Lagoon, but Katarina had planned ahead and made reservations for us. She wanted me to relax and enjoy the healing waters of Iceland's most famous spa right before leaving.

"Ari loved this place," Katarina said. We checked in and headed to the showers. Mary had already gone ahead, rushing around as though she wanted to hurry up and get going whereas I dawdled to take in every last moment.

"And what about you?" I asked. "Do you love it as well?"

"Yes. I love our geothermal spas. I couldn't imagine ever again living in a place that didn't have them."

The air was cool and the bluish-green water was almost fluorescent when we stepped outside to access the spa that looked more like a small lake. I dipped a toe then let my foot sink into the warmth that soon embraced me as I lay back.

"This is amazing." Scott put white silica sand on his face. "The water is so warm and relaxing."

"You should have seen Mom and Dad." Mary was already covered in the white silica. "They were nervous to get in the water, but once they were in, Karles and I thought we'd never be able to get them to leave."

Katarina took my hand as I floated. "Let yourself relax. Close your eyes and imagine you are drifting on a cloud."

I never could totally relax in water and felt tense as Katarina rubbed silica sand on my forehead. "What is that supposed to do?"

"It will help cleanse and re-energize you," she said. "I want you to be strong when you get back to Ottawa."

Nothing could have cleansed and re-energized me for life without Katarina and I felt the weight of defeat as my body went limp in the water.

"There, that's it." She continued to massage my forehead. "I'm excited for you and your new business. You'll be great at it and every little bit helps in the mitigation against climate change.

"Don't tell me you're talking about climate change again." Scott had wandered over. "This is supposed to be a relaxing day."

"She's programmed it into her system," Loki said. "You'd better get used to it."

"We all better get used to it," Katarina said. "Climate change is here to stay and mitigation is our only hope. "

"I agree that it's needed," Scott said, "but nobody's going to want to give up everything. You're doomed to failure if that's what you think."

"It's not what I think," Katarina said. "It's about balancing mitigation."

"Exactly," Scott said.

"Including mitigating life when things are tough," Katarina said. "In a way, coming out was about mitigating my life. I couldn't take it anymore. Trying to fit in with everyone else instead of myself."

"We've all been there," Scott said. "Try living with a crazy religious father."

"Or with strict parents who wanted to change me," Katarina said. "I don't know what I would have done if it wasn't for Ari. He was always there to help ease things when all I wanted to do was run away and never see them again. He was even there when I got my wish and they disappeared at sea."

The conversation went silent until Karles finally spoke, his words slow and carefully pronounced. "I have thought a lot about Ari's death. I think he did what he did for you, Katarina. He wanted to bring his family together."

"You are right," Loki said. "He knew the treatments weren't

helping and were too hard on him to make the trip to find Scott. That's why he stopped them."

"I could have come to him," Scott said.

"There wouldn't have been enough time to convince you," Katarina said. "Look at me. He couldn't convince me to come to Ottawa in time."

"Here we are," Scott said. "We have to make the best of it."

"That's right." Katarina flopped onto her back.

Scott turned to me. "You'll do well with your business even though I won't be around to keep tabs on you. Mary will have to do that for me."

"Yes, I will, since you and Katarina are abandoning her." Mary's green eyes glowed from her silica white face.

"We're not abandoning her," Scott said. "I'm coming back for my stuff and we'll be in touch over the year."

"And what about you?" Katarina asked Mary. "Aren't you abandoning Karles?"

"Of course not." Mary faced him. "He doesn't want all of my baggage, right Karles?"

"Maybe if they were full of money and we could retire on my boat." He gave a weak laugh.

"Ellen's going to pick us up at the airport." Mary said.

Red blotches shot up Scott's neck, giving his silica-covered face a pink tinge. "Who arranged that?"

"I did." Mary raised her shoulders out of the water. "Barbra's going to need some mitigation of her own to get through the next few months. Ellen can be her mitigation balance."

"That bitch won't give her any balance," Scott said.

"How do you know that?" Mary said. "I think she's changed. She's taking good care of Barbie and I think she's fallen in love with my cat."

"She's looking after Barbie?" Scott almost stood up.

"Yes," Mary said. "She seems very caring these days. Besides, it's not like Barbra's going to get some mitigation balance anywhere else."

There was another pause in the conversation. I should have said something, anything, because they were talking about me as though what I thought didn't matter, but I had nothing to say. What was supposed to have been a relaxing and re-energizing visit to the spa was turning into a hardened dose of reality.

This time Katarina broke the silence. She reached into her bathing suit top and pulled out a small plastic bag. "I saved some of Ari's ashes because I wanted him to be with us today."

"How nice," Scott said. "He would've loved this."

"Yes, he would have," Karles said. "He hoped that the rich mineral waters would help with his cancer and came here often."

"I bet he's watching us now and is smiling," Loki said.

Katarina opened the bag and started to cry. "I still can't believe he's gone."

I wanted to reach over to console her, but I couldn't. The warm water was doing nothing to curb the numbness I felt inside. Even tears wouldn't flow for me when a sobbing Katarina spread the ash dust on the water and mixed it in with her hand.

"Well Ari, this has been quite the journey you've taken us on," Scott sculled his hands through the water. "Black Rapids to the Blue Lagoon."

"Did you go canoeing down some rapids when he was in Canada?" Loki asked. "He would have loved that."

"No," Scott said. "Black Rapids is a small picnic area near one of the lock stations in Ottawa. Ari loved it, especially watching the boats go through. We spread some of his ashes there."

"The water here's not actually blue," Mary said. "If you cup it in your hands you can see that it's clear."

"You're right," Katarina said. "It's just an illusion, like many things in life." She had stopped crying. "Even Ari. It's like he was just an illusion."

"Don't ever say that," Loki said. "Ari was real and he would have done anything for you."

"I'm not an illusion," Scott said. "I'm going to be in your face for the next year to prove it."

"Yes, I'm glad you are here," Katarina said. "I think I will hit the showers now. We should probably head back soon so that Bebs and Mary can make sure they are ready for their flight tomorrow."

Katarina fell asleep during the drive back to Reykjavik. We were in the rear seats again and I was feeling a crater of sadness in my soul. I pretended to sleep too, but I felt each bump and turn, trying to cherish every last second.

Chapter Forty-two

I SPENT MY final night in Iceland in Katarina's arms. We went to bed early and clung to each other, Katarina rubbing the back of my head and telling me how grateful she was that we had shared this time together. I told her over and over again how much I loved her, but it didn't seem to matter. Her mind was made up and we were coming to the end of our relationship.

Mary spent the night with Karles, but he had to take another group of tourists out on his boat the next morning so he wouldn't be coming to the airport. He dropped her off at Katarina's early and was gone before I got out of bed. I noticed Mary's suitcase waiting by the front door when I dragged myself into the kitchen for a breakfast that I couldn't eat. Katarina brought my bag out and lined it up with Mary's while we waited for Scott and Loki to arrive to drive us to the airport.

"We should get going soon." Mary was full of energy. "I know there's lots of time, but I won't be able to relax until I'm through security and sitting at the boarding gate."

I didn't want to rush this last morning, but I had no fight left and didn't say anything.

"How was Karles this morning?" Katarina asked. She had bags under her eyes.

"He was busy getting ready for an excursion up north," Mary said. "He felt bad about not being able to come to the airport, but I think it's better this way."

"Me too," Katarina said.

"Aren't you coming to the airport?" Mary swung around to face her.

"Of course I am, but I think it would be hard for Karles."

"I know," Mary said. "I'm going to miss him, but my life is back in Ottawa and I don't think there'd be much work here for a lawyer who can't speak Icelandic."

"Scott can't speak Icelandic and he's going to work for me. But you are right, your life is back in Ottawa." Katarina looked at me. "And so is yours. You will do great things there with your business."

I started to cry.

Mary put her arms around me. "Maybe you shouldn't come with us to the airport."

Katarina looked at the floor. "Maybe I shouldn't."

"No," I said. "Please, you have to come."

THE RIDE TO the airport was sombre and painful. Katarina and I shared our seat with Mary, holding hands in silence. Mary chatted with Scott and Loki, but even they were subdued.

Scott pulled up in front of departures to drop us off with our bags before parking the vehicle and joining us inside. Mary pulled our suitcases out of the back before I even had a chance to undo my seat belt. I looked at Katarina, but she stared straight ahead and didn't move. Little creases appeared around her mouth and eyes before her face folded into her hands. She started to bawl.

"I can't go in. I'm so sorry." She struggled to get the words out as she sobbed. "Thank you for coming. Have a safe trip home."

I wrapped an arm around the love of my life and kissed her half-hidden cheek. "I love you, Katarina." I got out and stumbled to my suitcase on the curb.

Of all the times I had told Katarina I loved her, she never once admitted to having any feelings of love for me. Not even with her tears. Thanks for coming and have a safe trip home. Rejected, I stepped onto the curb and waited as Scott hugged Mary.

Loki pulled me into a hug. "I know it meant a lot to Scott for you to come here and Katarina too. I'm sorry things didn't work out, but I know you were a big help to her and Ari would have been pleased. Take care of yourself and I will see you soon."

I couldn't speak through my sobs. Scott took me into his arms and caressed the back of my head. "I'm so sorry that things turned out like this for you. It's going to be hard, but you're a trouper, Bebs. I know you can get through this and I'll be here for you. We can talk every day if you like and I'll see you again soon."

"Take care of yourself." I pulled out of Scott's embrace, grabbed the handle of my suitcase, and rushed into the airport.

The flight to Halifax was painfully long as I sat in silence and kept my eyes closed. Customs inspection into Canada and then the short wait for the brief flight to Ottawa seemed surreal as I followed along behind Mary. I went through the motions just to get to my bed, where I wanted to curl up into a ball and never leave.

"Barbra, you have to pull yourself together," Mary said.

The plane was about to land in Ottawa and I was crying again.

"Think of this as a fresh start," she said. "That's what I'm doing."

"It's different for you," I said. "You need a fresh start. I've just lost the love of my life."

"I've also lost the love of my life."

"I thought Karles was just a fling?" Could she have fallen in love with him?

"I'm not talking about Karles."

I didn't want to hear about it.

"I know it's hard for you to believe, but Jonathan was the love of my life." She squeezed my hand. "We can do this together, but I don't want to be known as the sad sisters."

I wiped my nose.

"I think you should have a fling of your own in Ottawa to get through this rough patch."

"I'm not like you," I said. "I can't just have a fling with anyone."

"Well, maybe you should try to be more like Katarina and me."

Mary was right. I had been nothing more than a fling to Katarina. I took a deep breath and blew my nose as the plane came to a stop at the gate. Mary insisted we stop by the washroom before heading to the arrivals area.

"You don't want Ellen to see you like this. She could be good for you now."

"Scott wouldn't like to hear you saying that." I splashed water on my face.

"He's already heard me say that. He can't expect you to sit around and be by yourself after everything."

We left the washroom and I checked my e-mail. There was nothing. We were walking toward the escalator to take us down to arrivals, down to Ellen, when I felt an e-mail pop in. My heart raced until I saw that it was from Scott. He wanted to know if we'd made it back okay. I replied to let him know that we had. We were getting closer to the escalator, but I wasn't ready to go down.

"I need to pop back into the washroom," I said.

"Really?"

"Yes. My stomach is upset so it's best if you wait for me out here."

I just wanted a few minutes to myself and couldn't let Ellen see me in a state of inconsolable rejection again. I looked at my fallen face in the mirror and suddenly realized I had forgotten my bamboo ski poles at Katarina's. Tears gushed again.

I splashed water against my red eyes and stood hunched over the sink as I tried to get hold of myself. My breathing was starting to steady when another message came in. My hands shook and my heart pounded as I reached for my phone. It was from Mary, asking if I was almost done.

She was pacing when I came out of the washroom. "We have to get going or someone else is going to take our luggage."

"Let's get this over with." I forced one foot in front of the other while Mary almost ran. She was waiting for me at the top of escalator when my phone rang. I looked at the number and my stomach twirled.

"Hi." My heart thumped.

"I love you, Bebs. I need you in my life." Katarina was crying. "I don't want Ellen to be your mitigation balance. I want it to be me and we can help balance each other. I think we can make it work. I know we can make it work."

I dropped to my knees and cried. "Yes. Oh, yes."

"Barbra, what's wrong?" Mary raced over and grabbed my arm to pull me up and lead me to the nearest seat. She sat beside me.

"It's Kat..." I put the phone on speaker.

"Is this you, Katarina?"

"Mary? What's happening?"

"You're on speaker phone," Mary said. "Barbra seems to be having a hard time talking right now. What's going on?"

"I have been so stupid and stubborn," Katarina said. "I love your sister and want to be with her."

"She can't move to Iceland." Mary's shoulders tensed.

"She won't have to," Katarina said. "I will move to Ottawa, if she'll have me."

"Of course I want you to come." I was afraid to wake up from a dream. "What happened? What made you change your mind?"

"Scott and Loki. They knew when we left the airport that I needed you. They're here with me now. I'll put my phone on speaker too."

"She can be stubborn," Scott said, "but we finally talked some sense into her. I told her that we couldn't have Ellen being your mitigation balance."

"And I couldn't have Katarina crying all the time," Loki said. "We're going to bring her to Ottawa with us."

"How's this going to work?" Mary asked. "What about Katarina's business?"

"I'm going to take it over," Scott said.

"Not exactly," Katarina said. "I can work remotely from Ottawa. Scott will be the contact in Iceland. I'll get him set up over the next few weeks. I think he will be good at it."

"Except that he can't speak Icelandic," Mary said.

"We'll figure it out," Katarina said. "Just like Bebs and I will figure things out. I want to help you get your business up and running. We'll fight climate change together."

"I can't believe this is happening." I pinched my arm. "I think I have a name for my business. Mitigation Balance Consulting."

"I like the sound of that," Katarina said. "There may be a glitch though. If you want me to stay in Canada for a long time, you might have to marry me."

"Yes, of course I'll marry you." I wanted to jump up and down.

"You forgot your ski poles," Katarina said. "I will pack them with mine."

"And I will buy you a pair of snowshoes," I said. "I can't wait until it snows."

About the Author

Karen has always loved daydreaming and making up imaginary worlds to create her own stories. Born and raised in Timmins, Ontario, Canada, she is a northerner at heart and loves the outdoors. She is especially fascinated with natural environments and can often be found wandering with her camera to capture the moment.

In 1998, Karen moved to Ottawa, Ontario and met the woman of her dreams during her first week in the city. Over twenty years later, they are still very much enjoying their journey through life together.

Karen is also the author of two novels published by Bella Books. *My Forever Hero* is a romantic thriller set in Australia and *Kindling for the Heart* is a winter romance set in Northern Ontario.

MORE REGAL CREST PUBLICATIONS

VISIT US ONLINE AT
www.regalcrest.biz

At the Regal Crest Website You'll Find

~ The latest news about forthcoming titles and new releases

~ Our complete backlist of titles

~ Information about your favorite authors

Regal Crest print titles are available from all progressive booksellers including numerous sources online. Our distributors are Bella Distribution and Ingram.

VISIT US ONLINE AT
www.regalcrest.biz

At the Regal Crest Website You'll Find

~ The latest news about forthcoming titles and new releases

~ Our complete backlist of titles

~ Information about your favorite authors

Regal Crest print titles are available from all progressive booksellers including numerous sources online. Our distributors are Bella Distribution and Ingram.